THE BESTSELLING NOVELS OF
Tom Clancy

RAINBOW SIX

Clancy's shocking story of international terrorism—closer to reality than any government would care to admit.

"GRIPPING . . . BOLT-ACTION MAYHEM."
—*People*

EXECUTIVE ORDERS

Jack Ryan has always been a soldier. Now he's giving the orders.

"AN ENORMOUS, ACTION-PACKED, HEAT-SEEKING MISSILE OF A TOM CLANCY NOVEL."
—*Seattle Times*

DEBT OF HONOR

It begins with the murder of an American woman in the backstreets of Tokyo. It ends in war . . .

"A SHOCKER CLIMAX SO PLAUSIBLE YOU'LL WONDER WHY IT HASN'T YET HAPPENED!"
—*Entertainment Weekly*

THE HUNT FOR RED OCTOBER

The smash bestseller that launched Clancy's career—the incredible search for a Soviet defector and the nuclear submarine he commands . . .

"BREATHLESSLY EXCITING!"
—*Washington Post*

continued . . .

P9-DHJ-957

RED STORM RISING

The ultimate scenario for World War III—the final battle for global control . . .

"THE ULTIMATE WAR GAME . . . BRILLIANT!"
—*Newsweek*

PATRIOT GAMES

CIA analyst Jack Ryan stops an assassination—and incurs the wrath of Irish terrorists . . .

"A HIGH PITCH OF EXCITEMENT!"
—*Wall Street Journal*

THE CARDINAL OF THE KREMLIN

The superpowers race for the ultimate Star Wars missile defense system . . .

"*CARDINAL* EXCITES, ILLUMINATES . . . A REAL PAGE-TURNER!" —*Los Angeles Daily News*

CLEAR AND PRESENT DANGER

The killing of three U.S. officials in Colombia ignites the American government's explosive, and top secret, response . . .

"A CRACKLING GOOD YARN!"
—Washington Post

THE SUM OF ALL FEARS

The disappearance of an Israeli nuclear weapon threatens the balance of power in the Middle East—and around the world . . .

"CLANCY AT HIS BEST . . . NOT TO BE MISSED!"
—Dallas Morning News

WITHOUT REMORSE

The Clancy epic fans have been waiting for. His code name is Mr. Clark. And his work for the CIA is brilliant, cold-blooded, and efficient . . . but who is he really?

"HIGHLY ENTERTAINING!"
—Wall Street Journal

Tom Clancy's
Op-Center

DIVIDE
AND
CONQUER

Created by
Tom Clancy and **Steve Pieczenik**

Written by
Jeff Rovin

B
BERKLEY BOOKS, NEW YORK

TOM CLANCY'S OP-CENTER: DIVIDE AND CONQUER

A Berkley Book / published by arrangement with
Jack Ryan Limited Partnership and S & R Literary, Inc.

PRINTING HISTORY
Berkley edition / June 2000

All rights reserved.
Copyright © 2000 by Jack Ryan Limited Partnership and
S & R Literary, Inc.
This book may not be reproduced in whole
or in part, by mimeograph or any other means,
without permission. For information address:
The Berkley Publishing Group, a division of Penguin Putnam Inc.,
375 Hudson Street, New York, New York 10014.

The Penguin Putnam Inc. World Wide Web site address is
http://www.penguinputnam.com

ISBN: 0-425-17480-8

BERKLEY®
Berkley Books are published by The Berkley Publishing Group, a
division of Penguin Putnam Inc., 375 Hudson Street, New York,
New York 10014.
BERKLEY and the "B" design are trademarks belonging to
Penguin Putnam Inc.

PRINTED IN THE UNITED STATES OF AMERICA

10 9 8 7 6 5 4 3 2 1

Acknowledgments

We would like to acknowledge the assistance of Martin H. Greenberg, Larry Segriff, Robert Youdelman, Esq., Tom Mallon, Esq., and the wonderful people at Penguin Putnam, including Phyllis Grann, David Shanks, and Tom Colgan. As always, we would like to thank Robert Gottlieb of The William Morris Agency, our agent and friend, without whom this book would never have been conceived. But most important, it is for you, our readers, to determine how successful our collective endeavor has been.

—Tom Clancy and Steve Pieczenik

PROLOGUE

Washington, D.C.
Sunday, 1:55 P.M.

The two middle-aged men sat in leather armchairs in a corner of the wood-paneled library. The room was in a quiet corner of a Massachusetts Avenue mansion. The blinds were drawn to protect the centuries-old art from the direct rays of the early-afternoon sun. The only light came from a dull fire that was smoldering in the fireplace. The fire gave the old, wood-paneled room a faintly smoky smell.

One of the men was tall, stout, and casually dressed with thinning gray hair and a lean face. He was drinking black coffee from a blue Camp David mug while he studied a single sheet of paper resting in a green folder. The other individual, seated across from him with his back to the bookcase, was a short bulldog of a man with a three-piece gray suit and buzz-cut red hair. He was holding an empty shot glass that, moments before, had been brimming with scotch. His legs were crossed, his foot was dancing nervously, and his cheek and chin bore the nicks of a quick, unsatisfactory shave.

The taller man shut the folder and smiled. "These are wonderful comments. Just perfect."

"Thank you," said the red-haired man. "Jen's a very good writer." He shifted slowly, uncrossing his legs. He leaned forward, causing the leather seat to groan. "Along with this afternoon's briefing, this is really going to accelerate matters. You know that, don't you?"

"Of course," the taller man said. He put his coffee mug on a small table, rose, and walked to the fireplace. He picked up a poker. "Does that scare you?"

"A little," the red-haired man admitted.

"Why?" the taller man asked as he threw the folder into the flames. It caught fire quickly. "Our tracks are covered."

"It's not us I'm worried about. There *will* be a price," the red-haired man said sadly.

"We've discussed this before," the taller man said. "Wall Street will love it. The people will recover. And any foreign powers that try to take advantage of the situation will wish they hadn't." He jabbed the burning folder. "Jack ran the psychological profiles. We know where all the potential trouble spots are. The only one who's going to be hurt is the man who created the problem. And he'll recover. Hell, he'll do better than recover. He'll write books, give speeches, make millions."

The taller man's words sounded cold, though the red-haired man knew they weren't. He had known the other man for nearly thirty-five years, ever since they served together in Vietnam. They fought side by side in Hue during the Tet offensive, holding an ammunition depot after the rest of the platoon had been killed. They both loved their country passionately, and what they were doing was a measure of that deep, deep love.

"What's the news from Azerbaijan?" the taller man asked.

"Everyone's in place." The red-haired man looked at his watch. "They'll be eyeballing the target close-up, showing the man what he has to do. We don't expect the next report for another seven hours or so."

The taller man nodded. There was a short silence broken only by the crackling of the burning folder.

The red-haired man sighed, put his glass on the table, and rose. "You've got to get ready for the briefing. Is there anything else you need?"

The taller man stabbed the ashes, destroying them. Then he replaced the poker and faced the red-haired man.

"Yes," he said. "I need you to relax. There's only one thing we have to fear."

The red-haired man smiled knowingly. "Fear itself."

"No," said the other. "Panic and doubt. We know what we want, and we know how to get there. If we stay calm and sure, we've got it."

The red-haired man nodded. Then he picked up the leather briefcase from beside the chair. "What was it that Benjamin Franklin said? That revolution is always legal in the first person, as in 'our' revolution. It's only illegal in the third person, as in 'their' revolution."

"I never heard that," said the taller man. "It's nice."

The red-haired man smiled. "I keep telling myself that what we're doing is the same thing the founding fathers did. Trading a bad form of government for a better one."

"That's correct," the other man said. "Now, what I want you to do is go home, relax, and watch a football game. Stop worrying. It's all going to work out."

"I wish I could be as confident."

"Wasn't it Franklin who also said, 'In this world nothing can be said to be certain, except death and taxes'? We've done the best we can, and we've done everything we can. We have to put our trust in that."

The red-haired man nodded.

They shook hands, and the shorter man left.

A young aide was working at a large, mahogany desk outside the library. She smiled up at the red-haired man as he strode down the long, wide, carpeted corridor toward the outside door.

He believed that this would work out. He truly did. What he didn't believe was that the repercussions would be so easy to control.

Not that it matters, he thought as a security guard opened the door for him and he stepped into the sunlight. He pulled sunglasses from his shirt pocket and slipped them on. *This has to be done, and it has to be done now.*

As he walked down the paved drive to his car, the red-haired man held tight to the notion that the founding fathers had committed what many considered to be treasonous acts when they forged this nation. He also thought of Jefferson Davis and the Southern leaders who formed the Confederacy to protest what they considered repression. What he and his people were doing now was neither unprecedented nor immoral.

But it *was* dangerous, not just for themselves but for the nation. And that, more than anything, would continue to scare the hell out of him until the country was firmly under their control.

ONE

Baku, Azerbaijan
Sunday, 11:33 P.M.

David Battat looked impatiently at his watch. They were over three minutes late. *Which is nothing to be concerned about*, the short, agile American told himself. A thousand things could have held them up, but they would be here. They would come by launch or motorboat, possibly from another boat, possibly from the wharf four hundred yards to his right. But they *would* arrive.

They had better, he thought. He couldn't afford to screw up twice. Not that the first mistake had been his fault.

The forty-three-year-old Battat was the director of the Central Intelligence Agency's small New York field office, which was located across the street from the United Nations building. Battat and his small team were responsible for electronic SOS activities: spying on spies. Keeping track of foreign "diplomats" who used their consulates as bases for surveillance and intelligence-gathering activities. Battat also had been responsible for overseeing the activities of junior agent Annabelle Hampton.

Ten days before, Battat had come to the American embassy in Moscow. The CIA was running tests in the communications center on an uplink with a new high-gain acoustic satellite. If the satellite worked on the Kremlin, the CIA planned on using it in New York to eavesdrop more efficiently on foreign consulates. While Battat was in Moscow, however, Annabelle helped a group of terrorists infiltrate the United Nations. What made it especially painful was that the young woman did it for pay, not principle. Battat could respect a misguided idealist. He could not respect a common hustler.

Though Battat had not been blamed officially for what Annabelle did, he was the one who had run the background check on her. He was the one who had hired her. And her "seconding action," as it was officially classified, had happened during his watch. Psychologically and also politically, Battat needed to atone for that mistake. Otherwise, chances were good that he would get back to the United States and discover that the field agent who had been brought in from Washington to operate the office in his absence was now the permanent New York field director. Battat might find himself reassigned to Moscow, and he didn't want that. The FBI had all the ins with the black marketeers who were running Russia and the Bureau didn't like to share information or contacts with the CIA. There wouldn't be anything to do in Moscow but debrief bored *aparatchiks* who had nothing to say except that they missed the old days and could they please get a visa to anywhere west of the Danube?

Battat looked out over the tall grasses at the dark waters of the Bay of Baku, which led to the Caspian Sea. He raised his digital camera and studied the *Rachel* through the telephoto lens. There was no activity on the deck of the sixty-one-foot motor yacht. A few lights were on below deck. They must be waiting. He lowered the camera. He wondered if the passengers were as impatient as he was.

Probably, he decided. Terrorists were always edgy but focused. It was an unusual combination, and one way that security forces zeroed in on potential troublemakers in crowds.

Battat looked at his watch again. Now they were five minutes late. Maybe it was just as well. It gave him a chance to get a handle on the adrenaline, to concentrate on the job. It was difficult.

Battat had not been in the field for nearly fifteen years. In the closing days of the war in Afghanistan, he had been a CIA liaison with the Mujahideen guerrilla fighters. He had reported from the front on Soviet troop strength, arms, deployment, tactics, and other battlefield details. Anything the military might need to know if the United States ever fought Soviet or Soviet-trained soldiers. That was back when the United States still had people on the ground collecting solid, firsthand intelligence instead of satellites gathering pictures and audio transmissions, which teams of experts then had to interpret. Former operatives like Battat who had been trained in HUMINT—human intelligence—called those experts "educated lucky guessers," since they were wrong just as often as they were right.

Now, dressed in black boots, blue jeans, leather gloves, a black turtleneck, and a black baseball cap, Battat was watching for a possible new enemy. One of those satellites Battat hated had picked up a communication during a test run in Moscow. For reasons as yet unknown, a group known as "Dover Street" was meeting on the *Rachel*, presumably a boat, to pick up "the Harpooner." If this was the same Harpooner the CIA had missed grabbing in Beirut and Saudi Arabia, they wanted him. Over the past twenty-five years, he had been responsible for the deaths of hundreds of Americans in terrorist bombings. After discussing the contents of the message with Washington, it was decided that Battat would photograph the individuals and return to the American consulate in Baku for positive ID. After that, the boat would be tracked by satellite, and a special ops team would be dispatched from Turkey to take him out. No extradition debate, no political hot potato, just a good, old-fashioned erasure. The kind the CIA used to do before Iran-Contra gave black ops a bad name. Before "do something" was replaced by "due process." Before good manners replaced good government.

Battat had flown to Baku. Clearing customs, he had taken the crowded but clean metro out to the Khatayi stop on the sea. The ride cost the equivalent of three cents, and everyone was exceedingly polite, helping one another on and off and holding the doors for late arrivals.

The United States embassy in Baku maintained a small CIA field office staffed by two agents. The agents were presumably known to the Azerbaijani police and rarely went into the field themselves. Instead, they brought in outside personnel whenever neccessary. The embassy would not be happy to be presented with the action as a fait accompli. But there were increasing tensions between the United States and Azerbaijan over Caspian oil. The republic was attempting to flood the market with inexpensive oil to bolster its weak economy.

That represented enormous potential damage to American oil companies, who were only marginally represented here—a holdover from the days of the Soviet Union. The CIA in Moscow did not want to inflame those tensions.

Battat spent the late afternoon walking around a section of beach, looking for a particular boat. When he found it, anchored about three hundred yards offshore, he made himself comfortable on a low, flat rock among a thatch of high reeds. With his backpack, water bottle, and bag dinner at his side and the camera hanging around his neck, he waited.

The smell of salty air and oil from the offshore rigs was strong here, like nowhere else in the world. It almost burned his nostrils. But he loved it. He loved the sand under his rubber soles, the cool breeze on his cheek, the sweat on his palms, and the accelerated beat of his heart.

Battat wondered how many foreign invaders had stood on these shores, perhaps in this very spot. The Persians in the eleventh century. The Mongols in the thirteenth and fourteenth centuries. The Russians in the eighteenth century, then the Persians again, then the Soviets. He couldn't decide whether he was part of a dramatic historical pageant or an ugly, unending rape.

Not that it matters, he told himself. He wasn't here to safeguard Azerbaijan. He was here to redeem himself and to protect American interests.

Crouched among the high reeds at this isolated section of beachfront, Battat felt as though he had never been away from the field. Danger did that. It was like a fond song or a familiar food smell, a bookmark in the soul. He loved that, too. He also felt good about what he was doing. Not just to atone for Annabelle but because it was right.

Battat had been here for nearly seven hours now. The cell phone communications they'd intercepted said that the pickup was scheduled for eleven-thirty P.M. The Harpooner was supposed to be there to examine the parcel, whatever it was, then pay for it and leave.

Just then, something happened on the boat. A hatch door opened, and a man climbed out onto the deck. Battat looked out at the water. The man turned on a radio. It was playing what sounded like local folk tunes. Maybe that was a signal. Battat's gaze swept across the water.

Suddenly, an elbow locked around Battat's throat from behind and yanked him to his feet. He gagged. He tried to tuck his chin into the elbow, to relieve the pressure on his throat so he could breathe, but the attacker was well trained. He had locked his right arm around his throat and was pushing Battat's head with his left hand so he couldn't turn it. Battat tried to drive an elbow back into the attacker's gut, but the man was standing to the side. Finally, he tried to reach back and grab the shoulder of the choking arm and pull the attacker over.

The attacker responded by tilting his own body back and lifting Battat from the ground. Although Battat was able to grab the man's shoulder, he couldn't throw the attacker. Battat's feet were in the air and he had no leverage.

The struggle lasted five seconds. The attacker's arm squeezed against the American's carotid arteries from the side, immediately cutting the blood supply to the head and causing Battat to black out. Taking no chances, the attacker kept pressing the arteries for another half minute. Then he dropped the unconscious body to the sand.

The Harpooner reached into the pocket of his windbreaker. He removed a syringe from his pocket, pulled off the plastic tip, and injected the man in the neck. After wiping away the small drop of blood, he took out a flashlight and flicked it on. He waved it back and forth several times. Another flashlight answered from the *Rachel*.

Then both lights went dark. Moments later, a motor dinghy lowered from the boat and headed toward shore.

TWO

Camp Springs, Maryland
Sunday, 4:12 P.M.

Paul Hood sat on an armchair in the corner of the small, TV-lit hotel room. The heavy shades were drawn and a football game was on, but Hood wasn't really watching it. He was watching reruns in his mind. Reruns of over sixteen years of married life.

Old pictures in my new home, he thought.

Home was an anonymous fifth-floor suite at the Days Inn on Mercedes Boulevard, located a short distance from Andrews Air Force Base. Hood had moved in late Saturday night. Though he could have stayed at a motel right next to the base where Op-Center was located, he wanted the option of being able to get away from work. Which was ironic. It was Hood's dedication to Op-Center that had cost him his marriage.

Or so his wife maintained.

Over the past several years, Sharon Hood had become increasingly frustrated by the long hours her husband kept at Op-Center. She grew tense and angry each time an international crisis caused him to miss one of their daughter Harleigh's violin recitals or their son Alexander's ball games. She was bitter that virtually every vacation they planned had to be canceled because of a coup attempt or assassination that demanded his attention. She resented how he was on the phone, even when he was with his family, checking with Deputy Director Mike Rodgers on how the mobile Regional Op-Center was performing in field tests or discussing with Intelligence Chief Bob Herbert what they could do to strengthen the new relationship with Op-Center's Russian counterpart in Saint Petersburg.

But Hood had never believed that work itself was really the problem. It was something older and deeper than that.

Even when he had resigned his position as director of Op-Center and went to New York for Harleigh's performance at a United Nations reception, Sharon still wasn't happy. She was jealous of the attention that other mothers on the junket gave him. Sharon realized that the women were drawn to Hood because he had been a highly visible mayor of Los Angeles. After that, he had held a powerful job in Washington, where power was the coin of the realm. It didn't matter to Sharon that Hood put no stock in fame and power. It didn't matter to her that his replies to the women were always polite but short. All Sharon knew was that she had to share her husband again.

Then came the nightmare. Harleigh and the other young musicians were taken hostage in the Security Council chambers by renegade United Nations peacekeepers. Hood had left Sharon at the State Department's understaffed crisis center so that he could oversee Op-Center's successful covert effort to rescue the teenagers and the captive foreign delegates. In Sharon's eyes, he had not been there for her again. When they returned to Washington, she immediately took the children to her parents' house in Old Saybrook, Connecticut. Sharon had said she wanted to get Harleigh away from the media zoo that had pursued the children from New York.

Hood couldn't argue with that. Harleigh had seen one of her friends seriously wounded and several other people executed. She was almost killed herself. She had suffered the clinical consequences of classic stressor triggers for post-traumatic stress disorder: threats to the physical integrity of herself and others; fear and helplessness; and a guilt response to survival. After all that, to have been surrounded by TV lights and shouting members of the press corps would have been the worst thing for Harleigh.

But Hood knew that wasn't the only reason his wife had gone back to Old Saybrook. Sharon herself needed to get away. She needed the comfort and safety of her childhood home in order to think about her future.

About *their* future.

Hood shut off the TV. He put the remote on the night table, lay back on the bunched pillows, and looked up at the white ceiling. Only he didn't see a ceiling. Hood saw Sharon's pale face and dark eyes. He saw how they had looked on Friday when she came home and told him she wanted a divorce.

That wasn't a surprise. It was actually a relief in some ways. After Hood had returned from New York, he met briefly with the president about repairing the rift between the United States and the UN. Being back at the White House, being plugged into the world, had made him want to withdraw his resignation from Op-Center. He *liked* the work he was doing: the challenge, the implications, the risk. On Friday evening, after Sharon had told him of her decision, he was able to withdraw his resignation with a clear conscience.

By the time Hood and Sharon talked again on Saturday, the emotional distancing had already begun. They agreed that Sharon could use their family attorney. Paul would have Op-Center's legal officer, Lowell Coffey III, recommend someone for him. It was all very polite, mature, formal.

The big questions they still had to decide were whether to tell the kids and whether Hood should leave the house immediately. He had called Op-Center's staff psychologist Liz Gordon, who was counseling Harleigh before turning her over to a psychiatrist who specialized in treating PTSD. Liz told Hood that he should be extremely gentle whenever he was around Harleigh. He was the only family member who had been with her during the siege. Harleigh would associate his strength and calmness with security. That would help to speed her recovery. Liz added that whatever instability was introduced by his departure was less dangerous than the ongoing strife between him and his wife. That tension would not show Hood in the light Harleigh needed to see him. Liz also told him that intensive therapy for Harleigh should begin as soon as possible. They had to deal with the problem, or she ran the risk of being psychologically impaired for the rest of her life.

After having discussed the situation with Liz Gordon, Hood and Sharon decided to tell the kids calmly and openly what was happening. For the last time as a family, they sat in the den—the same room where they had set up their Christmas tree every year and taught the kids Monopoly and chess and had birthday parties. Alexander seemed to take it well after being assured that his life wouldn't change very much. Harleigh was initially upset, feeling that what had happened to her was the cause. Hood and his wife assured Harleigh that was not the case at all, and they would both be there for her.

When they were finished, Sharon had dinner with Harleigh at home, and Hood took Alexander out to their favorite greasy pit, the Corner Bistro—the "Coroner Bistro" as the health-conscious Sharon called it. Hood put on his best face, and they had a fun time. Then he came back to the house, quickly and quietly packed a few things, and left for his new home.

Hood looked around the hotel room. There was a glass-covered desk with a blotter, a lamp, and a folder full of postcards. A queen-sized bed. An industrial-strength carpet that matched the opaque drapes. A framed print of a painting of a harlequin whose outfit matched the carpet. A dresser with a built-in cabinet for a minirefrigerator and another cabinet for the TV. And, of course, a drawer with a Bible. There was also a night table with a lamp like the one on the desk, four wastebaskets, a clock, and a box of tissues he had moved from the bathroom.

My new home, he thought again.

Except for the laptop on the desk and the pictures of the kids beside it—last year's school photos, still in their warping cardboard frames—there was nothing of home here. The stains on the carpet weren't apple juice Alexander had spilled as a boy. Harleigh hadn't painted the picture of the harlequin. The refrigerator wasn't stocked with rows of plastic containers filled with that wretched kiwi-strawberry-yogurt juice that Sharon liked.

The television had never shown home videotapes of birthday parties, pool parties, and anniversaries, of relatives and coworkers who were gone. Hood had never watched the sun rise or set from this window. He had never had the flu or felt his unborn child kick in this bed. If he called out to the kids, they wouldn't come.

Tears pressed against the backs of his eyes. He turned to look at the clock, anything to break the steady succession of thoughts and pictures. He would have to get ready soon. Time—and government—stopped for no man. He still had professional obligations. But lord God, Hood thought, he didn't feel like going. Talking, putting on a happy face the way he did with his son, wondering who knew and who didn't in the instant message machine known as the Washington grapevine.

He looked up at the ceiling. Part of him had wanted this to happen. Hood wanted the freedom to do his job. He wanted an end to being judged and criticized by Sharon. He also wanted to stop constantly disappointing his wife.

But another part of him, by far the largest part, was bitterly sad that it had come to this. There would be no more shared experiences, and the children were going to suffer for their parents' shortcomings.

As the finality of the divorce hit him, hit him hard, Hood allowed the tears to flow.

THREE

Washington, D.C.
Sunday, 6:32 P.M.

Sixty-one-year-old First Lady Megan Catherine Lawrence paused before the late-seventeenth-century gilded pier mirror over a matching commode. She gave her short, straight, silver hair and ivory satin gown one last check before picking up her white gloves and leaving her third-floor salon. Satisfied, the tall, slender, elegant woman crossed the South American rug collected by President Herbert Hoover and entered the private presidential bedroom. The president's private dressing room was directly across from her. As she stepped out, she looked out at the lamp-lit white walls and light-blue Kennedy curtains, the bed that was first used by Grover and Frances Cleveland, the rocking chair where delicate, devoted Eliza Johnson awaited word of her husband Andrew's impeachment trial in 1868, and the bedside table where each night the seventh president, Andrew Jackson, would remove a miniature portrait of his dead wife from its place beside his heart, set it on the table next to her well-read Bible, and made certain that her face was the first thing he saw each morning.

As she looked out at the room, Megan smiled. When they first moved into the White House, friends and acquaintances would say to her, "It must be amazing having access to all the secret information about President Kennedy's missing brain and the Roswell aliens." She told them the secret was that there *was* no secret information. The only amazing thing was that, after nearly seven years of living in the White House, Megan still felt a thrill to be here among the ghosts, the greatness, the art, and the history.

Her husband, former Governor Michael Lawrence, had been president of the United States for one term when a series of stock market tumbles helped the moderate conservative lose a close election to Washington outsiders Ronald Bozer and Jack Jordan. Pundits said it was as much the family lumber fortune of the Oregon redwood that had made the president a target, since he was largely unaffected by the downturn. Michael Lawrence didn't agree, and he was not a quitter. Rather than become a token partner in some law firm or join the board of directors of his family corporation, the former president stayed in Washington, set up a nonpartisan think tank, American Sense, and was a hands-on manager. He used the next eight years to find ways to fix or fine-tune what he perceived had been wrong with his first term, from the economy to foreign policy to social programs. His think tank members did the Sunday morning talk show circuit, wrote op-ed pieces, published books, and gave speeches. With a weak incumbent vice president to run against, and a new vice president on his own ticket—New York Senator Charles Cotten—Michael Lawrence decisively won reelection. His popularity rating remained in the 60 percent region, and reelection was considered a fait accompli.

Megan crossed the room to the president's dressing

room. The door was shut, which was the only way to keep the bathroom warm, since draftiness came with the old walls and history. That meant her husband was probably still in the shower, which was surprising. Selected guests would be arriving at the second-floor study for a small, private half-hour cocktail reception at seven. Her husband usually liked to be ready fifteen minutes before that to sit with his thick personnel folder and review the likes, dislikes, hobbies, and family data of foreign guests. Tonight, he had the newly appointed acting ambassadors from Sweden and Italy coming up before a state dinner for key United Nations delegates. Their predecessors had been assassinated during the recent siege, and the replacements had been named quickly to show the world that terrorism could not stop the pursuits of peace and diplomacy. The president wanted a chance to meet the two men privately. After that, they'd go down to the Blue Room for a formal predinner reception with other influential United Nations delegates. Then it was on to the dinner itself, which was designed to show unity and support after the attack the previous week.

The president had come up shortly before six o'clock, which should have given him plenty of time to shower and shave. Megan couldn't understand what was keeping him. Perhaps he was on the phone. His staff tried to keep calls to the private residence to a minimum, but he'd been getting more and more calls over the past few days, sometimes in the small hours of the morning. She did not want to sleep in one of the guest bedrooms, but she wasn't a youngster anymore. Years ago, when they first started campaigning for public office, she used to be able to get by on two or three hours of sleep. No more. It had to be even worse on her husband. He was looking more tired than usual and desperately needed rest. The crisis at the United Nations had forced them to cancel a planned vacation in the northwest, and they had not been able to reschedule it.

The First Lady stopped by the six-panel door and listened. The shower was not running. Neither was the water in the sink. And it didn't sound as if he was on the phone.

"Michael?"

Her husband did not answer. She turned the bright brass handle and opened the door.

There was a narrow anteroom before the bathroom. In an alcove to the right was a stand-alone cherry wood wardrobe where the president's valet left his clothes for the day. In an alcove to the left was a matching cherry wood dressing table with a large, brightly lit wall mirror above it. The president was dressed in a royal blue bathrobe. He was standing there, breathing heavily, a look of rage in his narrow blue eyes. His fists were white-knuckle tight at his sides.

"Michael, are you all right?"

He glared at her. She had never seen him look so angry and—disoriented was the word that came to mind. It frightened her deeply.

"Michael, what *is* it?"

He looked back at the mirror. His eyes softened and his hands relaxed. His breathing came more easily. Then he slowly lowered himself into a walnut side chair in front of the dressing table.

"It's nothing," he said. "I'm fine."

"You don't look fine," she said.

"What do you mean?"

"A moment ago, you looked like you wanted to take a bite out of something," Megan told him.

He shook his head. "That was just leftover energy from my exercises," he said.

"Your exercises? I thought you were at a meeting before."

"I was just doing isometrics," he told her. "Senator Samuels does them for ten minutes every morning and evening. He says they're a great tension releaser when you can't get to the gym."

Megan did not believe him. Her husband perspired easily when he exercised. His forehead and upper lip were dry. Something else was happening here. He had seemed increasingly distant the past few days, and it was starting to scare her.

She stepped forward, coming to his side, and touched his face.

"Something's bothering you, hon," she said. "Talk to me."

The president looked at her. "It's nothing," he said. "These past couple of days have been rough, that's all."

"You mean the calls at night—"

"That, plus everything else that's going on," the president said.

"Is it worse than usual?"

"In some ways," he said.

"Do you want to talk about it?"

"Not right now," he said, forcing a little smile. His deep voice had regained some of its vigor and confidence, and his eyes had a little sparkle now. The president took her hands in his and rose. He stood just over six-foot-four. He looked down at her. "You look beautiful."

"Thank you," Megan said. "But you've still got me worried."

"Don't be," he said. He looked to his right. There was a shelf with a gold clock that had belonged to Thomas Jefferson. "It's late," the president said. "I'd better get ready."

"I'll wait for you," she told him. "And you'd better do something about your eyes."

"My eyes?" he said, glancing at the mirror. He'd gotten up even earlier than she had that morning, and his eyes were severely bloodshot. It was bad for an individual in a position of great responsibility to look weak or tired.

"I didn't sleep very well last night," he said, touching and tugging on the skin around them. "A few eyedrops will take care of that." The president turned back to his wife and kissed her gently on the forehead. "It's all right, I promise," he said, then smiled again and turned away.

Megan watched as her husband walked slowly toward the bathroom and shut the door. She heard him turn on the shower. She listened. Michael usually hummed rock and roll oldies when he showered. Sometimes he even sang. Tonight he was silent.

For the first time in a long time, Megan didn't believe what her husband had told her. No politician was entirely truthful on the outside. Sometimes they had to say what voters and political rivals wanted to hear. But Michael was an honest man on the inside, at least with Megan. When she looked into his eyes, she knew whether or not he was hiding something. When he was, Megan could usually coax him into telling her about it.

But not today, and that bothered her deeply. She was suddenly very scared for him.

Slowly, Megan walked back toward her own dressing room. She pulled on her gloves and tried to concentrate on what she had to do for the next four hours. She had to be an outgoing hostess. She had to be gracious and complimentary to the delegates' wives. At least she would be with people she didn't know. It was easier to hide her feelings when she was with strangers. They would not know that she was putting on an act.

But it *would* be an act.

Megan went back into the bedroom. There was a small, early-nineteenth-century mahogany Tambour writing cabinet on her side of the bed. She picked up a folder from her executive secretary and went over the guest list, paying particular attention to the names of the foreign delegates and their wives. There was a phonetic guide beside each name, and she reviewed the pronunciation aloud. The names came easily to the First Lady. She had an affinity for language and had planned on becoming a translator when she met and married her husband. Ironically, she had wanted to work for the United Nations.

Megan closed the folder and set it down. She looked around the room. The magic was still here, the lurking spirits and the resonance of great drama. But she was also acutely aware of something she didn't often feel here. Here, in a house that was literally watched by every eye in the world.

She suddenly felt a great sense of isolation.

FOUR

Baku, Azerbaijan
Monday, 2:47 A.M.

David Battat awoke slowly.

The sea air was chilly and becoming raw. David was lying on his belly, his face turned to the reeds in front of the water. There was cool moisture on his cheeks, condensation from the Caspian.

He tried to move, but his head felt as if it were made of concrete. His throat was raw, and his neck hurt. He touched it gently and winced. The skin was bruised and extremely sore. His camera was gone. The CIA team back in Moscow wouldn't be able to study the photographs he took to see who else might have been on the boat, or calculate how much weight it was carrying by where the waterline reached. Artillery and missiles weighed a lot more than explosives, currency, or drugs.

Battat tried to push himself off the ground. As he did, he felt as though a spike had been hammered through the back of his neck. He dropped, waited a few seconds, then tried again even more slowly. He managed to get his knees under him, then sat looking out across the dark water.

The *Rachel* was gone. He'd blown this big time. Like it or not, he'd have to let Moscow know as soon as possible.

Battat's head throbbed, and he lowered himself back to the ground. He rested on his forearms, placed his forehead on the cool earth, and tried to get a handle on the pain. He also tried to make sense of what had happened.

Why was he still alive? Battat wondered. The Harpooner had never let anyone live. Why him?

Then it occurred to him that maybe he went down before the Harpooner even arrived. Maybe some waterfront thug had happened by, saw his camera and backpack, and decided to steal them. Battat couldn't decide which was worse: letting his target sneak up on him or being mugged. Not that it mattered. They were both bad.

The operative took a long breath, then rose slowly, first to his knees again and then to his feet. He stood unsteadily as his head pounded. He looked around for his backpack. That was gone, too. No flashlight, no chance to look around for footprints or other clues.

He looked at his watch. His wrist was trembling, and he used his free hand to steady it. It would be dawn in less than three hours. Fishermen would be setting out soon, and Battat didn't want to be seen here. Just in case he wasn't meant to survive, he didn't want anyone to know that he had. He walked slowly from the shore, his head drumming. Each swallow was painful, and the collar of his turtleneck chafed his bruised neck.

But the worst pain was none of those.

The worst pain was the knowledge that he'd failed.

FIVE

Washington, D.C.
Sunday, 8:00 P.M.

As he entered the White House through the East Appointment Gate, Paul Hood remembered the first time he brought his children here. Hood had come to Washington for a conference of mayors. Harleigh was eight at the time, and Alexander was six. Alexander was not impressed by the imposing G. P. A. Healy painting of Abraham Lincoln or the magnificent Blue Room chairs bought by James Monroe or even the secret service officers. Alexander had seen paintings and chairs and police officers in Los Angeles. The spectacular chandelier in the State Dining Room was barely worth an upward glance, and the Rose Garden was just grass and flowers. But as they crossed the lawn toward E Street, the young boy finally saw something that impressed him.

Horse chestnuts.

The dark green chestnuts growing from the stout trees resembled nothing so much as little floating mines with Herz horns projecting from all sides. Alexander was convinced that they were little bombs to keep prowlers out. They'd bump their heads, and the chestnuts would explode. Alexander's father played along with the idea, even snatching a few of the chestnuts—carefully, of course—so they could plant them in the ground back at home. Harleigh finally busted her dad by stepping on one of the newly planted chestnuts and failing to blow up.

Sharon had never approved of the deception. She felt that it encouraged militarism. Hood felt that it was just a boy's imagination at work, nothing more.

It was rare that Paul Hood came to the White House without thinking of the horse chestnut trees. Tonight was no different, except that for the first time in years, Hood had the strong desire to go out back and pluck a few. Bring them to his son as a token, a memory of a good time shared. Besides, walking around the grounds would have been preferable to what he was doing.

He had dressed in his tuxedo, driven to the White House, and presented his calligraphic invitation at the East Appointment Gate. A junior secret service agent met Hood there and escorted him to the Red Room, which adjoined the State Dining Room. The president and First Lady were still in the Blue Room, which was the next room over. Though no one said so, the smaller Red Room—typically used for entertaining by the first ladies—was for the B-level guests.

Hood recognized but did not really know many of the people who were there. He knew some of them from conferences, some from briefings, and many from other dinners he attended here. The White House had two hundred fifty state dinners every year, and he was invited to at least fifteen of those. His background in Los Angeles government—which really meant knowing movie stars—finance, and espionage made him an ideal dinner guest. He could talk to generals, world leaders, diplomats, reporters, senators, and their spouses, informing and entertaining them and also not offending them. That was important.

Sharon usually came with him to those dinners. Being in the health-food business, she was generally unhappy with the fare, though she always loved the settings, which were from different administrations, different centuries. When Sharon couldn't make it, Op-Center's press liaison Ann Farris went with Hood. She liked any food that was put in front of her and, unlike Sharon, enjoyed talking to whoever she was seated with.

This was the first time Hood had come stag. Regardless of how the White House might try to position it, Hood did not consider Mala Chatterjee as his date. The UN secretary-general was also coming alone and was assigned a seat at Hood's table, directly to his left.

Hood opened the door and looked into the long, chandelier-lit dining room. Fourteen round tables had been brought into the dining room. Each one was set for ten people. Hood's invitation had said that he was seated at table two, near the center of the room. That was good. He was rarely seated so close to the president. If things got tense between him and Chatterjee, Hood would be able to exchange knowing glances with the First Lady. Megan Lawrence had been raised in Santa Barbara, California. She had spent time with Hood when he was mayor of Los Angeles, and they got to know each other quite well. She was a smart, classy lady with a dry sense of humor.

While senior staff members watched, liveried White House waitstaff hurried around, making last-minute adjustments to the rose centerpieces. They were dressed in black jackets and were multiethnic, which was to be expected at an affair of this kind.

The White House selected from a large pool of security-cleared hourly employees. And though no one liked to admit it, the composition of the staff was determined by the nature of the dinner. The young and attractive personnel were filling crystal water glasses and making sure the flatware was spaced exactly alike from setting to setting.

Straight ahead was the towering 1869 portrait of Abraham Lincoln that hadn't impressed Alexander. It was the only painting in the dining room. Directly across from him, inscribed on the mantel, was a passage written by John Adams to his wife Abigail before they moved into the newly completed executive mansion. Franklin Roosevelt had read the lines and liked them so much that they became the official White House prayer. The inscription read:

```
I pray Heaven to bestow the best of
blessings on this house and all
that shall hereafter inhabit it.
May none but honest and wise men
ever rule under this roof.
```

Sorry, Mr. Adams, Hood thought. *We managed to blow that one*.

One of the senior attendants walked over. Dressed in white trousers and a white waistcoat with gold braid, he politely but insistently shut the door. Hood stepped back into the Red Room. It had grown noisier and more crowded as people began filing in from the Blue Room.

He couldn't imagine what it was like in here before air-conditioning.

Hood happened to be facing the door to the Blue Room as Mala Chatterjee entered. She was on the arm of the president, who was followed by the First Lady and two delegates. The vice president and Mrs. Cotten came in next followed by California Senator Barbara Fox. Hood knew Fox well. She looked uncharacteristically confused. Hood didn't get to ask why. At almost exactly that moment, the door to the State Dining Room opened. There was no more rushing around inside the hall. The twenty members of the waitstaff were lined up along the northwest wall, while attendants stood in a row by the door to show guests to their tables.

Hood made no effort to link up with Chatterjee. She was an intense woman, and she seemed caught up in her conversation with the president. He turned and went back into the dining hall.

Hood watched as the glitterati entered beneath the golden light of the chandelier. There was something almost ghostly about the procession: people moving slowly, stiffly dignified, and without much expression; voices low and hollow in the echoing chamber, with only occasional polite laughter; chairs soundlessly lifted and moved by attendants so they didn't drag on the hardwood floor; and a sense that this scene had been repeated over and over throughout the years, throughout the centuries, with the same people: those who had power, those who wanted it, and people like Hood who were the buffers between them.

Hood took a sip of water. He wondered if divorce turned all men into cynics.

Chatterjee had left the president's side and was being shown to the table. Hood rose as the New Delhi native neared. The attendant pulled out her chair. The secretary-general thanked him and sat down. Without obviously ignoring Hood, the forty-three-year-old woman managed not to look at him. Hood had no patience for that.

"Good evening, Madam Secretary-General," Hood said.

"Good evening, Mr. Hood," she replied, still without looking at him.

Other people began arriving at the table. Chatterjee turned and smiled at Agriculture Secretary Richard Ortiz and his wife. That left Hood staring at the back of the secretary-general's head. He exited the awkward moment by reaching for his napkin, putting it on his lap, and looking the other way.

Hood tried to put himself in Chatterjee's position. The attorney-turned-diplomat had only been on the job for a short while when the terrorists struck. She had joined the United Nations as an avowed peacekeeper, and here were terrorists executing diplomats and threatening to shoot children. Chatterjee's negotiating tactics had failed, and Hood had embarrassed her publicly by infiltrating the Security Council and ending the crisis with quick, violent action. Chatterjee was further humiliated by the way many member nations loudly applauded Hood's attack.

But Hood and Secretary-General Chatterjee were supposed to be putting that ill will behind them, not nurturing it. She was an avowed advocate of first move détente, in which one party demonstrated trust by being the first to lay down arms or surrender land.

Or maybe she only believes in that when she advocates others to make the first move, Hood thought.

Suddenly, someone appeared behind Hood and spoke his name. He turned and looked up. It was the First Lady.

"Good evening, Paul."

Hood rose. "Mrs. Lawrence. It's good to see you."

"It's been too long," she said, taking his hand in hers and holding it tight. "I miss those Los Angeles fundraisers."

"We had fun," Hood said. "We made some history, and hopefully we did some good, too."

"I like to think so," the First Lady said. "How is Harleigh?"

"She took a very hard hit, and is having a rough time," Hood admitted.

"I can't even imagine," the First Lady said. "Who's working with her?"

"Right now, it's just Liz Gordon, our staff psych at Op-Center," Hood said. "Liz is getting a little trust going. Hopefully, in a week or two, we can bring in some specialists."

Megan Lawrence smiled warmly. "Paul, maybe there's something we can do to help each other. Are you free for lunch tomorrow?"

"Sure," he said.

"Good. I'll see you at twelve-thirty." The First Lady smiled, turned, and went back to her table.

That was strange, Hood thought. *"Maybe there's something we can do to help each other."* What could she possibly need his help for? Whatever it was, it must be important. A First Lady's social calendar was usually well-booked months in advance. She would have had to move her engagements around to make room for him.

Hood sat back down. The table had been joined by Deputy Secretary of State Hal Jordan and his wife Barri Allen-Jordan as well as two diplomats and their spouses who Hood did not know. Mala Chatterjee did not introduce him, so he introduced himself. The secretary-general continued to ignore him, even after the president rose at his table to offer a toast and say a few words about how he hoped this dinner and its show of unity would send a message to terrorists that the civilized nations of the world would never yield to them. As the White House photographer took pictures and a C-SPAN camera unobtrusively recorded the event from the southwest corner of the hall, the president underscored his faith in the United Nations by announcing officially, and to great applause, that the United States was about to retire its nearly two billion dollar debt to the United Nations.

Hood knew that paying off the debt had very little to do with terrorists. The United Nations didn't scare them, and the president knew it, even if Mala Chatterjee didn't. What the two billion dollars did was get the United States out of the doghouse with poor countries like Nepal and Liberia. With thawed economic relations in the Third World, we could then convince them to take loans with the provision that they buy American goods, services, and military intelligence. That would become a self-perpetuating source of income for American companies, even when other nations started putting money into those countries. That was the great thing about a government budgetary surplus and a politically expedient moment. When they came together, an administration could look benevolent and score points on the stock exchange.

Hood was only half listening to the speech when the president said something that drew him back in.

"Finally," the president said, "I am happy to inform you that American intelligence leaders are presently earmarking personnel and resources for a vital new initiative. It is their intention to work closely with governments around the world and guarantee that attacks against the United Nations cannot, do not, and *will not* happen again."

There was mild applause from tables where there were delegates. But the statement had caught Hood's attention because he knew something that the president apparently did not.

It wasn't true.

SIX

Hellspot Station, the Caspian Sea
Monday, 3:01 A.M.

The white Cessna U206F flew low over the dark Caspian Sea, its single engine roaring loudly. Its only occupants were a Russian pilot and the man seated beside him, an Englishman of average build and average appearance.

This trip had started out off the coast of Baku. After taking off, the seaplane had headed northeast and had traveled nearly two hundred miles in the past ninety minutes. It had been a smooth, quiet ride. Neither the pilot nor his passenger spoke a word the entire time. Though forty-one-year-old Maurice Charles spoke Russian—along with nine other languages—he did not know the pilot well and did not trust even those people he did know well. That was one reason he'd managed to survive as a mercenary for nearly twenty years.

When they finally arrived, all the pilot said was, "Below, four o'clock."

Charles looked out his window. His pale blue eyes fixed on the target. It was a beautiful thing. Tall, brightly lit, majestic.

And alone.

The semisubmersible offshore oil drilling platform stood approximately 150 feet above the water and was surrounded by sea. There was a helipad on the north side of the platform, a 200-foot-tall derrick beside it on the northwest side, and a network of tanks, cranes, antennae, and other equipment in the oil processing area.

The rig was like a lady standing on a deserted avenue under a streetlamp late at night by the Mersey back home. Charles could do what he wanted with it. And he would.

Charles picked up a camera that was sitting in his lap. He popped the button on the tan leather carrying case and removed the top. The camera was the same thirty-five-millimeter reflex that he had used in his first assignment, back in Beirut in April 1983. He began snapping pictures. A second camera, the one he had taken from the CIA operative on the beach, lay on the floor of the cabin between his feet along with the man's backpack. There might be names or numbers in there that would prove useful. Just like the operative himself would be useful, which was why Charles had left him alive.

The airplane circled the oil platform twice, once at 600 feet and once at 300 feet. Charles exposed three rolls of film, then indicated to the pilot that it was all right to leave. The seaplane swung back to its cruising altitude of 2000 feet and headed to Baku. There, Charles would rejoin the crew of the *Rachel*, which by now would have removed the white banner with the fake name. They had ferried him to the plane and would be his partners in the next part of the undertaking.

But that would only be the start. His employers in America had very specific goals, and the team Charles had put together were experts in achieving those goals:

turning neighbor against neighbor, nation against nation, through acts of terrorism and assassination. Before they were finished, the region would be awash in fire and blood from around the world.

And though he had already made a lot of money in the terrorist game, he had spent a lot of that wealth buying weapons, passports, transportation, anonymity. With this job, he would be richer than he had ever dared to imagine. And he had a fertile imagination.

When he was growing up in Liverpool, Charles had often dreamed about wealth and how he might obtain it. He thought about it when he swept the train station where his father sold tickets. He thought about it when he slept with his two brothers and grandfather in the living room of their one-bedroom flat, a flat that always smelled of perspiration and trash from the adjoining alley. He thought about it when he helped his father coach the local men's football team. The elder Charles knew how to communicate, how to strategize, how to win. He was a natural leader. But Maurice's father, his family, his working-class people were held down by the upper class. They were not permitted to go to the better schools, even if they could have afforded them. They weren't allowed to work in the upper levels of banking, of communications, of politics. They had funny, common accents and brawny shoulders and weather-beaten faces and weren't taken seriously.

Charles grew up feeling bad that the only outlet, the only joy his father had was football. Charles also idolized the Beatles because they had made it out—the same reason, ironically, his father and so many of his contemporaries hated "those young punks." Charles realized that he could not escape poverty musically because he had no talent for that and it had already been done. He had to get out his way, make a mark that was uniquely his own. How could he have known that he would find his hidden skills by joining the Royal Marines, 29 Commando Regiment, Royal Artillery, and learning to work with explosives? By discovering the pleasure and genius involved in tearing things down?

It was a glorious feeling to put events like this in motion. It was the creation of art: living, breathing, powerful, bleeding, changing, utterly unforgettable art. There was nothing else like it in the world, the aesthetics of destruction. And what was most rewarding was that the CIA had inadvertently helped him by sending that man to watch for him. The agency would conclude that it couldn't be the Harpooner who had attacked their man. No one had ever survived an encounter with the Harpooner.

Charles settled comfortably into his seat as the Cessna left the lights of the rig behind.

That was the beauty about being an artist, he told himself.

It gave him the right and privilege to surprise.

SEVEN

Camp Springs, Maryland
Monday, 12:44 A.M.

Throughout the Cold War, the nondescript two-story building located near the Naval Reserve flight line at Andrews Air Force Base was a staging area for pilots and their crews. In the event of a nuclear attack, their job would have been to evacuate key officials from the government and military to a safe compound in the Blue Ridge Mountains.

But the ivory-colored building with its neat, green lawn was not just a monument to the Cold War. The seventy-eight full-time employees who worked there now were employed by the National Crisis Management Center, familiarly known as Op-Center, an independent agency that was designed to collect, process, and analyze data on potential crisis points domestically and abroad. Once that was done, Op-Center then had to decide whether to defuse them preemptively through political, diplomatic, media, economic, legal, or psychological means or else—after gaining the approval of the Congressional Intelligence Oversight Committee—to terminate them through military means. To this end, Op-Center had at its disposal a twelve-person tactical strike team known as Striker. Led by Colonel Brett August, Striker was based at the nearby Quantico FBI Academy.

In addition to the offices upstairs, a secure basement had been built into the facility to house the more sensitive intelligence retrieval systems and personnel. It was here that Paul Hood and his top advisers worked.

Hood came directly from the White House affair. He was still dressed in his tuxedo, which earned him a "Good morning, Mr. Bond" greeting from the Naval officer at the gate. It made him smile. It was the only thing that had done that for days.

A strange uneasiness had settled over Hood after the president made his comments. He couldn't imagine *why* the president had said the United States would offer intelligence assistance to the United Nations. If there was one thing many member nations feared, it was that the United States was already using the international organization as a means of spying on them.

The president's short speech had pleased some people, most notably delegates who were targets for acts of terrorism. But it struck some other attendees as odd. Vice president Cotten appeared surprised, as did Secretary of State Dean Carr and America's United Nations Ambassador Meriwether. And Mala Chatterjee had been openly bothered by the comment. So much so that she'd actually turned to Hood and asked if she had understood the president correctly. He told her that he believed she had. What he didn't tell her was that Op-Center would almost certainly have been involved in or briefed about any such arrangement. Something might have been arranged during the time that he was away, but Hood doubted it. When he visited his office the day before to catch up on business he had missed, he saw no reference to a multinational intelligence effort.

Hood didn't bother talking to anyone after the dinner. He left promptly and went to Op-Center, where he did additional digging into the matter. This was the first time he had seen the weekend night crew since his return. They were glad to see him, especially weekend night director Nicholas Grillo. Grillo was a fifty-three-year-old former Navy SEAL intelligence expert who had moved over from the Pentagon around the same time Hood had first joined Op-Center. Grillo congratulated him on the fine job he and General Rodgers had done in New York and asked how his daughter was. Hood thanked him and told him that Harleigh would be all right.

Hood began by accessing the files of the DCI—the Director of Central Intelligence. This independent body was a clearinghouse of information for four other intelligence departments: the Central Intelligence Agency; Op-Center; the Department of Defense, which included the four branches of the military, the National Reconnaissance Office, the National Security Agency, and the National Imagery and Mapping Agency; and Department Intelligence, which consisted of the Federal Bureau of Investigation, the Department of State, the Department of Energy, and the Department of Treasury.

Once Hood was into the DCI database, he asked for recent agreements or initiatives pertaining to the United Nations. There were nearly five thousand listings. He eliminated those that did not involve intelligence-gathering for the United Nations and its members. That reduced the list to twenty-seven. Hood browsed those quickly. The last was filed a week before, a preliminary report about the failure of the CIA field office to catch Annabelle Hampton's terrorist-support activities in New York. Blame was placed on New York field office head David Battat and his supervisor in Washington, Deputy Assistant Director Wong. Wong was given a written warning, which was not entered into his record. Battat was given a sterner reprimand, which did not become part of his permanent dossier. But Battat would be hung out to dry for a while, doing what Bob Herbert had once described as "sewer rat-a-tat" jobs—dirty work in the line of fire. The kind of work that freshmen agents usually had to perform.

There was nothing about a United Nations operation involving any of the fourteen intelligence agencies. Given the new détente the president was trying to establish with the United Nations, it wasn't surprising that Lawrence would look for a way to help them. But presenting a desire or opportunity as a done deal was mystifying.

The president would have needed the cooperation of the head of at least one of these agencies just to undertake a *study* for such a proposition, and that wasn't anywhere in the files. There wasn't even any correspondence, electronic or otherwise, requesting such a study. The only answer Hood could think of was a handshake deal between the president and the CIA, FBI, or one of the other groups. But then one of those persons would have been there at tonight's dinner, and the only representative from the intelligence community was Hood. Perhaps the president was trying to force the issue, the way John F. Kennedy did when he announced, publicly, that he wanted Congress to give NASA the funds to put a man on the moon. But United States involvement in international intelligence-gathering was an extremely sensitive area. A president would be reckless to attempt a wide-ranging operation like this without assurances from his own team that it was possible.

It could all be the result of a series of misunderstandings. Maybe the president thought he had the support of the intelligence community. Confusion was certainly not uncommon in government. The question was what to do now that the idea had been presented to the world body. The United States intelligence community was sure to be torn. Some experts would welcome the opportunity to plug directly into resources in nations like China, Colombia, and several former Soviet republics where they currently had very restricted access. Others—Hood included—would be afraid of joining forces with other nations and being fed false data, data that would then become part of U.S. intelligence gospel with potentially disastrous results. Herbert once told him about a situation in 1978, just before the overthrow of the shah of Iran, when antiextremist forces provided the CIA with a code used by supporters of the Ayatollah Khomeini to communicate via telefax. The code was accurate—then. Once the ayatollah assumed power, the shah's files were raided, and the code was found to be in American hands. The code remained in the CIA's system and was used to interpret secret communiqués. It wasn't until the ayatollah's death in 1989—when the secret communiqués said he was recovering—that the CIA went back and took a close look at the code and the disinformation they'd received. Ten years of data had to be reviewed and much of it purged.

Hood could just imagine what Teheran would say about joining this new antiterrorism network. *"Sure, sign us up. And don't forget to use this new code to monitor the Sunni terrorists working out of Azerbaijan."* It could be a real code for real transmissions, or the Iranians could use false transmissions to create deeper mistrust of the Sunnis. The United States could not refuse to help them, because the president had offered; we could not trust the code; and yet what if it turned out to be real and we ignored it?

The whole thing was a potential for disaster. For his part, Hood intended to contact Burton Gable, the president's chief of staff, to find out what he knew about the situation. Hood didn't know Gable well, but he had been one of Lawrence's think tank geniuses and was instrumental in getting the president reelected. Gable hadn't been at the dinner, but there was no policy undertaking in which he was not involved.

Hood went back to the motel, napped, then was back at Op-Center at five-thirty. He wanted to be there when his staff arrived.

Hood had spoken to psychologist Liz Gordon about Harleigh, and to attorney Lowell Coffey about the divorce, so both of them knew he was coming back. Hood had also informed General Rodgers, who had let intelligence chief Bob Herbert know.

Herbert rolled in first. He had lost his wife and the use of his legs in the American embassy bombing in Beirut in 1983. But he had turned that setback into an advantage: Herbert's customized wheelchair was a mini–communications center with phone, fax, and even a satellite uplink that helped to make him one of the most effective intelligence collectors and analysts in the world.

Rodgers followed him in. Though the gray-haired officer had played a key role in ending the terrorist standoff at the United Nations, he was still recovering emotionally from the torture he'd suffered at the hands of Kurdish terrorists in the Middle East. Since his return, there hadn't been quite the same fire in his eyes or bounce in his walk. Though he hadn't broken, some proud, vital part of him had died in that cave in the Bekaa Valley.

Rodgers and Herbert were happy to see him. The two men stayed long enough to welcome him back and for Hood to brief them on what had happened at the state dinner. Herbert was blown away by what the president had said.

"That's like the Goodyear Blimp saying it's going to watch the stands for rowdy fans instead of watching the Super Bowl," Herbert said. "No one would believe that. No one."

"I agree," Hood said. "Which is why we've got to find out why the president said it. If he has a plan that we don't know about, we need to be brought into the loop. Talk to the other intel people and find out."

"I'm on it," Herbert said as he wheeled out.

Rodgers told Hood that he would get in touch with the heads of Army, Navy, Air Force, and Marine intelligence to find out what their knowledge of the situation was.

When Herbert and Rodgers left, Hood was visited by the only key members of the team who hadn't known about Hood's return, FBI and Interpol liaison Darrell McCaskey and press liaison Ann Farris. McCaskey was just back from a stay in Europe, working with his Interpol associates and nurturing a romance with Maria Corneja, an operative he had worked with in Spain. Hood had a good sense about people, and his instincts told him that Darrell would be handing in his resignation before long to return to Maria. Since McCaskey was gone while Hood's retirement was briefly in effect, he had not missed his boss.

Ann Farris was a different story. The five-foot, seven-inch-tall divorcée had always been close to Hood and had hated to see him leave. Hood knew that she cared for him, though no one could have told that just by looking at her. The thirty-four-year-old woman had developed the perfect poker face for reporters. No question, no revelation, no announcement made her jump. But to Hood, her large, dark-rust eyes were more articulate than any speech-maker or television moderator he had ever heard. And right now, her eyes were telling Hood that she was happy, sad, and surprised all at once.

Ann walked toward the desk. She was dressed in what she called her "uniform," a black pantsuit and white blouse with a pearl necklace. Her brown hair was shoulder length and held back from her face with a pair of clips. Hood's office was stripped of his personal touches. He hadn't had time to put the photographs and mementos back. Yet after the struggles with Sharon and the coldness of his hotel room, Ann's arrival suddenly made this place seem like home.

"Mike just told me," she said.

"Told you what?"

"About Sharon," Ann replied. "About your coming back. Paul, are you all right?"

"I'm a little banged up, but I'll be okay."

Ann stopped in front of the desk. *Was it only just ten days ago that she had stood there while I packed?* Hood thought. It seemed so much longer. Why did pain stretch time while happiness made it feel so short?

"What can I do, Paul?" Ann asked. "How are Sharon and the kids?"

"We're all reeling. Liz is helping Harleigh, Sharon and I are pretty civil, and Alexander is Alexander. He's okay." Hood dragged a hand through his wavy black hair. "As for what you can do, I just realized we're going to have to send out a press release about my return."

"I know." She smiled. "A head's-up *would* have been a big help."

"I'm sorry," Hood said.

"That's all right," Ann replied. "You had other things on your mind. I'll write something up and show it to you."

Ann looked down at him, her shoulder-length brown hair framing her angular features. Hood had always felt the sexual tension between them. Hell, he thought. Everyone around them did. Bob Herbert and Lowell Coffey used to tease Hood about it. Hood's unwillingness to give in to that tension had always kept Ann at a distance. But he could feel that distance closing.

"I know you have a lot to do," Ann said, "but if you need anything, I'm here. If you want to talk or don't want to be by yourself, don't be shy. We go back quite a few years."

"Thanks," Hood said.

Ann's eyes held him for a long moment. "I'm sorry for what you and your family are going through, Paul. But you've done an amazing job here, and I'm glad you're back."

"It's good to be back," Paul admitted. "I think that frustrated me more than anything else."

"What did?" she asked.

"Not being able to finish the work I started," he said. "It may sound corny, but the teamwork of exceptional men and women built this nation. Op-Center is a part of that tradition. We have a great team here doing important work, and I hated leaving that."

Ann continued to look at him. She seemed to want to say something more but didn't. She stepped back from the desk.

"Well, I've got to get to work on the press release," she said. "Do you want me to say anything about the situation with Sharon?"

"No," Hood said. "If anyone wants to know, tell them. Otherwise, just say I had a change of heart."

"That's going to make you sound wishy-washy," she said.

"What the *Washington Post* thinks isn't going to affect my job performance," he said.

"Maybe not now," Ann said. "But it might if you ever decide to run for public office again."

Hood looked at her. "Good point," he said.

"Why don't we tell them that the president asked you to return?" she said.

"Because he didn't," Hood said.

"You two had a private meeting when you came back from New York," she said. "He won't deny asking you

to return. It shows loyalty on his part. Everyone benefits."

"But it isn't true," Hood said.

"Then let's just say this," Ann said. "After meeting
with the president, you decided to reconsider your resignation. That's true."

"You really want to get the president in there."

"Whenever I can," Ann said. "It gives us weight."

"Weight?" Hood said. "You mean suction."

"Excuse me?"

"Nick Grillo said that the word-de-jour is *suction*."

"Actually, that's not quite right," Ann informed him.
"*Weight* is when someone has credibility. *Suction* is
when they have considerable influence. There's a difference."

"I see," Hood said. They smiled at each other. Hood
looked away. "I'd better get to work," he said. "There's
a lot of catching up to do."

"I'm sure," Ann said. "I'll e-mail you a copy of the
press release before it goes out."

"Thanks again," Hood said. "For everything."

"Sure." Ann hesitated. She looked at Hood for a long
moment more and then left.

Hood turned to the computer monitor on his right. He
did not want to watch Ann go. Ann Farris was a beautiful, intelligent, very sexual woman. For the five years
they had known each other, they had flirted, she more
openly than he. Now that Hood was going to be single,
he felt uneasy about continuing the game. There was no
longer someone between them. Flirting no longer felt
like a game.

But Hood did not have time to think about that now.

There *was* a lot to do. He had to review the daily briefings that had gone to Mike Rodgers during the past
week, which included intelligence data collected from
around the world as well as ongoing covert operations.
He also had to look at reports from the rest of the staff
and have a glance at the schedule for the upcoming week
before he went to see the First Lady. He noticed that
Rodgers was going to be interviewing the final candi-
dates to replace Martha Mackall, the political liaison
who had been assassinated in Spain, as well as candi-
dates for the new post of economic adviser. With more
and more nations linked together financially—"Siamese
megatuplets" was how Lowell Coffey had put it—politics was becoming a troublesome sideshow to the force
that really drove the world.

Hood decided to let Mike make those hires. Not only
had he started the process, but Hood was going to be
too busy with everything else. But with all that was going on, one thing remained true.

Paul Hood loved this work, this place.

It was good to be back.

EIGHT

Baku, Azerbaijan
Monday, 4:00 P.M.

Azerbaijan is a nation in flux.

Because of political conflict in the Nagorno-Karabakh region, twenty percent of the country—mostly in the southwest, along the borders with Armenia and Iran— are occupied by rebel forces. Though a cease-fire has been observed since 1994, firefights occur with some regularity. Privately, diplomats fear that the self-proclaimed Republic of Nagorno-Karabakh will become the next Kosovo. Protests, often violent, erupt in Baku and other cities without warning. Some of them pertain to politics, others to general unrest. Since the breakup of the Soviet Union, there has been an extreme shortage of staples such as medical supplies, produce, and new technology. Cash—preferably U.S. dollars—is the only form of exchange recognized in most areas of the country, including the capital.

The United States has managed to openly support the legitimate government of Azerbaijan without alienating the powerful insurgent forces. Loans have been granted to Baku, while goods have been sold directly to "the people"—primarily the rebels. In the event of widespread revolt, the United States wants to have open lines of communication on both sides.

Maintaining that balance is the primary task of the small American embassy. Since March 1993, the fifteen employees and ten marine guards have operated from a small stone building at 83 Azadlig Prospect. In the back of that building, in a windowless, wood-paneled room, is the Department of News Services. Unlike the small press department, which issues news releases and arranges for interviews and photo ops with U.S. congressmen, senators, and other government leaders, officially the job of the DNS is to collect news clippings from around Russia and keep them on file for reference.

Officially.

In fact, the DNS is staffed by one CIA operative who gathers intelligence from around the nation. Most of the information comes from electronic surveillance that is conducted both from the office via satellite and from vans. Some of it comes from personnel who are paid to watch, listen to, and photograph government officials— sometimes in compromising situations. Some of those situations are also arranged by the DNS.

Because he was hurt, David Battat did not want to attempt returning to Moscow. Instead, he made his way to the embassy on foot. He was taken to see Deputy Ambassador Dorothy Williamson, who brought in Senior Researcher Tom Moore. Williamson was a large woman with curly black hair. Battat guessed her to be about forty. Moore was a lean giant in his thirties with a long, gaunt face and a lugubrious expression. If Battat had to be stranded in Baku, his expression would be gloomy as well.

Williamson's aide was a smart veteran named Ron

Friday. He was the only one who gave Battat an encouraging smile. Battat appreciated that.

While Battat gave Moore a quick rundown on what had happened, Williamson had the Marine medic take a look at Battat's wounds. There was swelling in his throat and traces of blood in his saliva, though the damage did not appear to be serious. When the medic was finished with him, Battat was taken to the DNS room. He was given privacy while he called Moscow. He spoke to Pat Thomas, the assistant director of public information at the embassy. Thomas was also an OTR—off the record—field director for the CIA. That meant there was no record of him at agency headquarters. His reports were delivered directly to Washington in the diplomatic pouch.

Thomas did not take the news well. If Battat had succeeded in identifying the Harpooner, Thomas would have been a hero. Instead, he would have to explain to his counterpart in Baku and his superior in Washington how they had managed to blow the relatively simple job of surveillance.

Thomas said that he would think about their next step and let him know. Food was brought in. Battat ate, even though he had left his appetite back at the beach, along with his self-esteem, his energy, the mission, and his career. Then he sat in a chair resting until Williamson and Moore arrived for a second, more thorough, conversation. Moore looked grim. This was going to be painful.

Acoustic devices planted in the walls caused conversations to sound like static to the electronic eavesdropping devices that the Azerbaijanis had placed on surrounding buildings.

Battat told them that Moscow had suspected the Harpooner was in Baku, and he had been sent to try and identify him. This news did not meet with the approval of the senior researcher.

"The field office in Moscow obviously didn't feel it was necessary to involve us in this operation," Moore complained. "Do you want to tell me why?"

"They were afraid that our target might have people watching the embassy," Battat said.

"Not all of our people are *in* the embassy," Moore pointed out. "We have external resources."

"I understand," Battat said. "But Moscow felt that the fewer people who were in the loop, the better our chances of surprising the target."

"Which didn't really help, did it?" Moore said.

"No."

"Whoever attacked you obviously knew you were coming."

"Apparently, though I don't understand how," Battat said. "I was well hidden, and I wasn't using anything that gave out an electronic pulse. The camera was one of the digital seventies. No flash, no glass in front to reflect light, no moving parts that clicked."

"Couldn't this Harpooner or his people have done a routine sweep of the shore?" the deputy ambassador asked.

"I was watching for that," said Battat. "I got to the site early, at a spot we'd selected through satellite imaging. We chose it specifically so that I could see and hear people coming and going."

"Then why didn't you see or hear the goddamned assailant coming?" asked Moore.

"Because they hit me just when something started to happen out on the boat I was watching," he said. "Someone came from below and turned on a radio. It was a perfect distraction."

"Which suggests that someone knew you were in that spot, Mr. Battat," Moore said.

"Probably."

"Possibly even before you got there," Moore went on.

"I don't see how, but I can't rule it out," Battat agreed.

"What I really want to know, though, is whether this was even the Harpooner," Moore went on.

"What do you mean?" the deputy ambassador asked.

"The Harpooner has been a terrorist for over two decades," Moore told her. "He has personally run or been a part of at least fifteen terrorist strikes that we know of and probably many more that we don't know about. He's eluded countless efforts to trap him thanks, in large part, to his ability to stay mobile. He has no permanent address that we know of, hires whoever he needs, and rarely uses the same people twice. We only know what he looks like because one of his arms suppliers once snuck a photo to us. The supplier's body was found a few months later on a sailboat, slit from chin to belly with a fish-gutting knife—*after* we'd relocated him and given him a new ID."

"I see," the deputy ambassador said.

"He left the knife behind," Moore said. "He always leaves his weapons behind, from spearguns to bowline stirrups."

"Sea-related things," said Williamson.

"Often," Moore said. "We suspect he was in the naval service somewhere—not a big leap of faith, though we haven't been able to trace him. But in all that time, the Harpooner never left a witness. Which means that either it wasn't the Harpooner who attacked Mr. Battat or the Harpooner wanted him alive."

The deputy ambassador regarded Battat. "For what reason?"

"I can't think of one," Battat admitted.

The three were silent for a moment. The only sound was the hum of the air vent.

"Mr. Battat, the presence of a man like the Harpooner in this region could have terrible ramifications for all of us," said the deputy ambassador.

"Which is another reason why we should have been in the loop on this!" Moore said angrily. "Hell, we *know* who the undercover guys are that are watching us, and they haven't been around for days. They're too busy trying to find a Russian spy who slipped out of jail two days ago."

"Again, I'm sorry," said Battat.

"Would you mind staying in Baku while we try to make sense of all this?" the deputy ambassador asked.

"Not at all," said Battat. "I want to help."

"Hopefully, it's not too late for that," Moore said.

They rose. "What about the *Rachel?*" Battat asked.

"I've sent a small plane out to look for it," Moore told him. "But they've had several hours head start, and God knows which direction they went. I'm not optimistic."

"Can't you trace the name?" Battat asked. "Isn't there a local registry?"

"There is," Moore told him, "and the *Rachel* isn't in

it. We're checking records in Dagestan, Kalmyk, and other republics on the Caspian, but my guess is she's a rogue."

Moore showed Battat to a small guest room on the second floor of the building. There was a cot in the corner, and Battat lay down to think. The boat, the music they played, the brief glimpse he had of the man on deck—he replayed the sounds and images over and over, looking for more information. Something that might tell him who the crew of the *Rachel* were, how they were dressed, or where they might have come from. In SD sessions—subconscious debriefing—trained interviewers would walk agents through experiences to help them remember lost details. The interviewers would ask about the color of the sky, the look of the water, the force of the wind and the smells riding it. Once the agent was reimmersed in the scene, the interviewer would move him around, ask him to describe distinctive markings on the hull of the boat or whether there were banners on the stern or mast or sounds coming from the deck or below. It always surprised Battat how much information the brain stored that was not always immediately accessible.

Though Battat closed his eyes and breathed slowly and deeply and went through the SD checklist, he could not remember anything that brought him closer to whoever was on the boat or from what direction his assailant might have come. He could not even remember the feel of the fabric on the arm that had been choking him or the smell of the man who had attacked him. He couldn't remember if the man's cheek had touched him and whether he was bearded or clean-shaven. Battat had been too focused on trying to survive.

Battat's eyes remained shut. They stopped looking into the past and gazed ahead. He would stay in Baku, but not just because the deputy ambassador had asked. Until Battat found whoever had attacked him, his confidence was broken and his life belonged to them.

Which, he realized, could be why he was left alive.

NINE

Washington, D.C.
Monday, 11:55 A.M.

It had always amazed Hood how different Washington looked during the daytime. At night, the white facades were brightly lit and appeared to stand alone, shining with Olympian grandeur. In the day, situated between modern office buildings, vending carts, and glossy restaurant logos, beneath loud and ever-present jet traffic and security barricades of concrete and steel, the landmarks seemed almost antique instead of timeless.

Yet both were Washington. They represented an old, increasingly monolithic bureaucracy that had to be dealt with, and a vision of greatness that could not be ignored or diminished.

Hood parked in the Ellipse on the southern side of the grounds. He crossed E Street and walked up East Executive to the East Appointment Gate. He was buzzed through the iron gate and, after passing through a metal detector, waited inside the East Wing for one of the First Lady's aides.

Of all the landmarks in Washington, Hood had always been partial to the Capitol. For one thing, it was the guts of the government, the place where Congress put wheels on the president's vision. They were often square wheels or wheels of different sizes, but nothing could move without them. For another thing, the building itself was a vast museum of art and history, with treasures everywhere. Here a plaque indicating where the desk of Congressman Abraham Lincoln was located. There a statue of General Lew Wallace, the onetime governor of the territory of New Mexico and the author of *Ben-Hur*. Somewhere else a sign indicating the status of the search for the cornerstone of the building, which was laid over two hundred years before in a little-noted ceremony and was somehow buried and then lost under numerous modifications to the foundation.

The White House wasn't as imposing as the Capitol. It was a much smaller structure, with peeling paint and warping wood on the exterior. But its grounds and columns, its rooms and many familiar angles were intertwined in American memory with images of great leaders doing great things—or, sometimes, infamous, very human things. It would always be the symbolic heart of the United States.

A young male assistant to the First Lady arrived. He brought Hood to the elevator that led to the third floor. Hood was somewhat surprised that the First Lady wanted to see him upstairs. She had an office on the first floor and typically received visitors there.

Hood was taken to the First Lady's sitting room, which adjoined the presidential bedroom. It was a small room with a main door that led to the corridor and another, he assumed, that opened into the bedroom. There was a gold settee against the far wall, two matching wing chairs across from it, and a coffee table between them. A tall secretary with a laptop sat on the opposite wall. The Persian rug was white, red, and gold; the drapes were white, and they were drawn. A small chandelier threw bright shards of light around the room.

Hood looked at the two portraits on the wall. One was of Alice Roosevelt, daughter of Theodore. The other was a painting of Hannah Simpson, mother of Ulysses S. Grant. He was wondering why they were here when the First Lady entered. She was dressed casually in beige slacks and a matching sweater. Her aide shut the door behind her, leaving the two of them alone.

"Nancy Reagan found them in the basement," Megan said.

"I beg your pardon?"

"The portraits," she said. "She found them personally. She hated the idea of women being left to gather dust."

Hood smiled. They embraced lightly, and then Megan gestured toward the settee.

"There are still wonderful things down there," Megan said as they sat. "Furnishings, books, documents, *things* like Tad Lincoln's writing slate and a diary that belonged to Florence Harding."

"I thought most of that memorabilia was in the Smithsonian."

"A lot of it is. But many of the family-related things are still here. People have gotten jaded by all the scandals over the years," Megan said. "They forget how much the White House was and is a home. Children were born and raised here, there were weddings, birthdays, and holidays."

Coffee arrived, and Megan was silent as it was served. Hood watched her as the White House steward quietly and efficiently set out the silver service, poured the first cup, then left.

The passion in Megan's voice was exactly as Hood remembered. She never did anything she didn't care deeply about, whether it was addressing a crowd or advocating greater education spending on TV talk shows or discussing the White House with an old friend. But there was something in her expression he had never seen before. The old enthusiasm stopped short of her eyes. When he looked in them, they seemed frightened. Confused.

Hood picked up his cup, took a sip of coffee, then turned to Megan.

"I appreciate your coming," the First Lady said. Her cup and saucer were on her lap, and she was looking down. "I know you're busy and that you have problems of your own. But this isn't just about me or the president, Paul." She looked up. "It's about the nation."

"What's wrong?" Hood asked.

Megan breathed deeply. "My husband has been behaving strangely over the last few days."

Megan fell silent. Hood didn't push her. He waited while she drank some of her coffee.

"Over the past week or so, he's been more and more distracted," she said. "He hasn't asked about our grandson, which is very unusual. He says that it's work, and maybe it is. But things got very strange yesterday." She regarded Hood intently. "This remains between us."

"Of course."

Megan took a short, reinforcing breath. "Before the dinner last night, I found him sitting at his dressing table. He was running late. He wasn't showered or dressed. He was just staring at the mirror, flushed and looking as though he'd been crying. When I asked him about it, he said he'd been exercising. He told me that his eyes were bloodshot because he hadn't been sleeping. I didn't believe him, but I let it be. Then, at the predinner reception, he was flat. He smiled and was pleasant, but there was no enthusiasm in him at all. Until he received a phone call. He took it in his office and returned about two minutes later. When he came back, his manner was entirely different. He was outgoing and confident."

"That's certainly how he seemed at dinner," Hood said. "When you say the president was flat, what exactly do you mean?"

Megan thought for a moment. "Do you know how someone gets when they're really jet-lagged?" she asked. "There's a glassiness in their eyes and a kind of delayed reaction to whatever is said?"

Hood nodded.

"That's exactly how he was until the call," Megan said.

"Do you know *who* called?" Hood asked.

"He told me it was Jack Fenwick."

Fenwick was a quiet, efficient man who had been the president's budget director in his first administration. Fenwick had joined Lawrence's American Sense think tank, where he added intelligence issues to his repertoire. When the president was reelected, Fenwick was named the head of the National Security Agency, which was a separate intelligence division of the Department of Defense. Unlike other divisions of military intelligence, the NSA was also chartered to provide support for nondefense activities of the Executive Branch.

"What did Fenwick tell the president?" Hood asked.

"That everything had come together," she told Hood. "That was all he would say."

"You have no idea who or what that is?"

Megan shook her head. "Mr. Fenwick left for New York this morning, and when I asked his assistant what the phone call was about, she said something very strange. She asked me, 'What call?'"

"Did you check the log?"

Megan nodded. "The only call that came into that line at that time was from the Hay-Adams Hotel."

The elegant old hotel was located on the other side of Lafayette Park, literally across the street from the White House.

"I had a staff member visit the hotel this morning," Megan went on. "He got the names of the night staff, went to their homes, and showed them pictures of Fenwick. They never saw him."

"He could have come in a back entrance," Hood said. "Did you run a check of the registry?"

"Yes," she said. "But that doesn't mean anything. There could have been any number of aliases. Congressmen often use the hotel for private meetings."

Hood knew that Megan wasn't just referring to political meetings.

"But that wasn't the only thing," Megan went on. "When we went downstairs to the Blue Room, Michael saw Senator Fox and went over to thank her. She seemed very surprised and asked *why* he was thanking her. He said, 'For budgeting the initiative.' I could see that she had no idea what he was talking about."

Hood nodded. That would explain the confusion he had noticed when Senator Fox entered the room. Things were beginning to fall into place a little. Senator Fox was a member of the Congressional Intelligence Oversight Committee. If any kind of intelligence operation had been approved, she would have to have known about it. Apparently, she was as surprised to learn about the international intelligence-sharing operation as Hood had been. Yet the president either assumed or had been told, possibly by Jack Fenwick, that she had helped make it happen.

"How was the president after the dinner?" Hood asked.

"That's actually the worst of it," Megan said. Her composure began to break. She set her coffee cup aside and Hood did likewise. He moved closer. "As we were getting ready for bed, Michael received a call from Kirk Pike."

The former chief of Navy Intelligence, Pike was the newly appointed director of the CIA.

"He took the call in the bedroom," Megan went on. "The conversation was brief, and when Michael hung up, he just sat on the bed, staring. He looked shell-shocked."

"What did Pike tell him?"

"I don't know," Megan told him. "Michael didn't say. It may have been nothing, just an update that got his mind working. But I don't think he slept all night. He wasn't in bed when I got up this morning, and he's been in meetings all day. We usually talk around eleven o'clock, even if it's just a quick hello, but not today."

"Have you talked to the president's physician about this?" Hood asked.

Megan shook her head. "If Dr. Smith can't find anything wrong with my husband, he might recommend that Michael see Dr. Benn."

"The psychiatrist at Walter Reed," Hood said.

"Correct," Megan said. "Dr. Smith and he work closely together. Paul, you know what will happen if the president of the United States goes to see a psychiatrist. As much as we might try to keep something like that a secret, the risks are much too high."

"The risks are higher if the president isn't well," Hood said.

"I know," Megan said, "which is why I wanted to see you. Paul, there are too many things going on that don't make sense. If there's something wrong with my husband, I'll insist that he see Dr. Benn and to hell with the political fallout. But before I ask Michael to submit to that, I want to know whether something else is going on."

"Glitches in the communications system or a hacker playing tricks," Hood said. "Maybe more Chinese spies."

"Yes," Megan said. "Exactly."

He could see Megan's expression, her entire mood, lighten when he said that. If it were something from the outside, then it could be fixed without hurting the president.

"I'll see what I can find out," Hood promised.

"Quietly," Megan said. "Please, don't let this get out."

"I won't," Hood assured her. "In the meantime, try and talk to Michael. See if you can get him to open up somehow. Any information, any names other than what you've told me, will be a big help."

"I'll do that," Megan said. She smiled. "You're the

only one I can trust with this, Paul. Thank you for being there."

He smiled back. "I get to help an old friend and my country. Not a lot of people get that chance."

Megan rose. Hood stood, and they shook hands. "I know this is not an easy time for you, either," the First Lady said. "Let me know if there's anything *you* need."

"I will," Hood promised.

The First Lady left, and her aide returned to show Hood out.

TEN

Baku, Azerbaijan
Monday, 9:21 P.M.

Pat Thomas experienced two miracles in one day.

First, the Aeroflot TU-154 that was scheduled to leave Moscow at six P.M. did so. On time. With the possible exception of Uganda Royal Airways, Aeroflot was the most notoriously late carrier Thomas had ever flown on. Second, the airplane landed in Baku at 8:45 P.M.—five minutes ahead of schedule. During his five years of service at the American embassy in Moscow, Thomas had never experienced either of those events. What was more, despite a relatively full aircraft, the airline had not double- or triple-booked his seat.

The slim, nearly six-foot-tall, forty-two-year-old Thomas was assistant director of public information at the embassy. What the title of ADPI really meant was that Thomas was a spy: a diplomatic private investigator was how he viewed the acronym. The Russians knew that, of course, which was the reason one or two Russian agents always shadowed Thomas in public. He was certain that someone in Baku would be waiting to tail him as well. Technically, of course, the KGB was finished. But the personnel and the infrastructure of the intelligence operation were still very much in place and very much in use as the Federal Security Service and other "services."

Thomas was dressed in a three-piece gray winter suit that would keep him warm in the heavy cold that always rolled in from the Bay of Baku. Thomas knew he would need more than that—strong Georgian coffee or even stronger Russian cognac—to warm him after the reception he expected to receive at the embassy. Unfortunately, keeping secrets from your own people was part of the spy business, too. Hopefully, they would vent a little, Thomas would act contrite, and everyone could move on.

Thomas was met by a staff car from the embassy. He didn't rush tossing his single bag in the trunk. He didn't want any Russian or Azerbaijani agents thinking he was in a hurry. He paused to pop a sucker into his mouth, stretched, then climbed into the car. Be boring. That was the key when you thought you were being watched. Then, if you had to speed up suddenly, chances were good you might surprise and lose whoever was trailing you.

It was a thirty-minute drive from Baku International Airport to the bay-side region that housed the embassies and the city's commercial district. Thomas never got to spend more than a day or two at a time here, though that was something he still meant to do. He had been to the local bazaars, to the Fire Worshipper's Temple, to the State Museum of Carpets—a museum with a name like that demanded to be seen—and to the most famous local landmark, the Maiden Tower. Located in the old Inner City on the bay and at least two thousand years old, the eight-story tower was built by a young girl who either wanted to lock herself inside or throw herself into the sea—no one knew for certain which version was true. Thomas knew how she felt.

Thomas was taken to see Deputy Ambassador Williamson, who had returned from dinner and was sitting behind her desk, waiting for him. They shook hands and exchanged a few banal words. Then she picked up a pen and noted the time on a legal pad. Moore and Battat came to her office moments later. The agent's neck was mottled black and gunmetal gray. In addition to the bruises, he looked exhausted.

Thomas offered Battat his hand. "Are you all right?"

"A little banged up," Battat said. "I'm sorry about all this, Pat."

Thomas made a face. "Nothing's guaranteed, David. Let's see how we can fix it."

Thomas looked at Moore, who was standing beside Battat. The men had met several times at various Asian embassy conferences and functions. Moore was a good man, what they called a twenty-four/seven—an agent who lived and ate his work twenty-four hours a day, seven days a week. Right now, Moore was making no attempt to conceal his dark, unforgiving mood.

Thomas extended his hand. Moore accepted it.

"How have you been?" Thomas asked.

"That isn't important," Moore said. "I'm not happy now. There was no reason for this to go down the way it did."

"Mr. Moore, you're correct," Thomas said as he released his hand. "In retrospect, we should have done this all differently. The question is, how do we fix it now?"

Moore sneered. "You don't get off that easily," he

said. "Your team mounted a small operation here and didn't tell us. Your man says you were worried about security risks and other factors. What do you think, Mr. Thomas—that the Azerbaijani are wet-wired into the system? That we can't conduct a surveillance without them finding out?"

Thomas walked to an armchair across from Williamson. "Mr. Moore, Ms. Williamson, we had a short time to make a quick decision. We made a bad one, a wrong one. The question is, what do we do now? If the Harpooner is here, can we find him and stop him from getting away?"

"How do we bail you out, you mean?" Moore asked.

"If you like," Thomas conceded. Anything to get this out of reverse and moving ahead.

Moore relaxed. "It isn't going to be easy," he said. "We've found no trace of the boat Mr. Battat says he saw, and we have a man watching the airport. No one who fits the description of the Harpooner has left today."

"What about working backward?" Thomas said. "Why would the Harpooner be in Baku?"

"There are any number of targets a terrorist for hire could hit," Moore said. "Or he may just have been passing through on his way to another republic or to the Middle East. You know these people. They rarely take a direct route anywhere."

"If Baku was just a layover, the Harpooner is probably long gone," Thomas said. "Let's concentrate on possible targets in the region and reasons for hitting those targets."

"The Nagorno-Karabakh and Iran are our biggest concerns," Williamson said. "The people in NK have voted themselves an independent republic, while Azerbaijan and Armenia are both fighting to claim it. The whole region will probably explode when Azerbaijan gets enough money to buy more advanced weapons for its military. That would be bad enough for both nations, but with Iran just fifteen miles to the south, it could end up being quite an explosion. As for Iran, even without the NK situation, Teheran and Baku have been gnawing at each other for years over access to everything from offshore oil to Caspian sturgeon and caviar. When the Soviet Union watched over the Caspian, they took what they wanted. And not only are there problems, but the problems overlap," Williamson added. "Sloppy drilling by Azerbaijan has caused a quarter-inch-thick oil film in parts of the sea where Iran fishes for sturgeon. The pollution is killing the fish."

"What is the oil situation, exactly?" Thomas asked.

"There are four major oil fields," Williamson said. "Azeri, Chirag, Guneshli, and Azerbaijan. Azerbaijan and the Western Consortium members that underwrite the drilling are convinced that international law protects their exclusive rights to the sites. But their claim is based on boundaries that are defined by fishing rights, which both Iran and Russia insist do not apply. So far, the arguments have all been diplomatic."

"But if someone perpetrated a new action somewhere," Thomas said, "such as an embassy explosion or an assassination—"

"There could be a disastrous chain reaction reaching into a half-dozen surrounding nations, affecting oil supplies worldwide, and drawing the United States into a major foreign war," Williamson said.

Moore added sarcastically, "That's why we like to be kept informed about covert actions in our backward little outpost."

Thomas shook his head. "*Mea culpa*. Now, can we all agree to look ahead instead of back?"

Moore regarded him for a moment, then nodded.

"So," Williamson said, looking down at her notes. "As I understand this, there are two possible scenarios. First, that the individual who attacked Mr. Battat was not the Harpooner, in which case we may have nothing more than a drug smuggler or gunrunner on our hands. One who managed to get the drop on Mr. Battat and then slip away."

"Correct," said Thomas.

"What are the chances of that?" Williamson asked.

"They're unlikely," Thomas said. "We know that the Harpooner is in the region. An official from the Department of State Bureau of Intelligence and Research was on a Turkish Airlines flight from London to Moscow and made a tentative ID of the Harpooner. He tried to follow the target but lost him."

"You're saying an INR guy and the world's most wanted terrorist just happened to be on the same flight?" Moore said.

"I can't speak for the Harpooner, only for the DOS official," Thomas replied. "But we're finding that more and more terrorists and spies take the diplomatic routes. They try to pick up intel from laptops and phone calls. DOS has issued several alerts about that. Maybe it was a coincidence; maybe there was a diskette or phone number the Harpooner wanted to try and steal when the official went to the rest room. I don't know."

"The official was able to identify the Harpooner based on what?" Williamson asked.

"The only known photograph," Thomas told him.

"It was a good picture, reliable," Moore assured her.

"We were notified and did some checking," Thomas went on. "It fit with some intel we had picked up independently. The passenger was traveling under an assumed name with a fake British passport. We checked taxi records, found that he had been picked up at the Kensington Hilton in London. He'd only been there for one night, where he met with several people who, according to the concierge, looked and sounded Middle Eastern. We tried to track the individual in Moscow, but no one saw him leave the terminal. So we checked flights to other areas. Someone matching his description had shown a Russian passport in the name of Gardner and flown to Baku."

"It *is* the Harpooner's boat," Deputy Ambassador Williamson said suddenly. "It has to be."

The others looked at her.

"You've heard of it?" Thomas asked.

"Yes. I went to college," Williamson said. "Gardner is the captain of the *Rachel* in *Moby-Dick*. It's one of the ships that was chasing the elusive white whale. She failed to capture him, I might add."

Thomas regarded Battat unhappily. "The Harpooner," Thomas said. "Dammit. Of course. He planted that for us to find."

"Now, there's a smart terrorist," Moore said. "If you recognize the allusion, you would have thought it a joke and wouldn't have bothered to pursue. If you thought it was real, then the Harpooner knew just where you'd be looking for him. And he would be there, waiting to stop you."

"But the boat *was* real," Battat said. "I saw the name—"

"A name that was put there to hold your attention for a while," Thomas said. "Shit. We fell for that one, big time."

"Which brings us to the second and suddenly very likely scenario," Williamson said. "If the Harpooner has been in Baku, there are two things we need to find out pretty damn quick. First, what he wanted and second, where he is now. Is that about right?"

Thomas nodded.

Moore rose. "I'm betting he's no longer using the Russian passport. I'll get into the hotel computers and check the names of the guests against our passport registry database. See if any new names pop up."

"He may also be working with people here, in which case he may not be staying at a hotel," Thomas said.

"I'll give you a list of known or suspected foreign cells," Moore told him. "You and Mr. Battat can cross-check those with people the Harpooner might have worked with before."

Battat said he would do that.

"There's one other thing we should try," Thomas said. "We pretty much tapped out our Moscow-based sources on this before Mr. Battat came down. It wasn't very productive, but that was all we had time for. What about other governments in the region?"

"We haven't made any significant intelligence inroads with any of them," the deputy ambassador admitted. "We don't have the personnel to nurse the relationships, and a lot of the republics, including Azerbaijan, have had their resources strained with internal problems.

Everyone is busy spying on each other, especially on Chechnya."

"Why there?" Battat asked.

"Because despite the coalition government that exists on paper, Chechnya is really controlled by Islamic militias intent on destabilizing and bringing down the other republics, including Russia," she said. "I'm hoping that the initiative the president announced last night in Washington will remedy that."

"What initiative?" Battat asked.

"An intelligence cooperative with the United Nations," Moore told him. "He announced it last night in Washington."

Battat rolled his eyes.

"You know, there *is* one place we might be able to try," Thomas said. "A couple of years ago I remember hearing that the National Crisis Management Center was involved with a Russian group based in Saint Petersburg."

"A Russian crisis management group," Moore said. "Yeah, I remember hearing about that."

"I can call Washington and have them contact Op-Center," Moore said. "See if they still have a relationship with the Russians."

"When you do, have them contact Bob Herbert over there," Thomas suggested. "He's the head of intelligence—a really capable guy from what I hear. I understand that the new guy running the place, General Rodgers, is something of a hard-ass."

"He's not running Op-Center," the deputy ambassador said.

"Who is?" asked Thomas.

"Paul Hood," said the deputy ambassador. "We got a directory update this morning. He withdrew his resignation."

Moore snickered. "I'll bet he won't be involved in the UN intelligence program."

"Regardless," Thomas said, "have them contact Herbert. The Harpooner may try to slip out of the region by heading north, into Scandanavia. If he does, the Russians may be able to help us up there."

Thomas agreed. Everyone rose then, and Thomas offered his hand to the deputy ambassador. "Thank you for everything," Thomas said. "I'm truly sorry about all this."

"So far, no real harm has been done."

"We're going to see that it stays that way," Thomas said.

"I'll have a room prepared for the two of you," Williamson said. "It's not fancy, but it's a place to crash."

"Thanks," Thomas said. "But until we find our man, I have a feeling I won't be getting a lot of sleep."

"None of us will, Mr. Thomas," Williamson assured him. "If you'll excuse me, Ambassador Small is due back from Washington at ten P.M. He'll want to be briefed on this as soon as possible."

Thomas left and walked down the corridor to Moore's office. The ADPI hated having lost the Harpooner. But he also hated the fact that the bastard was probably laughing at them for taking the whale bait. He also wondered if the Harpooner might somehow have known that Battat had come from Moscow. Maybe that was why he'd let the agent live, to create conflict between the CIA office in Moscow and Baku. Or maybe he did it just to confuse them, have them waste time wondering why he hadn't killed Battat.

Thomas shook his head. *Your mind is all over the damn place*, he chided himself. *Stop it. You've got to focus.* But that was going to be tough, Thomas knew, because the Harpooner was obviously a man who liked to keep his trackers off balance by mixing games with reality.

And so far, he was doing a helluva job.

ELEVEN

Washington, D.C.
Monday, 3:00 P.M.

The cell phone rang in the office of the red-haired man. He shooed out two young assistants who closed the door behind them. Then he swiveled his chair so the high leather back was facing the door. He looked out the window, drew the cell phone from his inside jacket pocket, and answered on the fifth ring. If the phone had been stolen or lost and someone answered before that, the caller had been instructed to hang up.

"Yes?" the red-haired man said softly.

"He's completed phase one," said the caller. "Everything is exactly on schedule."

"Thank you," said the red-haired man and clicked off. He immediately punched in a new number. The phone was answered on the fifth ring.

"Hello?" said a gravelly voice.

"We're on track," said the red-haired man.

"Very good," said the other.

"Anything from Benn?" asked the red-haired man.

"Nothing yet," said the other. "It will come."

The men hung up.

The red-haired man put the phone back in his jacket pocket. He looked out across his desk and the office beyond. The photographs with the president and foreign heads of state. The commendations. A seven-by-ten-inch American flag that had been given to him by his mother. The red-haired man had carried it, folded, in his back pocket during his tour of duty in Vietnam. It was framed on the wall, still creased and soiled with sweat and mud, the lubricants of combat.

As the red-haired man called his two aides back to the office, the ordinary nature of that act, the return of routine, underscored the extreme and complex nature of what he and his partners were undertaking. To remake the international political and economic map was one thing. But to do it quickly, in a stroke such as this, was unprecedented.

The work was daunting, and it was exciting. If the operation ever were to become publicly known, it would be considered monstrous by some. But to many, so were the American Revolution and the Civil War in their day. So was the involvement of the United States in World War II, before Pearl Harbor. The red-haired man only hoped that if their actions were ever revealed, people would understand *why* they had been necessary. That the world in which the United States existed was radically different from the world into which the United States had been born. That in order to grow it was sometimes necessary to destroy. Sometimes rules, sometimes lives.

Sometimes both.

TWELVE

Camp Springs, Maryland
Monday, 3:14 P.M.

Paul Hood called Senator Fox after returning from the White House. She admitted being totally confused by the president's remarks and had put in a call to him to talk about it. Hood asked her to hold off until after he had had a chance to review the situation. She agreed. Then Hood called Bob Herbert. Hood briefed the intelligence chief on his conversation with the First Lady, after which he asked Herbert to find out what he could about the phone call from the hotel and whether anyone else had noticed any odd behavior from the president. Because Herbert stayed in touch with so many people—never asking them for anything, just seeing how they were doing, what the family was up to—it was easy for him to call and slip in important questions among the chitchat without making it seem as though he were fishing.

Now the two men were back in Hood's office. But the Herbert who wheeled through the door was different than before.

"Is everything all right?" Hood asked.

The usually outgoing Mississippi native didn't answer immediately. He was extremely subdued and staring ahead at something only he could see.

"Bob?" Hood pressed.

"They thought they had him," Herbert said.

"What are you talking about?"

"A friend of mine at the CIA slipped me some news from the embassy in Moscow," Herbert said.

"Why?"

Herbert took a long breath. "Apparently, they had a solid lead that the Harpooner was in Baku."

"Jesus," Hood said. "What for?"

"They don't know," Herbert said. "And they lost him. They sent one freakin' guy to do the recon and—surprise!—he got clocked. I can't blame them for wanting to be low profile, but with a guy like the Harpooner, you have to have backup."

"Where is he now?" Hood asked. "Is there anything we can do?"

"They don't have a clue where he went," Herbert said. He shook his head slowly and swung the computer monitor up from the armrest. "For almost twenty years what I've wanted most out of life is to be able to hold the bastard's throat between my hands, squeeze real hard, and look into his eyes as he dies. If I can't have that, I want to know that he's decaying in a hole somewhere with no hope of ever seeing the sun. That's not a lot to ask for, is it?"

"Considering what he did, no," Hood said.

"Unfortunately, Santa's not listening," Herbert said bitterly. He angled the monitor so he could see it. "But enough about that son of a bitch. Let's talk about the president."

Herbert shifted in his seat. Hood could see the anger

in his eyes, in the hard set of his mouth, in the tense movements of his fingers. "I had Matt Stoll check the Hay-Adams phone log."

Matt Stoll was Op-Center's computer wizard.

"He hacked into the Bell Atlantic records," Herbert said. "The call came from the hotel, all right, but it didn't originate in any of the rooms. It originated in the system itself."

"Meaning?"

"Meaning someone didn't want to be *in* one of the rooms where they might have been seen coming or going," Herbert said. "So they got to the wires somewhere else."

"What do you mean 'got' to them?" Hood asked.

"They hooked in a modem to transfer a call from somewhere else," Herbert said. "It's called *dial-up hacking*. It's the same technology phone scammers use to generate fake dial tones on public phones in order to collect credit card and bank account numbers. All you need to do is get access to the wiring at some point in the system. Matt and I brought up a blueprint of the hotel. The easiest place to do that would have been at the phone box in the basement. That's where all the wiring is. But there's only one entrance, and it's monitored by a security camera—too risky. Our guess is that whoever hacked the line went to one of the two public phones outside the Off the Record bar."

Hood knew the bar well. The phones were right beside the door that opened onto H Street. They were in closetlike booths and there were no security cameras at that spot. Someone could have slipped in and gotten away without being seen.

"So, with the help of a dial-up hacker," Hood said, "Jack Fenwick could have called the president from anywhere."

"Right," Herbert told him. "Now, as far as we can tell, the First Lady is correct. Fenwick's in New York right now, supposedly attending top-level meetings with UN ambassadors. I got his cell phone number and called several times, but his voice mail picked up. I left messages for him to call me, saying it was urgent. I left the same message at his home and office. So far, I haven't heard from him. Meanwhile, Mike and I checked with the other intel departments. The president's announcement was news to each of them. Only one of them was involved in this cooperative effort with the United Nations."

"The National Security Agency," Hood said.

Herbert nodded. "Which means Mr. Fenwick must have sold the president some bill of goods to convince him they could handle this operation solo."

Herbert was correct, though in one way the National Security Agency would have been the perfect agency to interface with new intelligence partners. The primary functions of the NSA are in the areas of cryptology and both protecting and collecting signals intelligence. Unlike the CIA and the State Department, the NSA is not authorized to maintain undercover personnel on foreign soil. Thus, they do not generate the kind of knee-jerk paranoia that would make foreign governments nervous about cooperating with them. If the White House was looking for an intel group to pair with the United Nations, the NSA was it. What *was* surprising, though, was that the president didn't brief the other agencies.

And he should have at least notified Senator Fox. The Congressional Intelligence Oversight Committee is directly responsible for approving programs of counter-proliferation, counterterrorism, counternarcotics, counterintelligence, and covert activites abroad. What the president had proposed certainly fell under their jurisdiction.

But because the NSA *does* operate independently, and in very specific areas, it's also the least-equipped to organize and oversee a massive undertaking of the kind described by the president. That was the reason Hood didn't believe Lawrence when he announced the initiative at the dinner. It was why a large part of him still didn't believe it.

"Did you talk to Don Roedner about this?" Hood asked. Roedner was the Deputy National Security Adviser, second in command to Fenwick.

"He's with Fenwick, and I couldn't get him on the phone either," Herbert told him. "But I did talk to Assistant Deputy National Security Adviser Al Gibbons. And this is where things get a little weirder. Gibbons said that he was present at an NSA meeting on Sunday afternoon where Fenwick didn't mention a goddamn thing about a cooperative intelligence effort with other nations."

"Was the president at that meeting?"

"No," Herbert said.

"But just a few hours later, Fenwick called the president and apparently told him that they had an intelligence deal with several foreign governments," Hood said.

Herbert nodded.

Hood considered that. It was possible that the UN initiative was on a need-to-know basis and that Gibbons wasn't part of that loop. Or maybe there was a bureaucratic struggle between different divisions of the NSA. That wouldn't have been unprecedented. When Hood first came to Op-Center, he studied the pair of 1997 reports that had effectively authorized the creation of Op-Center. Report 105-24 issued by the Senate Select Committee on Intelligence and 105-135 published by the House Permanent Select Committee on Intelligence— the two arms of the Congressional Intelligence Oversight Committee—both proclaimed that the intelligence community was extremely top-heavy with "*intramural struggles, waste, and uninformed personnel lacking depth, breadth, and expertise in political, military, and economic analysis*," as the SIC report summed it up. Congressional reports didn't get much rougher than that. When Op-Center was chartered by act of Congress, Hood's mandate had been to hire the best and the brightest while the CIA and other intelligence groups worked on cleaning house. But the current situation was unusual, even by intelligence community standards, if the NSA's senior staff didn't know what was going on.

"This whole thing just doesn't make sense," Herbert said. "Between Op-Center and the CIA, we already have official cooperative intelligence plans with twenty-seven different nations. We have intelligence relationships with eleven other governments unofficially, through connections with high-ranking officials. Military intelligence has their hands in seven other nations. Whoever talked the president into this wants their own discreet, dedicated intelligence line for a reason."

"Either that, or they wanted to embarrass him," Hood said.

"What do you mean?"

"Sell him a project, tell him it's been cleared with other agencies and foreign governments, and then have him make a big public stumble."

"Why?"

"I don't know," Hood said.

He didn't, but he didn't like where this was leading him. Op-Center had once run a psy-ops game called Alternate Reality on how to make Saddam Hussein so paranoid that he would turn on his most trusted advisers. What if a foreign government were doing something like that to the president?

It was a far-fetched idea, but so was the KGB killing a dissident by poking him with a poisoned umbrella, and the CIA attempting to slip Fidel Castro a poison cigar. Yet these things had happened.

Then there was another option he didn't want to consider: that it wasn't a foreign government but our own. It was possible.

It could also be less sinister than that. The First Lady said her husband wasn't himself. What if she was right? Lawrence had spent four tough years in the White House and then eight tough years winning it back. Now he was in the hot seat again. That was a lot of pressure.

Hood was aware of several presidents who had showed signs of breaking during extended periods of stress: Woodrow Wilson, Franklin Roosevelt, Richard Nixon, and Bill Clinton. In the case of Nixon, his closest advisers encouraged him to resign not just for the health of the nation but for his own mental well-being. With Clinton, the president's staff and friends decided not to bring in doctors or psychiatrists but to keep a careful watch and *hope* he came through the impeachment crisis. He did.

But in at least two cases, allowing the president to carry the full burden of decision making and politicking was not the best policy. Wilson ended up with a stroke trying to push the League of Nations through Congress. And toward the end of World War II, burdened by the pressure of winning the war and drawing up plans for a postwar world, Roosevelt's closest advisers feared for his health. Had they impressed on him the absolute need to slow down, he might not have died of a cerebral hemorrhage.

Any of those scenarios could be correct, or they could all be dead wrong. But Hood had always believed that it was better to consider every option, even the least likely, rather than be surprised. Especially when the result of being right could be cataclysmic. He would have to proceed carefully. If he could get to see the president, he would have an opportunity to lay his few cards on the table and also observe Lawrence, see whether Megan's concerns had merit. The worst that could happen was the president would ask for his resignation. Fortunately, he still had his last one on file.

"What are you thinking?" Herbert asked.

Hood reached for the telephone. "I've got to see the president."

"Excellent," Herbert said. "Straight ahead has always been my favorite way, too."

Hood punched in the president's direct line. The phone beeped at the desk of his executive secretary, Jamie Leigh, instead of going through the switchboard. Hood asked Mrs. Leigh if she could please squeeze him in for a few minutes somewhere. She asked him for a log line for the calendar to let the president know what this was about. Hood said that it had to do with Op-Center having a role in the United Nations intelligence program.

Mrs. Leigh liked Hood, and she arranged for him to see the president for five minutes, from four-ten to four-fifteen.

Hood thanked her then looked at Herbert. "I've got to get going," Hood said. "My appointment's in forty minutes."

"You don't look happy," Herbert said.

"I'm not," Hood said. "Can we get someone to nail down who Fenwick is meeting in New York?"

"Mike was able to connect with someone at the State Department when you two were up there," Herbert said.

"Who?"

"Lisa Baroni," Herbert told him. "She was a liaison with the parents during the crisis."

"I didn't meet her," Hood said. "How did Mike find her?"

"He did what any good spymaster does," Herbert said. "When he's someplace new, he looks for the unhappy employee and promises them something better if they deliver. Let's see if she can deliver."

"Good," Hood said as he rose. "God. I feel like I do whenever I go to Christmas Eve Mass."

"And how is that?" Herbert asked. "Guilty that you don't go to church more often?"

"No," Hood replied. "I feel like there's something going on that's much bigger than me. And I'm afraid that when I figure out what that is, it's going to scare the hell out of me."

"Isn't that what church is supposed to be about?" Herbert asked.

Hood thought about that for a moment. Then he grinned as he left the office. "Touché," he said.

"Good luck," Herbert replied as he wheeled out after him.

THIRTEEN

Gobustan, Azerbaijan
Monday, 11:56 P.M.

Gobustan is a small, rustic village located forty-three miles south of Baku. The region was settled as far back as 8000 B.C. and is riddled by caves and towering outcroppings of rock. The caves boast prehistoric art as well as more recent forms of expression—graffiti left two thousand years ago by Roman legionnaires.

Situated low in the foothills, just beneath the caves, are several shepherds' shacks. Spread out over hundreds of acres of grazeable land, they were built early in the century and most of them remain in use, though not always by men tending their flocks. One large shack is hidden behind a rock that commands a view of the entire village. The only way up is along a rutted dirt road cut through the foothills by millennia of foot traffic and erosion.

Inside, five men sat around a rickety wooden table in the center of the small room. Another man sat on a chair by a window overlooking the road. There was an Uzi in his lap. A seventh man was still in Baku, watching the hospital. They weren't sure when the patient would arrive, but when he did, Maurice Charles wanted his man to be ready.

The window was open, and a cool breeze was blowing

in. Except for the occasional hooting of an owl or rocks dislodged by prowling foxes in search of field mice, there was silence outside the shack—the kind of silence that the Harpooner rarely heard in his travels around the world.

Except for Charles, the men were stripped to their shorts. They were studying photographs that had been received through a satellite uplink. The portable six-inch dish had been mounted on the top of the shack, which had an unobstructed view of the southeastern sky and the GorizonT3. Located 35,736 kilometers above twenty-one degrees twenty-five minutes north, sixty degrees twenty-seven minutes east, that was the satellite the United States National Reconnaissance Office used to keep watch on the Caspian Sea. Charles's American contact had given him the restricted web site and access code, and he had downloaded images from the past twenty-four hours.

The decoder they used, a StellarPhoto Judge 7, had also been provided by Charles's contact through one of the embassies. It was a compact unit roughly the size and configuration of a fax machine. The SPJ 7 printed photographs on thick sublimation paper, a slick, oil-based sheet that could not be faxed or electronically transmitted. Any attempt to do so would be like pressing on a liquid crystal display. All the receiver would see was a smudge. The unit provided magnification with a resolution of ten meters. Combined with infrared lenses on the satellite, he was able to read the numbers on the wing of the plane.

Charles smiled. His plane was on the image. Or rather, the Azerbaijani plane that they had bought.

"Are you certain the Americans will find that when they go looking for clues?" asked one of the men. He was a short, husky, swarthy man with a shaved head and dark, deep-set eyes. A hand-rolled cigarette hung from his downturned lips. There was a tattoo of a coiled snake on his left forearm.

"Our friend will make sure of it," Charles said.

And they would. That was the reason for staging this attack on the Iranian oil rig. Once the incident occurred, the United States National Reconnaissance Office would search the satellite database of images from the Guneshli oil region of the Caspian. Surveillance experts would look back over the past few days to see who might have been reconnoitering near the rig. They would find the images of Charles's plane. Then they would find something else.

Shortly after the attack, a body would be dropped into the sea—the body of a Russian terrorist, Sergei Cherkassov. Cherkassov had been captured by Azerbaijan in the NK, freed from prison by Charles's men, and was presently being held on the *Rachel*. Cherkassov would be killed shortly before the attack, shot with a shell from an Iranian-made Gewehr 3 rifle. That was the same kind of bullet that would have been fired by security personnel on the rig. When the Russian's body was found— thanks to intelligence that would be leaked to the CIA—the Americans would find photographs in the terrorist's pockets: the photographs Charles had taken from the airplane. One of those photographs would show portions of the airplane's wing and the same numbers seen in the satellite view. Another of the photographs would have markings in grease pencil showing the spot that particular terrorist was supposed to have attacked.

With the satellite photographs and the body of the terrorist, Charles had no doubt that the United States and the rest of the world would draw the conclusion that he and his sponsors wanted them to draw.

The wrong one.

That Russia and Azerbaijan had united to try to force Iran from its lucrative rigs in Guneshli.

FOURTEEN

New York, New York
Monday, 4:01 P.M.

The State Department maintains two offices in the vicinity of the United Nations Building on New York's East Side. One is the Office of Foreign Missions and the other is the Bureau of Diplomatic Security.

Forty-three-year-old attorney Lisa Baroni was the assistant director of diplomatic claims for the Diplomatic Liaison Office. That meant whenever a diplomat had a problem with the United States' legal system, she became involved. A legal problem could mean anything from an allegedly unlawful search of a diplomat's luggage at one of the local airports, or a hit-and-run accident involving a diplomat, to the recent seizure of the Security Council by terrorists.

Ten days before, Baroni had been on hand to provide counsel for diplomats but found herself giving comfort to parents of children who were held hostage during the attack. That was when she'd met General Mike Rodgers. The general talked with her briefly when the siege was over. He said he was impressed by the way she had remained calm, communicative, and responsible in the midst of the crisis. He explained that he was the new head of Op-Center in Washington and was looking for good people to work with. He asked if he could call her and arrange an interview. Rodgers had seemed like a no-nonsense officer, one who was more interested in her talent than her gender, in her abilities more than in the length of her skirt. That appealed to her. So did the prospect of going back to Washington, D.C. Baroni had grown up there, she had studied international law at Georgetown University, and all her friends and family still lived there. After three years in New York, Baroni could not wait to get back.

But when General Rodgers finally called, it was not quite the call Baroni had been expecting.

It came early in the afternoon. Baroni listened as Rodgers explained that his superior, Paul Hood, had withdrawn his resignation. But Rodgers was still looking for good people and offered her a proposition. He had checked her State Department records and thought she would be a good candidate to replace Martha Mackall, the political officer who had been assassinated in Spain. He would bring her to Washington for an interview if she would help him with a problem in New York.

Baroni asked if the help he needed was legal. Rodgers assured her it was. In that case, Baroni told him, she would be happy to help. That was how relationships were forged in Washington. Through back-scratching.

What Rodgers needed, he explained, was the itinerary of NSA Chief Jack Fenwick who was in New York for meetings with United Nations delegates. Rodgers said he didn't want the published itinerary. He wanted to know where Fenwick actually ended up.

That should have been relatively easy for Baroni to find. Fenwick had an office in her building, and he usually used it when he came to New York. It was on the seventh floor, along with the office for the secretary of state. However, Fenwick's New York deputy said that he wasn't coming to the office during this trip but was holding all of his meetings at different consulates.

Instead, Baroni checked the file of government-issued license plates. This listing was maintained in the event of a diplomatic kidnapping. The NSA chief always rode in the same town car when he came to New York. Baroni got the license number and asked her friend, Detective Steve Mitchell at Midtown South, to try to find the car on the street. Then she got the number of the car's windshield-mounted electronic security pass. The ESP enabled vehicles to enter embassy and government parking garages with a minimum of delay, giving potential assassins less time to stage ambushes.

The ESP didn't show up on any of the United States checkpoints, which were transmitted immediately to State Department security files. That meant that Fenwick was visiting foreign embassies. Over one hundred nations also transmitted that data to the DOS within minutes. Most of those were close U.S. allies, such as Great Britain, Japan, and Israel. Fenwick had not yet gone to visit any of them. She used secure e-mail to forward to Rodgers the information where Fenwick hadn't been.

Then, just after four P.M., Baroni got a call from Detective Mitchell. One of his squad cars spotted the chief

of staff's car leaving a building at 622 Third Avenue.
That was just below Forty-second Street. Baroni looked
up the address in her guide to permanent missions.

The occupant surprised her.

FIFTEEN

Washington, D.C.
Monday, 4:03 P.M.

Paul Hood arrived at the west wing of the White House at four o'clock. Even before he had finished passing through the security checkpoint, a presidential intern had arrived to show him to the Oval Office. Hood could tell he had been here at least several months. Like most seasoned interns, the freshly scrubbed young man had a slightly cocky air. Here he was, a kid in his early twenties, working at the White House. The ID badge around his neck was his trump card with women at bars, with chatty neighbors on airplanes, with brothers and cousins when he went home for the holidays. Whatever anyone else said or did, he was interacting with the president, the vice president, cabinet, and congressional leaders on a daily basis. He was exposed to real power, he was plugged into the world, and he was moving past the eyes and ears of all media where the expressions and casual utterances of even people like him could cause events that would ripple through history. Hood remembered feeling a lot of that when he was a kid working in the Los Angeles office of the governor of California. He could only imagine how much more extreme it was for this kid, the sense of being at the center of the universe.

The Oval Office is located at the far southeast corner

of the West Wing. Hood followed the young man in silence as they made their way through the busy corridors, passed by people who did not seem at all self-important. They had the look and carriage of people who were very late for a plane. Hood walked past the office of the national security adviser and the vice president, then turned east at the vice president's office and walked past the office of the press secretary. Then they turned south past the cabinet room. They walked in silence all the while. Hood wondered if the young man wasn't speaking to him because the kid had a sense of propriety or because Hood wasn't enough of a celebrity to merit talking to. Hood decided to give him the benefit of the doubt.

The office past the cabinet room belonged to Mrs. Leigh. She was seated behind her desk. Behind it was the only door that led to the Oval Office. The intern excused himself. Hood and the president's tall, white-haired secretary greeted each other with smiles. Mrs. Leigh was from Texas, with the steel, poise, patience, and dry, self-effacing humor required for the guardian of the gate. Her husband was the late Senator Titus Leigh, a legendary cattleman.

"The president's running a few minutes late," Mrs. Leigh said. "But that's all right. You can tell me how you are."

"Coping," Hood said. "And you?"

"Fine," she replied flatly. "My strength is the strength of ten because my heart is pure."

"I've heard that somewhere," Hood said as he continued toward the secretary's desk.

"It's Lord Tennyson," she replied. "How is your daughter?"

"She's strong, too," Hood said. "And she has an awful lot of people pulling for her."

"I don't doubt that," Mrs. Leigh said, still smiling. "Let me know if there's anything I can do."

"I absolutely will," Hood said. He looked into her gray eyes. "There is something you can do for me, though."

"And that is?"

"Off the record?"

"Of course," she assured him.

"Mrs. Leigh, has the president seemed all right to you?" Hood asked.

The woman's smile wavered. She looked down. "Is that what this meeting is about?"

"No," Hood said.

"What makes you ask a question like that?"

"People close to him are worried," Hood said.

"And you're the one who's been asked to bell the cat?" she asked.

"Nothing that calculated," Hood said as his cell phone beeped. He reached into his jacket pocket and answered the phone.

"This is Paul."

"Paul, it's Mike."

"Mike, what's up?" If Rodgers was calling him here, now, it had to be important.

"The target was seen leaving the Iranian mission to the UN about three minutes ago."

"Any idea where he was the rest of the time?" Hood asked.

"Negative," said Rodgers. "We're working on that. But apparently, the car didn't show up at the embassies of any of our top allies."

"Thanks," Hood said. "Let me know if you find out anything else."

Hood hung up. He put the phone back in his pocket. That was strange. The president had announced an intelligence initiative involving the United Nations, and one of the first missions the national security adviser visits belongs to Iran. As a sponsor of the kind of terrorism the United Nations opposed, that did not make sense.

The door to the Oval Office opened.

"Mrs. Leigh, would you do me a favor?" Hood said.

"Yes."

"Would you get me Jack Fenwick's itinerary in New York?"

"Fenwick? Why?"

"He's one of the reasons I asked you the question I did," Hood replied.

Mrs. Leigh looked at Hood. "All right. Do you want it while you're with the president?"

"As soon as possible," Hood said. "And when you get the file number, let me know what else is in the file. I don't need specific documents, just dates when they were filed."

"All right," she said. "And Paul—what you asked before? I have noticed a change."

He smiled at her. "Thanks. If there's a problem, we're going to try and fix it quickly and quietly, whatever it is."

She nodded and sat at her computer as the

vice president emerged from the Oval Office. Charles Cotten was a tall, stout man with a thin face and thinning gray hair. He greeted Paul Hood with a warm handshake and a smile but didn't stop to talk. Mrs. Leigh punched the phone intercom. The president answered. She told him that Paul Hood was here, and the president asked her to send him in. Hood went around the desk and walked into the Oval Office.

SIXTEEN

Baku, Azerbaijan
Tuesday, 12:07 A.M.

David Battat lay on the flimsy cot and stared at the dark ceiling of the damp basement storehouse. Pat Thomas slept on his back in a cot on the other side of the small room, breathing softly, regularly. But Battat couldn't sleep.

His neck still ached, and he was angry at himself for having gotten cold-cocked, but that wasn't what was keeping him awake. Before going to sleep, Battat had reviewed the original data the CIA had received about the Harpooner. He could not put it out of his mind. All signs, including a reliable eyewitness, pointed to it having been the terrorist that was being met by the *Rachel*. And if that were so, if the Harpooner had passed through Baku on his way to somewhere else, Battat was deeply troubled by one question: *Why am I still alive?*

Why would a terrorist with a reputation for scorched-earth attacks and homicidal behavior leave an enemy alive? To mislead them? To make them think it wasn't the Harpooner who was there? That had been his initial reaction. But maybe the terrorist had left him alive for another reason. And Battat lay there, trying to figure out what that reason could be.

The only reason he could think of would be to carry

misinformation back to his superiors. But he had not carried any information back, other than what was already known: that the *Rachel* was where it was supposed to be. And without knowing who got on or where it went, that information did them no good.

Battat's clothes had been gone over carefully for an electronic bug or a radioactive tracer of some kind. Nothing had been found, and the clothes were subsequently destroyed. If one had been located, it would have been used to spread disinformation or to misdirect the enemy. Moore had gone through Battat's hair, checked under his fingernails, looked in his mouth and elsewhere for a microtransmitter that could be used to locate Battat or eavesdrop on any conversations he might have. Nothing had been found.

There wasn't a damn thing, he thought. And it gnawed at him because he didn't think this was a screw-up. He was alive for a reason.

He shut his eyes and turned on his side. Thinking about this while he was dead tired would get him nowhere. He had to sleep. He forced himself to think about something pleasant: what he would do when he found the Harpooner.

The thought relaxed him. As he lay there, Battat began to feel warm. He attributed that to the poor ventilation in the room and the distress he was feeling over everything that had happened.

A few minutes later, he was asleep.

A few minutes after that, he began to perspire.

A few minutes after that, he was awake and gasping for breath.

SEVENTEEN

Washington, D.C.
Monday, 4:13 P.M.

The president was writing on a white legal pad when Hood entered. The president told Hood to have a seat; he needed to make a few notes before they talked. Hood quietly shut the door behind him and walked toward a brown leather armchair in front of the desk. He turned off his cell phone and sat down.

The president was dressed in a black suit and silver and black striped tie. A rich yellow light gleamed off the panes of bulletproof glass behind the president. Beyond it, the Rose Garden looked rich and alive. Everything seemed so right here, so healthy and normal, that for a moment Hood doubted himself.

But only for a moment. Hood's instincts got him where he was; there was no reason to start doubting them now. Besides, the battle was always somewhere else, never in the command tent.

The president finished writing, put down his pen, and looked at Hood. His face was drawn and wan, but his eyes had their usual gleam.

"Talk to me, Paul," the president said.

Hood grew warm behind the ears. This wasn't going to be easy. Even if he were correct, it wasn't going to be easy convincing the president that members of his staff might be running an operation of their own. Hood did not have a lot to go on, and part of him wished that he had gone to the First Lady before coming here. It would have been better to let her talk to him in private. But if the intelligence Herbert had received was right, there might not be time for that. Ironically, Hood would have to keep Megan Lawrence out of this. He did not want the president to know that his wife had been talking about him behind his back.

Hood leaned forward. "Mr. President, I have some concerns about the United Nations intelligence operation."

"Jack Fenwick is setting it all up," the president said. "There'll be a comprehensive briefing when he returns from New York."

"Will the NSA be running the project?"

"Yes," the president informed him. "Jack will be reporting directly to me. Paul, I hope this visit isn't about some kind of territorial pissing contest between Op-Center and the NSA—"

"No, sir," Hood assured him.

The intercom beeped. The president answered. It was Mrs. Leigh. She said she had something for Paul Hood. The president frowned and asked her to bring it in. He looked at Hood.

"Paul, what's going on?"

"Hopefully, nothing," Hood said.

Mrs. Leigh walked in and handed Hood a single sheet of paper.

"Is this all?" Hood asked.

She nodded.

"What about the file itself?"

"Empty," she said.

Hood thanked Mrs. Leigh, and she left.

"What file is empty?" the president asked irritably. "Paul, what the hell is going on?"

"I'll tell you in a moment, Mr. President," Hood said. He looked down at the paper. "From eleven A.M. this morning until four P.M., Jack Fenwick was scheduled to meet with representatives of the government of Iran at their permanent mission in New York."

"Impossible," said the president.

"Sir, Mrs. Leigh obtained this from the NSA office," Hood said. He handed the president the paper. "It has their file number on top. And according to intel we received, Fenwick did spend a good part of the afternoon at the Iranian mission."

The president looked at the paper and was still for a long moment. Then he shook his head slowly. "Fenwick was supposed to be meeting with the Syrians, the Vietnamese, a half-dozen others," he said. "That's what he told me last night. Hell, we aren't even close to reaching an intelligence agreement with Iran."

"I know," Hood said. "But Fenwick was there. And except for this document, the file is empty. As far as the NSA is concerned, there is no such thing as the UN initiative."

"This has to be bullshit," the president said dismissively. "More bullshit." The president jabbed the intercom button on his phone. "Mrs. Leigh, get me Jack Fenwick—"

"Sir, I don't think you should talk to anyone at the NSA," Hood said.

"Excuse me?"

"Not yet, at least," Hood said.

"Hold on, Mrs. Leigh," the president said. "Paul, you just told me my national security adviser is way off the playbook. Now you're telling me not to bother finding out if that's true?"

"Before you do that, we need to talk," Hood said.

"About what?"

"I don't believe this situation with Fenwick is a miscommunication," Hood said.

"Neither do I," the president said. "My conversations with him were very explicit. That's why he and I need to talk."

"But what if something is very wrong?" Hood asked.

"Explain."

"What if this is a rogue operation of some kind?" Hood asked.

"You're out of your mind," the president said. He appeared stunned. "Christ, Paul, I've known most of these people for fifteen, twenty years—they're good friends!"

Hood understood. And all he could think to say was, " 'Et tu, Brute?' "

The president looked at him. "Paul, what are you talking about?"

"When Julius Caesar was killed by republicans in the senate, it was his closest and oldest friend who organized the assassination," Hood said.

The president looked at him. A moment later, he told Mrs. Leigh to forget the call. Then he shook his head slowly. "I'm listening," the president said. "But this better be good."

Hood knew that. What he didn't know was where to

begin. There was a possible conspiracy and possible mental illness. Perhaps both. He decided to start at the beginning and work his way through.

"Mr. President, why did Fenwick call you last night?" he asked.

"He had finished a day of meetings with ambassadors at the Hay-Adams," the president said. "There was strong opposition to the intelligence initiative from several key governments. He was supposed to let me know if and when he finally pulled it all together."

"Mr. President," Hood said, "we don't believe that Jack Fenwick was at the Hay-Adams Hotel last night. The call he made to you was apparently routed to the hotel from somewhere else."

"From where?" the president asked.

"I don't know," Hood admitted. "Perhaps he was already in New York. Was Fenwick also liaising with the CIOC?"

"No," the president said. "Getting approvals from the Oversight Committee was the responsibility of Fenwick's deputy, Don Roedner, and Red Gable on this end."

Hood didn't know Roedner any better than he knew Gable. He didn't even know Gable *had* a nickname.

"Sir," Hood continued, "last night, when you thanked Senator Fox for budgeting Mr. Fenwick's initiative, that was the first she'd heard about it."

President Lawrence froze, but only for a moment. His expression changed slowly. He looked very strange for a moment, both twenty years older and like a lost boy. He sat back.

"Gable wouldn't go behind my back on something,"

the president said faintly. "He wouldn't. And if he did, I'd read it in his face."

"When was the last time you saw him?" Hood asked.

The president thought. "Friday, at the cabinet meeting."

"There were a lot of people there, a lot of issues on the table," Hood said. "You might have missed it. Or maybe he was snookered by the NSA."

"I can't believe that, either," the president said.

"I see," Hood said. "Well, if Fenwick and Gable aren't rogue, there's only one other option I can think of."

"Which is?"

Hood had to be careful how he said this. He was no longer floating ideas about the president's staff but about the president himself.

"Maybe none of this happened," Hood said. "The UN initiative, the meetings with foreign governments—none of it."

"You mean I imagined it all," the president said.

Hood didn't answer.

"Do you believe that?" the president asked.

"I do not," Hood replied truthfully. If nothing else, there was the rerouted phone call from the Hay-Adams, and the president didn't imagine that. "But I won't lie to you, Mr. President," Hood went on. "You do seem tense, guarded, distracted. Definitely not yourself."

The president took a long breath. He started to say something and then stopped. "All right, Paul. You've got my attention. What do we do next?"

"I suggest we proceed under the assumption that

we've got a serious problem," Hood said. "I'll continue the investigation from our end. We'll see what we can find out about the Iranian connection. Check on what else Fenwick has been doing, who he's been talking to."

"Sounds good," Lawrence said. "Fenwick is due back late tonight. I won't say anything to him or to Red until I hear from you. Let me know as soon as you learn anything else."

"I will, sir."

"Will you also bring Senator Fox up to speed?"

Hood said he would and then stood. So did the president. He seemed a little stronger now, more in command. But the things Megan had told Hood still troubled him.

"Mr. President," Hood said, "I do have one more question."

The president looked at Hood intently and nodded once.

"A few minutes ago, you said that this was 'more bullshit,' " Hood said. "What did you mean?"

The president continued to regard Hood. "Before I answer that, let me ask you a question."

"All right."

"Don't you already know the answer to that?" the president asked.

Hood said that he did not.

"You came to see me only because of what happened last night?" the president asked.

Hood hesitated. The president knew that he and the First Lady were old friends. It was not Hood's place to tell the president that his wife was worried about him.

But Hood also did not want to be just one more person who was lying to the president.

"No," Hood answered truthfully. "That is not the only reason."

The president smiled faintly. "Fair enough, Paul. I won't press you."

"Thank you, sir."

"But I will tell you one thing about the bullshit," the president said. "This is not the only mix-up we've had here over the past few weeks. It's been frustrating." The president extended his hand across his desk. "Thanks for coming, Paul. And thanks for pushing me."

Hood smiled and shook the president's hand. Then he turned and left the Oval Office.

There was a group of eager-looking Boy Scouts waiting outside with a photographer. The young men were award-winners of some kind, judging by their sashes. Hood winked at them, taking a moment to savor their openmouthed awe and innocence. Then he thanked Mrs. Leigh as he passed her desk. She flashed a concerned look at Hood, and he indicated that he would call her. She mouthed a thank-you and then showed the Boy Scouts inside.

Hood walked briskly to his car. He started the engine, then took out his cell phone and checked his messages. There was only one. It was from Bob Herbert. As Hood headed toward Fifteenth Street, he called Herbert back.

"Bob, it's Paul," said Hood. "What's up?"

"Plenty," Herbert said. "First of all, Matt traced the call that came from the Hay-Adams."

"And?"

"The call originated on Fenwick's cell phone."

"Bingo!" Hood said.

"Maybe, maybe not," Herbert replied.

"Explain," Hood said.

"I got a call a few minutes ago, one I didn't expect to get," Herbert said.

"From?"

"Fenwick," Herbert replied. "He was open and sounded surprised by what I had to say. He told me he didn't speak to the president last night. He said his briefcase was stolen, which is why he didn't get the calls I left on his cell phone. He only got the one I left at his office."

"I'm not ready to buy that," Hood replied. "The president did receive a call, and it was routed through the hotel."

"True," Herbert said. "But do you remember Marta Streeb?"

"The woman who had the affair with Senator Lancaster?" Hood asked.

"Right."

"What about her?"

"Her calls were run through a phone bank at Union Station so they couldn't be traced," Herbert said.

"I remember," Hood said. "But the president isn't having an affair."

"Are you sure?" Herbert asked. "His wife said he was acting strange. That could be guilt—"

"It could be, but let's rule out the national security issues first," Hood snapped.

"Sure," Herbert replied.

Hood took a moment to calm down. His anger surprised him. Hood had never had an affair, but for some reason, Herbert's comment made him feel guilty about Sharon.

"What else did Fenwick have to say?" Hood asked.

"That he doesn't know a damn thing about any UN initiative," Herbert said. "He didn't get any calls about it and didn't read about it in the paper. He told me he was sent to New York to help the Iranians with the situation involving the Harpooner and possible Azerbaijani terrorists in the Caspian. And there could be some truth to that," Herbert pointed out. "If the CIA was compromised over there, the Iranians might need to turn to someone else for help. Someone that could get them signal intelligence capacity ASAP."

"Were the Iranians working with the CIA on this?"

"I'm trying to find that out," Herbert said. "You know those Company guys. They don't like to share. But think about it. Op-Center's worked with other governments, some of them hostile. We'd get in bed with Teheran if all we were going to do was snuggle a little."

That was true, Hood had to admit.

"And Fenwick was at the mission," Herbert continued. "That much is pretty clear."

"It's about the only thing that is," Hood replied. "Bob, you said that Fenwick was sent to New York. Did he say who sent him?"

"Yes," Herbert replied, "and I don't think you're going to like this. Fenwick says the president was the one who sent him."

"Triple-O?" Hood asked. Triple-O was *oral orders only*. They were given when an official didn't want to leave a paper trail to or from a potentially explosive situation.

"Triple-O," Herbert told him.

"Jesus," Hood said. "Look—someone else would have to have been in this Iranian loop."

"Sure," Herbert agreed. "The veep, probably. The chief of staff—"

"Call Vice President Cotten's office," Hood said. "Find out what he has to say. I'll be there as soon as possible."

"I'll call out for pizza," Herbert told him.

Hood hung up and concentrated on getting himself through the maddening rush-hour traffic.

At the moment, it was a welcome diversion.

EIGHTEEN

Gobustan, Azerbaijan
Tuesday, 1:22 A.M.

The other men had gone to sleep on threadbare bed-rolls they had bought secondhand in Baku. But Maurice Charles was still awake, still sitting at the wooden table in the shepherd's shack. Though he never had trouble sleeping before a mission, he did have trouble waiting for other people to do things. Things on which the mission depended. Until then, he would not—could not—rest.

When the phone finally beeped, he felt a nearly electric shock. This was it. The last unfinished business before H-hour.

Charles went to the equipment table. Beside the StellarPhoto Judge 7 was a Zed-4 unit, which had been developed by the KGB in 1992. The secure phone system was the size and general shape of an ordinary hardcover book. The small, flat receiver fit neatly into the side. It was a remarkable improvement over the point-to-point radios Charles had used when he was first starting out. Those had a range of two and one-half miles. The Zed-4 utilized a series of satellite links to pick up cellular transmissions from around the world. A series of internal audio enhancers and boosters virtually eliminated breakup and lost signals.

The Zed-4 was also quite secure. Most secure-phone calls, including the United States Tac-Sat units, were encrypted with a 155-digit number. In order to crack the code, eavesdroppers had to factor that into its two-component prime numbers. Even using sophisticated computers like the Cray 916, that could take weeks. The CIA had managed to cut that time into days by stealing computer time from personal computers. In 1997, the agency began using Internet servers to piggyback the numbers into home computer systems. Small amounts of memory were appropriated to work on the problem without the user being aware of it. Networked throughout a system of millions of PCs, the CIA was able to add gigabytes of computation power to the problem. It also created a problem for counterprogrammers, since it was not possible to shut down the CIA's so-called Stealth Field System. Thus, the Zed-4 was created using a complex encryption code of 309 digits. Even the SFS lacked sufficient power to break that code in a timely fashion.

Charles answered on the third ring. "B-sharp," he said. That was the receiver code name.

"C-natural," said the caller.

"Go ahead," said Charles.

"I'm across the street from the target," said the caller. "They're bringing him out the side door."

"No ambulance?"

"No," said the caller.

"Who's with him?" Charles asked.

"Two men," said the caller. "Neither of them in uniform."

Charles smiled. Americans were so predictable. If there were more than one operative, they invariably went to the user's manual. "How to Be a Soldier or Spy," Rule Fifty-three: Put the man above the mission. That thinking went at least as far back as the United States cavalry out West. Whenever the more aggressive Native American tribes like the Apaches were being pursued, they would stop to attack homesteaders. The warriors would always rape one of the women, leaving her where the cavalry was certain to find her. Invariably, the soldiers would send the woman back to the fort with an escort. That would not only delay the pursuing column but leave them depleted.

"Is backup in place?"

"Yes, sir."

"Then take them," Charles said.

"It's done," the caller said confidently. "Out."

The phone went dead. Charles hung up.

That was it. The last piece. He'd allowed the one agent to live to draw the others out. An injection in the neck, a fast-acting bacterial pneumonia, and the entire local cast was out of commission. Now there would be no one to put pieces together, to stop him from completing the mission.

Charles had one more call to place before he went to bed. It was to a secure line in Washington, to one of the few men who knew of Charles's involvement in this operation.

To a man who didn't follow the rule book.

To a man who helped devise one of the most audacious schemes of modern times.

NINETEEN

Baku, Azerbaijan
Tuesday, 1:35 A.M.

The ride to the VIP Hospital took just under ten minutes. The VIP was the only hospital the American embassy deemed to be up to the standards of western health care. They had an arrangement with Dr. Kanibov, one of the city's few English-speaking physicians. The fifty-seven-year-old Kanibov was paid off the books to be available for around-the-clock emergencies and to recommend qualified specialists when necessary.

Tom Moore didn't know if a specialist was going to be necessary. All he knew was that Pat Thomas had woken him twenty minutes earlier. Thomas had heard David Battat moaning on his cot. When Thomas went over to check on Battat, he found him soaked with perspiration and trembling. The embassy nurse had a look at him and took Battat's temperature. He had a fever of 105. The nurse suggested that Battat may have hit his head or suffered capillary damage when he was attacked. Rather than wait for an ambulance, Thomas and Moore loaded Battat into one of the embassy staff cars in the gated parking lot and brought him to the hospital themselves. The medic called ahead to let Dr. Kanibov know that they had a possible case of neurogenic shock.

This is all we need, to be down a man, Thomas

thought as he drove through the dark, deserted streets of the embassy and business district. It was bad enough to have too few people to deal with normal intelligence work. But to find the Harpooner, one of the world's most elusive terrorists, was going to take more. Thomas only hoped that his call to Washington would get them timely cooperation on a Saint Petersburg connection.

Dr. Kanibov lived just a block from the hospital. The tall, elderly, white-goateed physician was waiting when they arrived. Battat's teeth were chattering, and he was coughing. By the time a pair of orderlies put him on a gurney just inside the door, the American's lips and fingernail beds were rich blue.

"Very restricted blood flow," said Kanibov to one of the orderlies. "Oxygen." He looked in Battat's mouth. "Traces of mucus. Suction, then give me an oral temperature."

"What do you think is wrong?" Thomas asked.

"I don't know yet," Kanibov said.

"The nurse at the embassy said it could be neurogenic shock," Thomas said to the doctor.

"If it were, his face would be pale, not flushed," the doctor said with annoyance. He looked at Thomas and Moore. "You gentlemen can wait here or you can go back and wait—"

"We'll stay here," Thomas informed him. "At least until you know what's wrong."

"Very well," the doctor said as they wheeled Battat into the ward.

It seemed strangely quiet for an emergency room, Thomas thought. Whenever his three boys hurt themselves back in Washington or in Moscow, the ERs were like the West Wing of the White House: loud, purposeful chaos. He imagined that the clinics in the poorer sections of Baku must be more like that. Still, the silence was unnerving, deathlike.

Thomas looked at Moore. "There's no sense for both of us to be here," Thomas said. "One of us should get a little sleep."

"I wasn't sleeping," Moore said. "I was making those contacts we discussed and reviewing files."

"Did you find anything?" Thomas asked.

"Nothing," Moore said.

"All the more reason for you to go back to the embassy," Thomas said. "David is my responsibility. I'll wait here."

Moore considered that. "All right," he said. "You'll call as soon as you know something?"

"Of course," Thomas said.

Moore gave him a reassuring pat on the shoulder, then walked back through the lobby. He pushed the door open and walked around the front of the car to the driver's side.

A moment later, Tom Moore's head jerked to the right and he dropped to the asphalt.

TWENTY

Washington, D.C.
Monday, 6:46 P.M.

Paul Hood arrived at Op-Center, where he was to meet with Bob Herbert and Mike Rodgers. He also telephoned Liz Gordon. He asked her to wait around so he could talk to her later. He wanted to get her input on what, if anything, might be happening with the president from a clinical standpoint.

Hood bumped into Ann Farris on the way to his office. She walked with him through the tight, winding maze of cubicles to the executive wing. As Herbert had joked when he first went to work at Op-Center, that was where the cubicles had ceilings.

"Anything interesting going on?" Ann asked.

"The usual confusion," Hood said. "Only this time, it's happening in Washington, not overseas."

"Is it something really bad?"

"I don't know yet," Hood said. "There seems to be a loose cannon somewhere in the NSA." Hood didn't want to say anything about the president possibly having mental lapses of some kind. It wasn't that he didn't trust Ann, but Megan Lawrence had told him something in confidence. For now, he wanted to keep the number of people with whom he shared that as small as possible. "What's going on in your department?"

"The usual efficiency and expert coordination," she said with a disarming smile.

"You mean nothing's going on."

"Exactly," Ann said. She waited a moment, then asked, "Do you expect to be here long?"

"A couple of hours," he said. "There's no reason to go back to the hotel. I'd just sit there and watch some bad sitcom."

"Can I interest you in dinner?" she asked.

"It may be a long night," Hood said.

"I don't have any plans, either," she said. "My son is staying with his dad this week. There's nothing for me to go home to but a spoiled cat and those same sitcoms."

Hood's heart began thumping a little faster than usual. He very much wanted to say yes to Ann. But he was still a married man, and going out with a divorced female coworker could cause trouble, legally as well as ethically. And Op-Center did not need this distraction. The intelligence team was brilliant at uncovering information. Hood having dinner with Farris would be common knowledge by morning. Besides, if dinner with Ann was in the back of his mind, he would not be focusing on a crisis in the executive branch.

"Ann, I wish I could," he said sincerely. "But I don't know when I'll be finished here. Some other time?"

"Sure," she said with a small, sad smile. She touched the back of his hand. "Have a good meeting."

"Thanks," Hood said.

Ann left, and Hood continued on his way.

Hood felt terrible now. He had not done what he really wanted to do, which was have dinner with Ann. And he had hurt her feelings.

He stopped. He wanted to go after her and tell her he would have the dinner. But once he started down that road, there was no turning back. Hood continued toward his office.

Hood buzzed Rodgers and Herbert when he arrived. Rodgers said he would be right over. Herbert was on the computer and said he would be with them in a few minutes.

Rodgers was alert and professional when he arrived. The general had always wanted to run Op-Center. If he harbored any resentment about having it handed to him and then abruptly pulled away, it did not show. Above all, Rodgers was a good man and a team player.

General Rodgers had spent most of the day overseeing the activities of Op-Center while Paul Hood was involved with the president and the UN initiative. As Hood briefed his deputy director about Herbert's talk with Fenwick, Herbert wheeled in. The intelligence chief was flushed and perspiring slightly. He had hurried to get here.

"How's your relationship with Sergei Orlov at the Russian Op-Center?" Herbert asked breathlessly.

The question surprised Hood. "I haven't spoken to him in about six months. Why?"

"I just received a message that was forwarded from the U.S. embassy in Baku," Herbert said. "One of the CIA's people over there, Tom Moore, is now convinced that Baku has had a visit from the Harpooner. Moore doesn't know why the bastard's there—"

"It could have something to do with what you were just telling me about," Rodgers said to Hood. "Bob's conversation with Fenwick—"

"About Iran fearing terrorist attacks from Azerbaijan," Hood said.

Rodgers nodded.

"I agree that that's a possibility," Herbert said. "Paul, if it is the Harpooner, Moore wants to catch him going into or keep him from getting out of the former USSR. He's hoping that the Russian Op-Center can help."

"How?" Hood asked. "Orlov and I shared our files years ago. There was nothing on the Harpooner."

"Orlov's facility was new then," Herbert said. "He or his people may have found something in the old KGB files since then. Something they might not have told us about."

"It's possible," Hood agreed. Op-Center was understaffed, and the situation at their Russian counterpart was even worse. Keeping up a regular flow of information was difficult.

"In addition to intel on the Harpooner," Herbert said, "Moore was hoping that Orlov's people might be able to watch the northern and northwestern sections of Russia. He was thinking that the Harpooner might try to leave the region through Scandinavia."

Hood looked at his watch. "It's about three in the morning over there," he said.

"Can you reach him at home?" Herbert asked. "This is important. You know it is."

Herbert was right. Regardless of the intelligence chief's desire to see the terrorist captured, tried, and executed, the Harpooner was a man who deserved to be out of circulation.

"I'll call," Hood said.

"Before you do, what about President Lawrence?"

Rodgers asked. "How did things go over there?"

"I'll fill you in after I talk to Orlov," Hood said as he accessed his secure phone list on the computer. He found Orlov's number. "But from the look of it, we're facing a lose-lose situation. Either the president is suffering from some kind of mental fatigue, or we've got a group of top officials running a black ops action of some kind—"

"Or both," Herbert said.

"Or both," Hood agreed. "I've got Liz Gordon coming in later to talk about what the president might be experiencing."

Before punching in Orlov's home telephone number, Hood called Op-Center's linguistics office. He got Orly Turner on the line. Orly was one of Op-Center's four staff translators. Her area of expertise was Eastern Europe and Russia. Hood conferenced her in to the call. Though Orlov spoke English well enough, Hood wanted to make sure there were no misunderstandings, no delays if technical terms or acronyms had to be explained.

"You want to know what my gut tells me?" Herbert said.

"What?" Hood asked as he punched in Orlov's number.

"That all of this is related," Herbert said. "The president being out of the loop, Fenwick dealing secretly with Iran, the Harpooner showing up in Baku. It's all part of a big picture that we haven't figured out yet."

Herbert left the office. Hood didn't disagree with him. In fact, his own gut was willing to go one step further.

That the big picture was bigger than what they imagined.

TWENTY-ONE

Baku, Azerbaijan
Tuesday, 3:58 A.M.

When Tom Moore went down, Pat Thomas ran toward the hospital door. He was halfway out when he saw blood pulsing from the side of Moore's head. Thomas stopped and jumped back just as a shot blew out the glass in the door. The bullet punched into his left thigh and knocked him down. He landed in a sitting position and continued to scuttle back. A second bullet chewed up the green tile inches in front of his foot. Thomas hurried backward along the floor, propelled by his palms and right heel. The wound burned viciously, and each move was agony. He left a long smear of blood behind him.

It was a few moments before the hospital staff realized what had happened. One of the nurses, a young woman, ran forward and helped pull Thomas back. Several orderlies followed. They dragged him behind the admissions desk. Another nurse called the police.

A bald-headed doctor knelt beside Thomas. He was wearing off-white surgical gloves and shouted instructions in Azerbaijani to other hospital workers who were in front of the counter. As he did, he took a pocket knife from his white coat and carefully cut away the fabric around the wound.

Thomas winced as the khaki fabric came away. He

watched as the doctor exposed the wound.

"Will I live?" Thomas asked.

The doctor didn't answer. Suddenly, the bald man started to rise. But instead of getting up, he straddled the American's legs. He sat on the wound, sending fire up through his patient's waist. Thomas wanted to scream, but he could not. A moment later, the doctor slipped a hand behind the America's head, holding it in place, and pushed the knife blade through his throat. The metal entered the skin just behind Thomas's chin and pinned his mouth shut. The blade continued upward until Thomas could feel the point of the blade under his tongue.

Thomas choked as he coughed blood into his closed mouth. He raised his hands and tried to push the bald man back. But he was too weak. Calmly and quickly, the bald man angled the knife back. Then he drew the knife down until it reached Thomas's larynx. He cut swiftly to the left and right, following the line of the jaw all the way to the ears. Then he removed the blade, rose, and allowed Thomas to flop to the floor. The doctor pocketed the knife and walked away without a glance back.

The American lay there, his arms weak and his fingers moving aimlessly. He could feel the warm blood flowing from both sides of his throat as the flesh around it grew cold. He tried to call out, but his voice was a burbling whisper. Then he realized that his chest was moving but no air was going to it. There was blood in his throat.

Thomas's thoughts were confused. His vision swirled black. He thought about flying up to Baku, about meeting with Moore. He wondered how Moore was. And then he thought about his children. For a moment, he was back playing ball with them on the front lawn.

Then they were gone.

TWENTY-TWO

Saint Petersburg, Russia
Tuesday, 4:01 A.M.

General Sergei Orlov was standing in the snow in the small town of Nar'yan Mar on the Arctic Ocean when a peeping bird caused him to start. He turned to look for it and found himself staring at his alarm clock.

He was back in his one-bedroom apartment in Saint Petersburg.

"Damn you," Orlov said as the phone rang again. The former cosmonaut did not often dream of the town where he grew up. He hated being taken away from it and from his loving parents.

"Sergei?" his wife Masha said groggily beside him.

"I have it," Orlov told her. He picked up the receiver of the cordless phone. He held it to his chest to stifle the ringing. "Go back to sleep."

"All right," she said.

Orlov listened enviously to the cozy rustle of the sheets as his wife curled up on her side. He got out of bed, pulled a bathrobe from the edge of the door, and pulled it on as he stepped into the living room. Even if this were a wrong number, Orlov would have trouble getting back to sleep.

He finally answered the telephone. "Hello," Orlov said with a trace of annoyance.

"General Orlov?" said the voice on the other end. It was a man.

"Yes?" Orlov said as he rubbed his eyes vigorously with his free hand. "Who is this?"

"General, it's Paul Hood," said the caller.

Orlov was suddenly very much awake. "Paul!" he practically shouted. "Paul Hood, my friend. How are you? I heard that you resigned. And I heard about what happened in New York. Are you all right?"

Orlov walked over to an armchair while the woman translated. The general had a decent command of English, the result of the years he spent as a goodwill ambassador for the Russian space program after his flying days were finished. But he let the woman translate to be sure he didn't miss anything.

Orlov sat down. Standing just under five-foot-seven, he had the narrow shoulders and compact build that had made him an ideal cosmonaut. Yet he had presence. His striking brown eyes, high cheekbones, and dark complexion were, like his adventurous spirit, a part of his Manchu heritage. He walked with a significant limp due to a left leg and hip badly broken when his parachute failed to deploy in what turned out to be his last space mission.

"I'm fine," Hood said in reply. "I withdrew my resignation."

While Turner translated, Orlov turned on the lamp beside the chair and sat down. He picked up a pen and pad he kept on the small end table.

"Good, good!" Orlov said.

"Listen, General," Hood went on, "I'm very sorry to be calling you so early and at home."

"It's no bother, Paul," Orlov replied. "What can I do for you?"

"The terrorist who calls himself the Harpooner," Hood said. "You and I once spoke about him."

"I remember," said Orlov. "We've been looking for him in connection with the terror bombings in Moscow several years ago."

"General, we believe he is in Azerbaijan."

Orlov's full lips tightened. "That would not surprise me," he said. "We thought we had him located in Moscow two days ago. A guard near Lenin's Tomb was very confident in his identification. He summoned police assistance, but by the time it had arrived, the suspect had disappeared."

"Do you mean the police lost him, or the suspect knew he was being watched and managed to get away?" Hood asked.

"The police are generally good at surveillance," Orlov replied. "The subject went around a corner and was gone. He could have changed clothes somehow—I don't know. The Kievskaya metro stop is near where he was last seen. It is possible he went down there."

"It's more than possible," Hood said. "That was where one of our embassy people spotted him."

"Explain, please," Orlov said.

"We had heard that he was in Moscow," Hood said. "The embassy person followed the man he thought was the Harpooner onto the metro. They went to a transfer station, and the Harpooner got off. He boarded another train, left it at the Paveletskaya stop, then he literally vanished."

Orlov was now very interested. "You're sure it was Paveletskaya?" he asked.

"Yes," Hood asked. "Is that significant?"

"Perhaps," Orlov said.

"General Orlov," Hood said, "however the Harpooner left Moscow, it's possible that he may be headed back there or toward Saint Petersburg. Do you think you could help us try and find him?"

"I would love to capture that monster," Orlov replied. "I will contact Moscow and see what they have. In the meantime, please send whatever information you have to my office. I will be there within the hour."

"Thank you, General," Hood said. "And again, I'm sorry to have wakened you. I didn't want to lose any time."

"You did the right thing," Orlov assured him. "It was good speaking with you. I will talk to you later in the day."

Orlov rose and went back to the bedroom. He hung up the phone, kissed his precious, sleeping Masha on the forehead, then quietly went to the closet and removed his uniform. He carried it into the living room. Then he went back for the rest of his clothes. He dressed quickly and quietly, then left his wife a note. After nearly thirty years, Masha was not unaccustomed to his comings and goings in the middle of the night. When he had been a fighter pilot, Orlov was often called for missions at odd hours. During his spacefaring years, it was common for him to suit up while it was still dark. Before his first orbital flight he had left her a note that read, "My dearest—I am leaving the earth for several days. Can you pick me up at the spaceport on Sunday morning? Your loving husband, Sergei. PS: I will try to catch you a shooting star."

Of course, Masha was there.

Orlov left the apartment and took the stairs to the basement garage. The government had finally given him a car after three years, since the buses were unreliable. And with everything that was going on in and around Russia, from restless republics to rampant gangsterism in major cities, it was often imperative for Orlov to be able to get to his Op-Center's headquarters.

And it was imperative now. The Harpooner was back in Russia.

TWENTY-THREE

Washington, D.C.
Monday, 7:51 P.M.

Liz Gordon came to Hood's office after his conversation with Orlov. A husky woman with sparkling eyes and short, curly brown hair, Gordon was chewing nicotine gum and carrying her ever-present cup of coffee. Mike Rodgers remained for the talk.

Hood told Gordon how the president had seemed during their meeting. Hood also gave the woman a brief overview of the possible covert activities that might explain what appeared to be the president's delusions.

When Hood was finished, Gordon refilled her coffee cup from a pot in the corner of the office. Though Hood had been dubious of psychiatry when he had first come to Op-Center, Gordon's profiling work had impressed him. He had also been won over by her thoroughness. She brought a mathematician's prooflike manner to the process. That, coupled with her compassion, had made her an increasingly valuable and respected member of the team. Hood did not have any trouble entrusting his daughter to her.

"The president's behavior does not seem extreme," Gordon said, "so we can eliminate some very serious dementias, which would indicate a complete or near-complete loss of intellectual capacity. That leaves us with dangerous but more elusive delusions, of which there are basically six kinds. First there's organic, which is brought on by illness such as epilepsy or brain lesions. Second is substance-induced, meaning drugs. Third is somatic, which involves a kind of hyperawareness of the body—anorexia nervosa or hypochondria, for example. What you've described doesn't sound like any of those. Besides, they certainly would have been caught by the president's physician during one of his regular checkups. We can also rule out delusions of grandeur—megalomania—since that would show up in public. We haven't seen any of that.

"The only two possibilities are delusions of reference and delusions of persecution," she went on. "Delusions of reference is actually a mild form of delusions of persecution, in which innocent remarks are deemed to be critical. That doesn't seem to apply here. But I can't be as quick to rule out persecution delusions."

"Why not?" Hood asked.

"Because the sufferer will go to great pains to conceal them," she said. "He or she believes that others are trying to stop them or hurt them in some way. They often imagine a conspiracy of some kind. If the president fears that people are out to get him, he won't want to confide in anyone."

"But the stress might come out in little bursts," Rodgers said.

"Exactly," Gordon told him. "Crying, withdrawal, distraction, temper—all of the things Paul described."

"He seemed to want to trust me," Hood said.

"That's true and also characteristic of the illness," Gordon said. "Delusions of persecution is a form of paranoia. But as a sage once said, 'Sometimes even paranoids have enemies.' "

"Is there something we should do?" Hood asked. "The First Lady's feelings notwithstanding, we have to do something if the president can't continue to function under these circumstances."

"Whatever is going on sounds like it's in an advanced-early stage," Gordon said. "The effects are unlikely to be permanent."

Hood's phone beeped.

"If there is a conspiracy, and you can expose it quickly," Gordon went on, "there is every reason to believe the president can stay on the job after a short rest. Whatever has happened probably wouldn't have any effects, long-term or short."

Hood nodded as he answered the phone. "Yes?"

"Paul, it's Bob," said Herbert.

"What's up?"

"A major situation," he said. "I just got a call from the CIA suit who relayed Tom Moore's request to me from Baku. Moore and the CIA guy from Moscow, Pat Thomas, were just wasted. They were taking David Battat to the hospital—the guy the Harpooner attacked during the stakeout. Moore was tagged by a sniper outside the hospital, and Thomas had his throat cut in the lobby."

"By who?" Hood asked.

"We don't know."

"No one saw him?" Hood asked.

"Apparently not," Herbert replied. "Or if they did, they didn't see him again."

"Where is Battat?"

"He's still at the hospital, which is why the suit called me," Herbert said. "The embassy called for police protection, but we don't know whether they've been compromised or not. The CIA is out of people, and they're afraid Battat will be next, and soon. We don't have anyone in Baku, but I thought—"

"Orlov," Hood said urgently. "I'll call him now."

TWENTY-FOUR

Khachmas, Azerbaijan
Tuesday, 4:44 A.M.

Maurice Charles did not like to repeat himself.

If he arrived someplace by car, he liked to leave by bus or rail. If he went west by air, he liked to go east by car or bus. If he wore a hat in the morning, he took it off in the afternoon. Or else he wore a different one or dyed his hair. If he destroyed a car with a pipe bomb, he attacked the next target with C-4. If he had done surveillance along a coastline, he retreated inland for a short time. Repetition was the means by which entrepreneurs in any field were undone. Patterns enabled lesser thinkers to anticipate you. The only exceptions were densely populated cities where he might be seen. If he found a relatively obscure route through a place like that, he would use it more than once. The risk of being spotted and identified was greater than the risk of reusing an out-of-the-way road or tunnel.

Because Charles had surveyed the Caspian oil drilling site by plane, he decided to return to it by boat. The American and possibly Russian satellites would be looking for an aircraft by now. He and his team would take the motor yacht, which would have a different name on its side than it had the day before. One of the team members had made those arrangements in Baku. It would be waiting for them in Khachmas, a coastal town some fifty miles north of Baku. A freelance crew had been hired in Baku and sailed up with one of Charles's Iranian sailors. Not only was Khachmas closer to their target, it was unlikely that anyone would recognize them or the vessel.

After a short sleep, which was all he needed, Charles and his comrades had climbed into a van that was parked behind the shack. Their gear was already on board, and they drove from Gobustan back toward Baku. They traveled along roads that were utterly deserted at this time of night. Though Charles did not drive, he did not sleep. He sat in the backseat with a .45 in his lap. If anyone approached the van for any reason, he wanted to be awake.

The van arrived in sleepy Khachmas shortly before 4:30. They had driven the seventy miles nonstop. No one had approached them.

The *Rachel*—now the *Saint Elmo*—was waiting in a slip at a ramshackle marina. The berth was close to shore. The hired crew had been dismissed. They had departed in their own boat, a fishing vessel, which had accompanied the motor yacht north.

Wearing night-vision goggles, Charles stood watch while the equipment was transferred from the van to the *Saint Elmo*. When all the gear was on board, one of the team members drove off in the van. The vehicle would be painted locally and driven to another city. Finally, the motor yacht set off.

The trip to the target would take fifty minutes. The sun would just be coming up when they arrived. That was important. Working at sea, Charles did not like to use artificial lights. They were too easy to spot in the dark and reflected on the water. He also didn't like to work during bright daylight when the wet suits glistened. Early dawn was best. There would be just enough time to get the job done and depart without being seen.

Then he would leave Azerbaijan and do nothing but enjoy life for a month or two. Savor the international ramifications of what he had accomplished. Cherish the fact, as he always did, that no world leader, no army, no business, had a greater impact on international events than he did.

TWENTY-FIVE

Saint Petersburg, Russia
Tuesday, 4:47 A.M.

After the fall of the Soviet Union, many officials in Moscow were afraid of the Ministerstvo Bezopasnosti Ruskii, or MBR, the Security Ministry of Russia. They were even more afraid than when the intelligence agency had been known as the KGB and was routinely tapping their phone lines and opening their mail. The officials feared that leaders of the former Soviet intelligence group would either support ousted Communists in an effort to recapture power or attempt to seize power themselves. Because of this, the Kremlin's new regime had created an autonomous intelligence agency outside of Moscow, away from the immediate reach of the MBR. They based it in Saint Petersburg. And, following the adage of hiding in plain sight, they located the Op-Center in one of the most visited places in Russia: the Hermitage.

The Hermitage was built by Catherine the Great as a retreat. The towering, white, neoclassical building was formally known as the Winter Palace. It was a place where Catherine could enjoy the gems and great old masters paintings, drawings, and sculptures she had collected. She literally acquired them at a rate of one every other day from 1762 to 1772. When Catherine first opened her home to the patrician public, her only comments were that visitors should be joyful. However, she added, they "shall not try to damage, break, or gnaw at anything." The Hermitage remained a repository of the imperial collection until 1917. After the Russian Revolution, the Hermitage was opened to all the people. Its collection was expanded to include art from other schools as well as modern art. It currently houses over 8,000 paintings, 40,000 etchings, and 500,000 illustrations. Today, it is second only to the Louvre in Paris in terms of the size of its collection.

The Russian Op-Center was constructed underneath a fully operational television studio. Though the broadcast facility had been built as a cover for the construction of the intelligence center, satellite dishes beamed famed Hermitage programs around the world. Most of the time, however, the highly advanced uplinks allowed the Op-Center to interface with satellites for both domestic and international electronic communications. The comings and goings of museum staff and tourists helped to disguise the presence of Op-Center personnel. Also, the Kremlin had decided that in the event of war or revolution, no one would bomb the Hermitage. Even if an enemy had no use for art as an aesthetic possession, paintings and sculptures were always as negotiable as currency.

It was still dark when the fifty-three-year-old Orlov arrived at the museum. Because the Hermitage was still closed, he entered through an inconspicuous studio door on the northeastern side of the museum. As he did, he gazed north across the dark Neva River. Directly across the water were the stately Academy of Sciences and Museum of Anthropology. Nearby was the Frunze Naval College. In addition to training cadets, the college housed the dozen soldiers of the center's special operations force, Molot, which meant *Hammer*.

There was a guard seated behind a desk inside the TV studio. Orlov acknowledged him as he passed. The elderly guard stood and saluted. The general reached a door and used the keypad to enter. Once inside, he made his way through the dark reception area and down a short flight of stairs. At the far end, he punched the new day's four-digit code on a keypad, and the door popped open. The next day's number was always given to Orlov by the center's security chief at the end of each workday. When Orlov shut the door behind him, the overhead lighting snapped on automatically. There was another, longer set of stairs. He walked down where a second keypad gained him access to the Op-Center.

The facility consisted of a very long corridor with offices to the left and right. Orlov's office was at the end, literally at the shores of the Neva. There were times when he could hear barges passing overhead.

Ordinarily, Orlov did not arrive until nine o'clock. There was a skeletal night staff, and they were surprised to see the general. He greeted them without stopping. When he entered his small, wood-paneled office, he shut the door and walked over to his desk. The desk faced the door. On the walls were framed photographs Orlov had taken from space. There were no photographs of the general himself. Though he was proud of his accomplishments, he didn't enjoy looking at the past. All he saw was how short he fell of his goals. How he had hoped to walk on the moon and command a manned mission to Mars. How he had dreamed of seeing the cosmonaut corps grow and prosper. Perhaps if he had used his celebrity more constructively, more aggressively, he could have helped make that happen. Perhaps if he had spoken out against the war in Afghanistan. That struggle drained the nation's resources and pride and hastened the union's downfall.

There were no photographs of himself because General Orlov preferred to look ahead. The future held no regrets, only promise.

There was a voice mail from Paul Hood. The message did not say very much. Only that the matter was urgent. Orlov sat down and booted his computer. As he opened his secure phone list and auto-dialed Hood, he thought back to how the American Op-Center had helped him prevent a cabal of right-wing Russian officials from overthrowing the government. The counterattack had cost Hood one of his top field operatives, Lieutenant Colonel Charles Squires. Since then, the two Op-Centers had occasionally exchanged information. But they had never become fully integrated partners, which was something both Hood and Orlov had wanted. Unfortunately, like many of the progressive dreams Orlov had, the bureaucrats had not been ready for this. Distrust between the nations was still too deep.

The phone beeped once. Hood answered.

"Hello?" Hood said.

"Paul, it's Sergei," Orlov said.

Op-Center's translator was on standby. It only took her a moment to get on the line.

"General, I need your trust, and I need it fast," Hood said. His urgent tone left no room for discussion.

"Of course," Orlov said.

"Our team searching for the Harpooner suffered a catastrophic hit at a hospital in Baku," Hood informed him. "It happened a little over an hour ago. Two of our men were killed. The first was taken down by a sniper outside the hospital. The second had his throat cut inside the lobby. The last man is a patient. His name is David Battat, and he is ill with a fever of some kind."

Orlov took a moment to write the name down.

"The police are at the hospital, but we don't know who the killer is," Hood said. "He or she may still be in the hospital."

"The killer could be a police officer," Orlov pointed out.

"Exactly," Hood said. "General, do you have anyone in Baku?"

"Yes, we do," Orlov said without hesitation. "In what room is Mr. Battat located?"

"He's in one fifty-seven," Hood said.

"I will send someone at once," Orlov said. "Tell no one."

Hood gave him his word.

Orlov hung up.

The three most powerful Russian intelligence groups had their own personnel. These groups were the MBR; the military's Glavnoye Razvedyvatelnoye Upravlenie, or GRU, the Main Intelligence Directorate; and the Ministerstvo Vnutrennikh Del, or MVD, the Ministry of Internal Affairs. The Russian Op-Center did not have the financial resources to maintain its own network of intelligence and counterintelligence personnel, so it was necessary to share people with other relatively small

Russian agencies. These were administered by the Sisteme Objedinennovo Utschotya Dannych o Protivniki, or SOUD, the Interlinked System for Recognizing Enemies. SOUD also provided personnel for the Sluzhba Vneshney Razvedki, or SVR, the Foreign Intelligence Service; the Federal'naya Sluzhba Bezopasnosti, or FSB, the Federal Security Service; the Federal'naya Sluzhba Kontr-razvedky, or FSK, the Federal Counterintelligence Service; and the Federal'naya Sluzhba Okhrani, or FSO, the Federal Protective Service.

Orlov quickly accessed the SOUD files. He input the highest-priority code, Red Thirteen. This meant that the request was not only coming from a senior official—level thirteen—but involved a case of immediate national emergency: the apprehension of the Harpooner. The Red Thirteen code gave Orlov the names, locations, and telephone numbers of field personnel around the world. Even if the operatives were involved in other situations, he would be authorized to commandeer them.

Orlov went to the file for Baku, Azerbaijan.

He found what he was looking for.

He hesitated.

General Orlov was about to ask a deep-cover operative to try to help an American spy. If the Americans were planning an operation in Baku, this would be the quickest way to expose and neutralize Russian intelligence resources. But to believe that, Orlov would have to believe that Paul Hood would betray him.

Orlov made the call.

TWENTY-SIX

Washington, D.C.
Monday, 9:00 P.M.

Paul Hood was angry when he hung up with Orlov.

Hood was angry at the system, at the intelligence community, and at himself. The dead men were not his people. The man at risk was not his operative. But they had failed, and the Harpooner had succeeded, partly because of the way spies did business. The Harpooner commanded a team. Most American agents worked as part of a team. Theoretically, that should give the operatives a support system. In practice, it forced them to operate within a bureaucracy. A bureaucracy with rules of conduct and accountability to directors who were nowhere near the battlegrounds. No one could fight a man like the Harpooner with baggage like that. And Hood was guilty of supporting that system. He was as guilty as his counterparts at CIA, NSA, or anywhere else.

The irony was that Jack Fenwick had apparently done something off the books. It was Hood's job to find out what that was.

The bureaucrats are checking up on the bureaucrats, Hood thought bitterly. Of course, he probably should not be thinking at all right now. He was tired and frustrated about the situation with Battat. And he had not even called home to see how Harleigh was doing.

Rodgers had stayed with Hood between the time he first phoned Orlov and Orlov returned the call. While they waited for Bob Herbert to come back, Rodgers left to grab a soda. Hood decided to call home. It did not improve his mood.

He was doing just the thing that Sharon had always hated. Working late. Calling home as an afterthought. He could hear the anger in her throat, in the tightness of her mouth, in the brevity of her answers.

"I'm doing laundry," Sharon said. "Harleigh is in the den playing solitaire on the computer. Alexander is in his room doing homework and studying for a history test."

"How does Harleigh seem today?" Hood asked.

"How do you think?" Sharon said. "Your own psychologist said it's going to be a while before we see any kind of change. If we see any kind of change," Sharon added. "But don't worry, Paul. I'll handle whatever comes up."

"I'm not going anywhere, Sharon," Hood said. "I want to help."

"I'm glad. Do you want me to get Alexander?" she asked.

"Not if he's studying," Hood said. "Just tell him I called."

"Sure."

"Good night," Hood said.

He could feel Sharon hesitate. It was only a moment, but it felt much, much longer. " 'Night, Paul," she said, then hung up.

Hood sat there holding the phone for several moments. Now he was a bastard and a bureaucrat. He lay the phone in its cradle, folded his hands, and waited for Rodgers. As he sat there, something began to tick inside him. It wasn't a clock or a bomb. It was like a cam and rocker arm. And with each click of the arm, a spring grew tighter inside him. A desire to do something—and not just debate or call the Russians for help. Hood wanted to act. Something was not right, and he needed to know what it was.

Rodgers and Herbert arrived together. They found Hood staring at the back wall of his office where plaques and framed photographs once hung, the mementos of his years in government. Pictures with world leaders, with constituents. Photographs of Hood laying cornerstones or working in a Thanksgiving soup kitchen.

His life as a bloody goddamn bureaucrat. As part of the problem, not the solution.

"Are you all right?" Herbert asked.

"Fine," Hood said.

"Did you get news?" Herbert pressed.

"No," Hood said. "But I want to make some."

"You know where I stand on that," Herbert said. "What were you thinking of?"

"Battat," Hood said. That was not entirely true. He was thinking that he never should have withdrawn his resignation. He should have left Op-Center and never looked back. He wondered if resigning had actually been for him and not to spend more time with his family, as he had believed. But he was back, and he was not going to run away.

Battat was the next stop in his thought process. "This man was sent to the hospital with some kind of sickness where a pair of assassins were waiting," he said. "That doesn't sound like a coincidence."

"No, it doesn't," Herbert agreed. "My brain trust and I have been looking into that."

Herbert's brain trust consisted of four deputy intelligence directors who had been brought to Op-Center from military intelligence, the NSA, and the CIA. They were three men and one woman who ranged in age from twenty-nine to fifty-seven. With input from Darrell McCaskey, who liaised with the FBI and Interpol, Op-Center had the best per capita intelligence team in Washington.

"Here's what we've been thinking," Herbert said. "The CIA is ninety-nine percent certain the Harpooner passed through Moscow and went to Baku. A DOS agent thinks he saw him on a flight to Moscow, but that may have been intentional."

"Why?" Rodgers asked.

"It wouldn't be unprecedented for a terrorist to let himself be seen," Herbert said. "Back in 1959, the Soviet spy Igor Slavosk allowed himself to be seen at Grand Central Station in New York so he could draw police attention and bring FBI personnel to his apartment. When they got to the place down on Jane Street, it blew up. Slavosk came back, collected badges and IDs, and had perfect fakes made. He used them to get into FBI headquarters in Washington. So, yes, it's possible the Harpooner allowed his presence to be known through channels."

"Go on," Hood said quietly. He was getting impatient. Not at Bob Herbert; the intelligence chief was simply a

convenient target. Hood wanted Orlov to call him back.
He wanted to hear that everything was all right at the
hospital. He wanted some good news for a change.

"Sorry," Herbert said. "So the Harpooner somehow
lets it be known that he's going to Baku. He has some
kind of operation planned. He knows there are CIA personnel attached to the embassy. He also knows that the
CIA might not want to expose those people since police
from the Azerbaijani Ministry of Internal Security are
probably keeping an eye on embassy personnel, watching for foreign intelligence operations. So the CIA
brings someone in from Moscow."

"Battat," said Hood.

"Yes," Herbert said. He seemed a little uneasy. "David Battat was the head of the CIA's New York City
field office. He was the man who hired Annabelle Hampton."

"The junior officer we busted during the UN siege?"
Rodgers said.

Herbert nodded. "Battat was in Moscow at the time.
We checked him. He's clean. One of our CIA contacts
told me he was sent to Baku to do penance for the New
York screwup."

Hood nodded. "All right. You've got Battat in Baku."

"Battat goes out to a target area to watch for the Harpooner and gets taken down," Herbert said. "Not taken
out, which the Harpooner could have done with no problem. Battat was apparently infected with a virus or
chemical designed to drop him at a specific time. Something serious enough so that he'd be taken to the hospital."

"Under guard from his fellow CIA operatives," Hood said.

"Exactly," Herbert replied. "Pretty maids all in a row."

"Which leaves the Harpooner free of CIA interference to do whatever he's planning," Hood said.

"That's what it looks like," Herbert said. "No one but the United States, Russia, and probably Iran has any kind of intelligence presence in Baku."

"Because of the Caspian oil?" Rodgers asked.

Herbert nodded. "If the Harpooner also hit operatives from Moscow and Teheran, we haven't heard about it."

Hood thought about that. "Iran," he said softly.

"Excuse me?" Herbert said.

"That's the second time we've been talking about Iran today," Hood said.

"But not for the same—" Herbert said, then stopped.

"Not for the same reason?" Hood asked.

"Aw, no," Herbert said after a moment. "No."

"Hold on," Rodgers said. "What am I missing?"

"You're thinking the game of telephone could go from the Harpooner to Teheran to Jack Fenwick to the NSA to the CIA," Herbert said.

"It's possible," Hood said.

"That would put Fenwick in bed with them on something involving the Harpooner," Herbert said.

"Something he would not want the president to know about," Hood pointed out.

Herbert was shaking his head. "I don't want this to be happening," he said. "I don't want us working with the sonofabitch who killed my wife."

"Bob, I need you to calm down," Hood said.

Herbert was glaring at Hood's desk.

"If the Harpooner is up to something in Baku, we might still be able to get him," Hood said. "But only if we stay focused."

Herbert did not respond.

"Bob?"

"I hear you," Herbert said. "I'm focused."

Hood looked at Rodgers. A minute ago, Hood wanted to lash out. Now that one of his friends was hurting, the desire had subsided. All he wanted to do was help Herbert.

Why did he never feel that way about Sharon when she was angry?

"Mike," Hood said, "we really need to pin down what Fenwick's been up to and who, if anyone, he's been working with."

"I'll get that information," Rodgers said. "But I can tell you this much. I found two e-mails in my computer files from six months ago. They were written by Jack Fenwick and Burt Gable."

"What were the memos about?" Hood asked.

"They were responding to a Pentagon white paper," Rodgers said. "The paper was about the minimal threat of possible Russian military alliances with neighbors who were not part of the former Soviet Union. Fenwick and Gable took issue with that."

"The head of the National Security Agency and the president's chief of staff both took issue to the report, independently," Hood said.

"Correct," said Rodgers. "The memos were sent to all the members of congress and various military leaders."

"I wonder if the two men met philosophically on-line," Hood said. "What was the time code on the memos?"

"A few hours apart," Rodgers said. "They didn't appear to be part of a concerted effort. But they both shared an aggressive disapproval of the report."

"I guess it doesn't matter whether Fenwick and Gable issued those memos independent of one another or whether they found out they had something in common when they read them," Hood said. "The question is whether they did something about it. Whether they got together and did some plotting."

"What makes you think they might have?" asked Herbert, easing back into the conversation.

"Gable's name came up today in my talk with the president," Hood said. "He and Fenwick's assistant Don Roedner were responsible for keeping the CIOC in the loop about that UN initiative."

"And didn't," Herbert said.

"No, they didn't." Hood tapped the desk slowly. "We've got two issues here," he said a moment later. "Fenwick's activities in New York and the Harpooner's activities in Baku."

"Assuming they are separate," Herbert said. "The two operations do have Iran in common. The Harpooner has worked for Teheran before."

Hood nodded. "What if he's working for them again?"

"Against Azerbaijan," said Herbert.

"It's possible," Rodgers said. "The Iranians have two potential areas of conflict with Azerbaijan. The Caspian oil reserves and the bordering Nagorno-Karabakh region."

"But why would Fenwick want to be involved in something like that?" Herbert said. "Just to prove the Pentagon wrong? Then what?"

"I don't know," Hood said. He looked at Rodgers. "Get to him and make him open up. Not only about Iran but about why he lied to the president."

"Tell him you've got information you can only tell him face-to-face," Herbert said.

"Right," Hood said. "Have Liz work out a psych profile of the president. One based on firsthand observations, including my own, that makes it look as though Lawrence is losing his grip. Bring that to Fenwick, ostensibly on the Q.T. Ask if he's heard anything about this."

Rodgers nodded and left.

Hood looked at Herbert. "If Iran has any military adventures on the drawing board, they may have moved troops or matériel. The NRO may have noticed something. Has Stephen Viens gone back to work there?"

"Last week," Herbert said.

The NRO was the National Reconnaissance Office, the top-secret facility that manages most of America's spy satellites. An agency of the Department of Defense, the NRO is staffed by personnel from the CIA, the military, and civilian DOD personnel. The existence of the NRO was declassified in September of 1992, twenty years after it was first established. Stephen Viens was an old college buddy of Op-Center's computer chief Matt Stoll. He had been extremely helpful getting information to Op-Center when more established groups like military intelligence, the CIA, and the NSA were fighting for satellite time. Viens had been accused of hiding money in a black ops situation but was later vindicated.

"Good," Hood said. "See if Viens can find anything. The NRO may have spotted activity in Iran without perceiving any immediate danger."

"I'm on it," Herbert said.

The intelligence chief wheeled his chair from the office. Hood sat back. He looked at the phone. He wanted to hear from Orlov. He wanted to hear that the Russian had someone in place and that Battat would be all right. He wanted to hear that they had managed to put the brakes on the bad news and could start turning this situation around.

We have to, Hood thought. There was something out there. Something big and dangerous. He did not know what it was or who was behind it. He did not know if the pieces Op-Center had collected would fit together. He only knew one thing for certain: Whatever it was, it had to be stopped.

TWENTY-SEVEN

Baku, Azerbaijan
Tuesday, 5:01 A.M.

David Battat felt frigidly cold and light-headed. He could hear his heart in his ears, feel it in his throat. He was aware of being wheeled somewhere. There were faces over him. Lights flashed by. Then he felt himself being lifted. He was placed on a bed, still experiencing a sense of forward motion. He was not strapped down, but there were raised metal gates on the side of the bed.

Battat shut his eyes. He did not know what had happened to him. He remembered waking up at the embassy, perspiring and shaking. Moore and Thomas brought him to the car, and then he must have slept. The next thing he knew, he woke up on a gurney.

He heard people moving around him. He coughed and opened his eyes. There was a white-haired man looking down at him.

"Mr. Battat, can you hear me?" the man shouted.

Battat nodded.

"We are going to undress you and put you in a gown," the man said to him. "Then we need to get an IV into you. Do you understand?"

Battat nodded. "What . . . happened?"

"You're ill," the doctor told him as a pair of male nurses came over. They began lifting and undressing him. "You have a very high fever. We have to bring it down."

"Okay," Battat said. What else could he say? He could not have resisted if he wanted to. But he did not understand how he could have gotten sick. He had felt fine before.

The medical team worked on him for several minutes. Battat was not entirely aware of what they were doing. He only knew that he was being shifted and turned and poked. He felt a pinch in his right arm, at the elbow, and then there was no further pain. He was also shivering, and he felt cold. Sweat had soaked into Battat's pillow. His fever warmed it quickly. His head sank into the down, muffling the sounds of the people and whatever it was they were doing. He shut his eyes again and allowed his mind to go wherever it wanted.

Soon it was quiet and dark. Battat began to feel a little warmer, more comfortable. He no longer heard drumming in his ears. He was awake, but his thoughts were dreamlike. His mind went back over the days. He saw short, blurry visions of the embassy in Moscow, the trip to Baku, the seashore, the sudden pain of the attack. A pinch in his neck. He was unaware of time passing or the hospital room. There was just a strange, not unpleasant sense of drifting. There must be something in the IV. Something that was relaxing him.

Then Battat heard something click. It sounded like a gun hammer cocking. He opened his eyes. There was a window to the left of the bed, but it was shut. He glanced toward the foot of the bed. The last time he had looked, the door was ajar. Now it was shut. A doctor or nurse must have closed it. The room was even quieter than before. It was nice. He shut his eyes again. There were no more visions, only darkness. Battat slipped quickly into a dreamless sleep.

There was another click. The sound woke Battat, and he opened his eyes. The door was still closed. But now there was someone in the room. He could see a dark figure standing in front of the door. The figure was black against the darkness behind it.

Battat was not sure he was awake.

"Hi," he said. He heard his own voice. He was definitely awake.

Slowly, the shadow moved toward him. Someone must have come to check on him.

"It's all right," Battat said in a soft slur. "You can turn on the light. I'm awake."

The figure did not speak. Battat could not make out whether it was a man or a woman. It appeared to be wearing a medical robe of some kind. And it was holding something long and slender. Battat could see the silhouette low at its side. It looked like a knife.

"Do you speak English?" Battat asked.

There was a monitor on the wall behind Battat. The green glow threw a faint light on the figure as it stopped beside the bed. It was a man. And he was definitely holding a knife. The long blade gleamed in the dull light.

"What is this?" Battat asked. It was beginning to penetrate his foggy mind that the newcomer was not a doctor. Battat tried to move, but his arms felt like they were full of wet sand.

The man's arm went back.

"Someone!" Battat said, trying to raise his voice. "Help me—"

And then the man vanished.

A moment later, sounds came from the floor. There were low grunts, chattering, and then a long, slow groan. They were followed by silence.

Battat tried to raise himself on an elbow. His arm shook, and he fell back down.

Suddenly, someone rose beside the bed.

"There may be others," said the figure. "We have to leave."

The sharp, thickly accented voice belonged to a woman. There were an awful lot of people here.

"I thought this was a private room," Battat said.

With swift, sure movements, the woman lowered the gate beside the bed, unhooked the IV, and raised Battat to a sitting position. She kept her hand on his back.

"Can you walk?" she asked.

"If you let go . . . I'm not sure I can sit," he replied.

The woman lay Battat back down and stepped away from the bed. She was a tall, lean woman with broad shoulders. He could see now that she was wearing a police uniform. The woman went to the window and pulled the curtains aside. She turned the latch and raised the window. A cool, salty breeze blew in. It made him shiver. The woman looked outside. Then she grabbed a bathrobe from a hook behind the door and returned to the bed. She sat Battat up again and pulled the robe around his shoulders.

"What are we doing?" he asked. Without the IV in his arm, he was feeling a little more focused. His head was also hurting from sitting up.

"No talk," she said.

"But wait," he said.

"They've killed your companions, and they're trying to kill you," she snapped. "I was sent to get you out."

"Killed them?"

"Quiet!" she hissed.

Battat stopped talking.

His head ached as the woman helped him stand. She grabbed Battat's clothes, then slipped his left arm around her shoulder and helped him to the window. As they hobbled over, Battat tried to focus on what she had just told him. Were Moore and Thomas dead? If so, it had to be the Harpooner. Maybe he thought they knew more than they did. But if they were dead, who had sent this woman to help him? And how did he know that she was not working for the Harpooner? She might be taking him somewhere so the killer could finish the job.

But Battat knew he might as well trust her. He was certainly in no condition to resist. Besides, the woman was being gentle with him. And if she had wanted him dead, she could have killed him in the bed. Or she could have let the other intruder kill him.

When they reached the window, the woman told Battat to lean on the sill. He did, unsteadily. She kept a hand on him, helping to keep him upright as she slipped around him. She landed quietly among the hedges outside the window and then helped him down. She put his arm back around her shoulder and then crouched. They listened for several seconds.

Battat was shivering again, his teeth clattering. But at least he was more awake than before. After a moment, they were on the move again. He felt as if he was being carried through the night. They had emerged in back of the hospital and were making their way around to the north side. They stopped at a car. To Battat's surprise, it wasn't a police car but a small black Hyundai.

She probably was not a policewoman at all. Battat did not know if that were a good thing or a bad thing. But as she laid him across the backseat and climbed behind the wheel, he knew one thing for certain.

If he remained conscious, he would find out very soon.

TWENTY-EIGHT

Washington, D.C.
Monday, 10:03 P.M.

The red-haired man sat behind his large desk. The office was dark, save for the glow of a green-shaded desk lamp and the red light on top of the phone. That meant the scrambler function was engaged.

"People are asking about Fenwick's trip," said the red-haired man.

"What people?" said the man on the other end of the line.

"The intelligence unit at Op-Center."

"Op-Center is well removed from the president," the other man said. "They don't have the same clout as the CIA—"

"I'm not so sure about that," the red-haired man interrupted.

"What do you mean?"

"I was told that Director Hood asked for and received a private meeting with the president a few hours ago," said the red-haired man.

"I know."

"Do you know what they discussed?" asked the red-haired man.

"No. More fallout from the United Nations affair. I'd guess. Do you have reason to believe otherwise?" the man asked.

"Paul Hood spoke briefly with the First Lady last night." the red-haired man said. "I checked his file. They knew each other in the past."

"Knew each other in a way we can use?"

"No," said the red-haired man. "It was platonic. Anyway, she might have seen a change in the president. Maybe she said something to Hood. I just don't know."

"I see," said the other.

There was a long silence. The red-haired man waited. He was concerned about the unexpected presence of Op-Center. The other agencies had all been covered. He and his partners had been counting on the transition period between Paul Hood and General Rodgers to keep Op-Center's eyes looking inward. Unfortunately, that had not happened. But with H-hour approaching on the foreign operation, they could not afford to have anyone watching. Harpooner had seen to it on his end. They must see to it on their end.

"Is the other documentation ready?" the other man finally asked.

The red-haired man looked at his watch. He really needed glasses to read this close, but he was fighting that. He was fighting a lot of things. He moved his wrist back slightly. "In another hour or so," he replied.

"All right," said the other man. "I don't want to move against Op-Center directly. There isn't time. And without careful planning, we might do more harm than good."

"I agree," said the red-haired man.

"Let's continue with the plan," said the other man. "If Op-Center is watching Fenwick or the president without any real idea what we're up to, that should keep them busy enough. Just make sure Fenwick doesn't do or say anything that might give them more information."

"Understood," said the red-haired man. "I'll let Fenwick know."

The other man thanked him and hung up.

The red-haired man placed the receiver in the cradle. He would call Fenwick in a minute. This was serious, unprecedented business. He needed a moment to remind himself that this was all being done for a good reason: to make sure that the United States survived the new millennium.

Despite this small setback, everything was still working the way they had planned. Reporters had been calling his office to find out about the new UN initiative, an initiatve that only the president seemed to be aware of. Members of the CIOC and even people at the UN apparently had not known about it. One very dogged TV reporter had called this evening to ask if the president had imagined "this whole thing, too." And Red Gable, the president's chief of staff, had answered off the record, "I honestly don't know, Sam. I do not know what is wrong with the president."

Though the quote would be off the record, Gable knew that his sentiment would be mentioned in the broadcast. The reporter reminded Red that this was the third time in a week the president had gotten something seriously wrong. The first time was at a breakfast with reporters. The president commented about farm subsidy legislation that was supposedly before congress. It was not. The second time, just two days ago, was at a press conference. The president's opening remarks included comments about a civil rights case that was supposedly before the Supreme Court. No such case existed. What

Gable did not tell the reporter, of course, was that the set of documents the president had been given during his daily briefings was different from the set of documents that he should have seen. The real ones. Gable had slipped those documents into the president's files after he made the public misstatements. When the president had the files brought to him, he did not understand where the misinformation had come from. Investigations by Gable and his assistants failed to turn up any suspicious activity.

Gable did not smile. He could not. The situation was too serious. But he was gratified. The reporter and many of his colleagues were very concerned about the president's state of mind. By tomorrow afternoon, the rest of the nation would also be concerned. Events that were about to unfold a world away and in Washington had been very carefully orchestrated. Events that would be misinterpreted by everyone except the third and most important leader of their team: the vice president. The president would insist that Azerbaijan had attacked an Iranian oil rig. He would recommend staying out of the conflict because it was a local issue. As Iran built up its forces in the region, the vice president would publicly urge a different tack. He would say that he did not trust Iran and would strongly advise building up an American military presence in the Caspian. Fenwick would back up the vice president. He would report that during his meetings with the Iranians, they had spoken vaguely of events that were on the horizon. He would say that they asked the United States to do nothing while they strengthened their hold on oil reserves in the region.

The Iranians would deny that, of course. But no one in America would believe them.

The disagreement between the president and vice president would cause a very public rift.

And when the Harpooner's Iranian cohorts were found dead with photographs and other evidence of sabotage on their bodies—murdered by the Harpooner himself—the vice president and Fenwick would be vindicated.

Reporters would then openly discuss the president's questionable judgment. Washington would be abuzz with rumors that the president was unstable. Senators like Barbara Fox would have no choice but to support a motion to impeachment. Sex scandals were one thing. Mental illness was something much different. There would be calls for Lawrence to step down. For the good of the nation, Lawrence would have no choice but to resign.

Vice president Cotten would become president. He would ask Jack Fenwick to become his new vice president. Congress would quickly endorse his selection. Meanwhile, the American military would move into the Caspian. They would help the Azerbaijanis protect their rigs.

In the heat of rising tensions, President Cotten would remain strong.

And then something else would happen. Something that would demand an American response so firm, so devastating, that religious fanatics would never again attack a target under American protection.

In the end, Gable told himself, the career of a president was worth that sacrifice.

TWENTY-NINE

Baku, Azerbaijan
Tuesday, 6:15 A.M.

When forty-seven-year-old Ron Friday first arrived in Baku, he felt as though he had been dropped into medieval times.

It was not a question of architecture. Embassy row was in a very modern section of the city. The modern buildings could have been lifted whole from Washington, D.C., or London, or Tokyo, or any other modern metropolis. But Baku was not like those cities where he had spent so much time. Once you moved past the embassies and business center of Baku, there was a pronounced sense of age. Many of the buildings had been standing when Columbus reached the Americas.

No, the architecture was not what made Baku seem so old, so feudal. It was a sense of entropy among the people. Azerbaijan had been ruled from the outside for so long, now that the people were free and independent, they seemed unmotivated, directionless. If it were not for petrodollars, they would probably slip deep into the Third World.

At least, that was Friday's impression. Fortunately, when the former Army Ranger and his people were finished with what they were doing here, Azerbaijan would not be quite so independent.

Friday entered his seven-story apartment building. The ten-year-old brick building was located two blocks from the embassy. He made his way up the marble stairs. Friday lived on the top floor, but he did not like being in elevators. Even when he was with the other embassy workers who lived here, he took the stairs. Elevators were too confining, and they left him vulnerable.

Friday walked toward his apartment. He could not believe that he had been here nearly six months. It seemed much longer, and he was glad his tenure was coming to an end. Not because Deputy Ambassador Williamson didn't need him. To the contrary, Friday had proven valuable to the diplomat, especially in her efforts to moderate Azerbaijani claims on Caspian oil. Friday's years as an attorney for a large international oil company served him well in that capacity. But Friday's real boss would need him elsewhere, in some other trouble spot. He would see to it that Friday was transferred.

To India or Pakistan, perhaps. That was where Friday really wanted to go. There were oil issues to be dealt with there, in the Arabian Sea and on the border between the Great Indian Desert in the Rajasthan province of India and the Thar Desert in Pakistan. But more than that, the Indian subcontinent was the place where the next big war would begin, perhaps triggered by a nuclear exchange. Friday wanted to be in there, helping to manipulate the politics of the region. It had been a dream of his ever since he was in college. Since the day when he had first gone to work for the National Security Agency.

Friday put the key in the door and listened. He heard the cat cry. Her mewing was a normal welcome. That was a very good indication that no one was waiting for him inside.

Friday had been recruited by the NSA when he was in law school. One of his professors, Vincent Van Heusen, had been an OSS operative during World War II. After the war, Van Heusen had helped draft the National Security Act of 1947, the legislation that led to the founding of the Central Intelligence Agency.

Professor Van Heusen saw in Friday some of the same qualities he himself had possessed as a young man. Among those was independence. Friday had learned that growing up in the Michigan woods where he attended a one-room schoolhouse and went hunting with his father every weekend—not only with a rifle but with a longbow. After graduating from NYU, Friday spent time at the NSA as a trainee. When he went to work for the oil industry a year later, he was also working as a spy. In addition to making contacts in Europe, the Middle East, and the Caspian, Friday was given the names of CIA operatives working in those countries. From time to time, he was asked to watch them—to spy on the spies, to make certain that they were working only for the United States.

Friday finally left the private sector five years ago, bored with working for the oil industry. They had become more concerned with international profits than with the vitality of America and its economy. But that was not why he quit. He left the private sector out of patriotism. He wanted to work for the NSA full-time. He had watched as intelligence operations went to hell overseas. Electronic espionage had replaced hands-on human surveillance. The result was much less efficient mass intelligence gathering. To Friday, that was like getting meat from a slaughterhouse instead of hunting it down. The food didn't taste as good when it was mass-produced. The experience was less satisfying. And over time, the hunter grew soft.

Friday had no intention of growing soft. So when his Washington contact told him that Jack Fenwick wanted to talk to him, Friday was eager to meet. Friday went to see him at the Off the Record bar at the Hay-Adams Hotel. It was during the week of the president's inauguration, so the bar was jammed, and the men were barely noticed. It was then that Fenwick suggested a plan so bold that Friday thought it was a joke. Or a test of some kind.

Then Friday agreed to meet with some of the other members of the group. And he believed.

Oh, how he believed. They sent him here and, through contacts in Iran, he was put in touch with the Harpooner. Iran did not realize they were going to be double-crossed. That once they had an excuse to move into the Caspian Sea, a new American president would move against them.

And the Harpooner? He did not care. Friday and the Harpooner had worked closely organizing the attack against Battat and the program of disinformation to the CIA.

Friday was still dressed in yesterday's clothes. In case anyone saw him, that would support the story he would tell them. It was just one of the many stories he had perfected over the years to cover meetings he had to make with operatives.

Or targets.

Friday was glad the Harpooner had put one of his other men inside the hospital as backup. They had hoped that Friday would be able to get both Moore and Thomas while they were outside. But the way the ambulance was parked he did not have a clear shot at Thomas. Friday hoped the Iranian assassin had been able to get the other man. It would have been easier, of course, if Friday could have taken all three men out in the embassy. But that might have exposed him. The embassy was not that large, and someone might have seen them. And there were security cameras everywhere. This way had been cleaner, easier.

After firing the shot, Friday had dropped the rifle the Harpooner had given to him. It was a G3, a Heckler & Koch model, Iranian manufacture. He had others at his disposal if he needed them. Friday had tossed the weapon in a shallow pond near the hospital. He knew the local police would search the area for clues and would probably find it. He wanted it to be traced back to Teheran. Friday and his people wanted to make very sure that the world knew Iran had assassinated two officials of the United States embassy. The Iranians would disavow that, of course, but America would not believe the Iranians. The NSA would see to that.

The Iranians who were working with the Harpooner had made cell phone calls to one another during the past few days. They had discussed the attack on the oil rig and described the two pylons that had to be destroyed: "target one" and "target two." The Iranians did not know that the Harpooner made certain those calls were monitored by the NSA. That the conversations were recorded and then digitally altered. Now, on those tapes, the targets the Iranians were discussing were embassy employees, not pylons.

In a phone call of his own, the Harpooner had added that the deaths would be a warning, designed to discourage Americans from pursuing any action against Iran in the coming oil wars. The Harpooner pointed out in the call that if Washington insisted on becoming involved, American officials would be assassinated worldwide.

Of course, that threat would backfire. After President Lawrence resigned, the new president of the United States would use the brutal murders as a rallying cry. He was not a live-and-let-live leader like the incumbent. Someone who was willing to cooperate with the United Nations to the detriment of his own nation. The assassinations, like the attacks on the oil rigs, would underscore that the United States had unfinished business from the previous century: the need to strike a decisive, full-scale blow against terrorist regimes and terrorist groups that were being protected by those regimes.

Friday entered his apartment. He saw the red light on his answering machine flashing. He walked over and played the message. There was only one, from Deputy Ambassador Williamson. She needed him to come to the embassy right away. She said that she had tried his cell phone but could not reach him.

Well, of course she could not. His cell phone had been in his jacket, and his jacket had been slung over a chair in another room. He had not heard the phone because he was in the bedroom of a woman he had met at the International Bar.

Friday called her back at the embassy. Williamson did

not bother to ask where he had been. She just told him the bad news. Tom Moore had been shot and killed by a sniper outside the hospital. Pat Thomas's throat had been cut by an assassin inside the hospital.

Friday allowed himself a small, contented smile. The Harpooner's assassin had succeeded.

"Fortunately," Williamson went on, "David Battat was able to stop the man who tried to kill him."

Friday's expression darkened. "How?"

"His throat was cut with his own knife," she said.

"But Battat was ill—"

"I know," said the deputy ambassador. "And either Battat was delirious or afraid. After he stopped the killer, he left the hospital by the window. The police are out looking for him now. So far, all they've found was the rifle used to kill Mr. Moore. Metal detectors picked it up in a pond."

"I see," Friday said. The assassin did not speak English. Even if Battat were lucid, he could not have learned anything from the killer. But Fenwick and the Harpooner would be furious if Battat were still alive. "I'd better go out and join the search," Friday said.

"No," Williamson said. "I need you here at the embassy. Someone has to liaise between the Baku police and Washington. I've got to deal with the political ramifications."

"What political ramifications?" Friday asked innocently. This was going to be sweet. It was going to be very sweet.

"The police found the rifle they think was used in the attack on Moore," she said. "I don't want to talk about this on an open line. I'll tell you more when you get here."

That was good news, at least. The deputy ambassador had concluded that the killings were political and not random.

"I'm on my way," Friday said.

"Watch yourself," Williamson said.

"I always do," he replied. Friday hung up, turned around, and left the apartment. "I always do."

THIRTY

Baku, Azerbaijan
Tuesday, 6:16 A.M.

The Harpooner and his team reached the oil rig just before dawn. The boat cut its engines one thousand feet from the nearest of the four columns. Then the Harpooner and four members of his Iranian team slipped into the water. They were all wearing wet suits and compressed air cylinders. Slipping beneath the dark surface of the sea, the men swam toward the rig.

Two of them carried waterproof pouches containing watergel high-energy explosives. The Harpooner had carefully injected the blue sticks with heat-sensitive pentanitroaniline. As the sun rose, the heat would cause the foil packet to warm. The sunlight itself would detonate the explosion.

Two other men carried an inflatable raft. This would allow them some stability underneath the platform. Many rigs had sensors on the columns and motion detectors along the sea line. Avoiding the columns and going under the motion detectors was the safest way to get inside the perimeter. Once the explosives were placed, it would be virtually impossible for the crew of the rig to get to them in time.

The Harpooner carried a spear gun and night-vision glasses. He would use the gun to fire the watergel pack-

ets around the support struts beneath the platform. The
Harpooner had brought along only a dozen of the seven-
eighths-inch sticks of explosive. He had learned long
ago that the trick to destroying something big is not
necessarily to hit it with something big. In hand-to-hand
combat, a foe could be driven back with a powerful
roundhouse punch. He can be debilitated faster, more
efficiently, and with more control, with a finger pressed
against his throat, just below the larynx and above the
clavicle. Hooking the top of a foot behind the knee and
then stepping down with the side of the foot will drop
someone faster than hitting them with a baseball bat.
Besides, all it takes to neutralize a bat attack is to move
in close to the attacker.

The Iranian oil rigs in the Caspian Sea are mostly
semisubmersible platforms. They rest on four thick legs
with massive pontoons that sink below the waterline.
There is a platform on top of the legs. The riser system—the underwater component, which includes the
drill—descends from the derrick, which is mounted on
the platform. The key to destroying a platform like that
is not to take out the columns but to weaken the center
of the platform. Once that has happened, the weight of
the structures on top will do the rest. The Harpooner's
team had been able to get copies of the oil rig blueprints.
He knew just where to place the watergel.

The men reached the underbelly of the rig without
incident. Though it was dark in the water, the higher
struts of the rig caught the first glint of dawn. As the
Harpooner eyeballed the target, two men inflated the raft
while the other two attached a pair of watergel sticks
beneath the tip of three spears. The twelve-inch-long

sticks were carefully taped belly-to-belly. This configuration allowed the spear to be fitted into the tube muzzle. It also made sure that the sticks of watergel would not upset the balance of the spear. Though it would have been easier to assemble the package on the boat, the Harpooner had wanted to keep the watergel packets as dry as possible. Though moisture would not harm the explosives, wet foil would take longer for the sun to warm. These packets would only be exposed to direct sunlight for a half hour. He had to make certain they were dry enough—and thus hot enough—to explode within that time.

The raft was a six-man hexagonal platform. The Harpooner did not need it to hold six men. He wanted the larger size for stability. Larger rafts tended to ignore the smaller waves. That was important when he lay on his back to fire. He had removed the canopy to make it lighter. The large case in which it had been carried was discarded. The Harpooner climbed on board while the other men hung onto the sides to steady the raft even more.

The speargun was made of stainless steel. It was painted matte black to minimize reflected sunlight. The spears were also black. The weapon was comprised of a forty-inch-long black tube and a yellow grip and trigger at the end. Only a foot of spear protruded from the end. Normally, a rope was attached to the spears so that prey could be hauled back to the spearman. The Harpooner had removed these back on the boat.

There were six-inch-thick acoustic dampeners beneath the platform. They were located fifty feet above the sea. The hard rubber pads had been placed there to muffle the sounds of activity. This was done so that people who lived on the rig would suffer as little noise pollution as possible. The Harpooner had chosen his targets from the blueprints. He would fire two harpoons. The first would go into the padded area below and to the northeast of the derrick. The derrick was in the southwest corner of the platform. When the detonation occurred, the derrick would fall toward the center of the platform. A second harpoon would be fired into the platform at the point where the heavy center of the derrick would land. The second explosion, plus the impact of the derrick, would shatter the platform and cause it to collapse inward. Everything would slide to the center and tumble into the sea.

The Harpooner would not need the third harpoon to destroy the rig, though he did not tell his people that.

The terrorist donned night-vision glasses and lay on his back. The speargun had terrific recoil, equivalent to a twelve-gauge shotgun. That would give him quite a bump. But his shoulder could take it. He aimed the weapon and fired. There was a sound like a metallic cough and the spear flew through the dark.

It hit the target with a faint thunk. The Harpooner quickly repositioned himself to fire the second shaft. It, too, struck its target. He motioned the men to start back. As soon as the others ducked underwater, the Harpooner pulled the tape from the spear, grabbed one of the equipment bags, and slipped the watergel sticks inside. Then he slid into the water and followed his men back to the boat.

Upon boarding the vessel, the men dropped the remains of Sergei Cherkassov into the sea. On the way over, they had burned the body. It would look as though he had been killed in the blast. The photographs that had been taken from the airplane were already in his pocket. As far as the Iranians on board knew, the Russians and the Azerbaijanis would be blamed for the attack.

The Harpooner knew differently.

When Cherkassov was in the water, the boat departed. They were nearly out of visual range when the oil rig exploded.

The Harpooner was watching through high-powered binoculars. He saw the puff of yellow red smoke under the platform. He saw the tower shudder and then do a slow pirouette drop toward the center. A moment later, the muted pop of the first explosion reached the boat.

The Iranians on the deck all cheered. Which was odd, the Harpooner thought. Even though they thought they were doing this for the national good, they were happy about the deaths of at least one hundred of their countrymen.

A moment before the derrick hit, the second watergel packet exploded. The Harpooner had positioned the two to go off nearly at the same time. It would not have done for the derrick to crash, knock the spear from the rubber padding, and drop it into the sea. A second cloud of red and yellow smoke began to form, but it was flattened and disbursed when the derrick struck the platform. It hit with a small-sounding crunch. Debris flew into the morning sky, chasing away the distant gulls.

The entire rig shuddered. The whole thing reminded the Harpooner of a vignette he had seen as a child. A poplar tree had been split during a storm and fell across power lines. It hit them, bounced, then hit them again. The lines hung there for a moment before sagging and then ripping from the poles on the left and right. That was what happened here. The platform stood for a moment after the derrick struck. Then, slowly, the steel and concrete sagged where the second blast had weakened them. The platform bent inward. Sheds, cranes, tanks, and even the helicopter began sliding toward the crease. Their weight caused additional strain. The Harpooner could hear the ugly collisions in the distance, see the smoke and shattered pieces of wood and metal fly into the air.

And then it happened. The added weight was too much for the platform to bear. It cracked and dumped everything into the sea. The boat was now too far away for the Harpooner to make everything out. The collapse looked like a waterfall from this distance, especially when the cascade of white and silver debris hit the sea, sending up waves and spray.

As the rig disappeared beyond the horizon, all the Harpooner could see was a large ball of mist hanging in the new day.

He turned away, accepting the congratulations of the team. They were treating him like a football hero, but he felt more like an artist. Using the medium of explosives and a canvas of steel and concrete, the Harpooner had created a perfect destruction.

He went below to wash up. He always needed to wash after creation. It was a symbolic act of completion and of getting ready for the next work. Which would be soon. Very soon.

When the boat reached the docks, the Harpooner told

the crew he wanted to go ashore. He told the Iranians he wanted to make certain that the Azerbaijani police had not already learned of the blast. If they had, the police might be checking incoming vessels. They might be looking for possible terrorists and also for eyewitnesses to the explosion.

The men thought that was a good idea.

The Harpooner told them that if he did not come back in five minutes, they should leave the dock and head to the open sea. The Harpooner said that if the police were talking to people, stopping them from leaving the area, he would figure out a way to elude them.

The men agreed. The Harpooner went ashore.

Six minutes later, there was a massive explosion in the harbor. The Harpooner had stuck a timed detonator into one of the sticks of watergel. He had set it and then left it below, under one of the bunks. Evidence from the attack was still on board. It would take a while, but eventually the authorities would find traces of the watergel on the boat and on the rig and realize that the Iranians, aided by a Russian terrorist, had attacked their own operation. The Iranians would dispute that, of course, and tensions would rise even higher. The United States would suspect that the Russians and Iranians were working together to seize the Caspian oil wells. There would be no way to avoid what was coming.

The Harpooner got in the repainted van and drove it from the harbor. There were no police there. Not yet. At this hour, the Baku police force was involved primarily in traffic management and accident investigation. Besides, there was no indication that a boat had attacked the rig or that it had come to Baku. That would come later, when they found the Russian and the Americans had sent over satellite photographs of the region.

The Harpooner headed toward the Old City. There, he drove up Inshaatchilar Prospekti toward the hotels on Bakihanov Kuchasi. Two days before, he had taken a hotel room under an assumed name. Here he was Ivan Ganiev, a telecommunications consultant. It was a name and profession he had chosen with care. If he were ever stopped by customs agents or police, he could explain why he was traveling with high-tech equipment. And being Russian had another advantage, especially here. One that would help him get out of the country when the time came.

He had left clothing, gear, and cash in the room and a do not disturb sign on the door. He would clean himself up, dye his hair, and then take a long nap. When he woke, he would apply a fake mustache, slip colored contact lenses into his eyes, and call a cab to take him to the train station. A cabdriver was always a good hostage in case he was discovered and surrounded. He would use his fake passport to leave the city.

He parked the van in an alley near the hospital. Then he pulled a packet of dental floss from his pocket. He rubbed it deeply between two teeth until his mouth filled with blood. Then he spat on the floor, dashboard, and seat cushion. It was the fastest way to draw blood. It also left no scars, in case anyone decided to stop him and check for wounds. He did not need a lot of blood. Just traces for the forensics people to find. When he was finished with that, he slipped a plastic mircochip in the gas tank. Then he replaced the cap.

When he was finished dressing the van, the Harpooner

took the backpack containing the Zed-4 phone and left. When the authorities found the vehicle, they would also find evidence inside tying it to the Iranians in the boat. That would include their fingerprints on the wheel, glove compartment, and handles. They would assume that one or more of the men got away. The blood would suggest that he was injured. The police would waste time looking through hospital records for a possible perpetrator.

The Harpooner would return to Moscow. Then he would leave Russia and permit himself a rest. Possibly a vacation in some country where he had never committed terrorism. Some place where they would not be looking out for him.

Some place where he could sit back and read the newspapers.

Enjoy once again the impact his art had had on the world.

THIRTY-ONE

Washington, D.C.
Monday, 11:11 P.M.

Paul Hood was concerned, confused, and tired.

Bob Herbert had just spoken with Stephen Viens of the National Reconnaissance Office. Viens was working late to catch up on paperwork that had collected during his absence. While Viens was there, an NRO satellite had recorded an explosion in the Caspian Sea. He had called Herbert, who wanted to know if anything unusual had happened in the region. Then Herbert called Paul Hood.

"According to our files, the coordinates of the explosion match those of Iran's Majidi-2 oil rig," Herbert said.

"Could it have been an accident?" Hood asked.

"We're checking that now," Herbert said. "We've got some faint radio signals coming from the rig, which means there may be survivors."

"May be?"

"A lot of those rigs have automatic beacons to signal rescue craft in the area," Herbert said. "That may be what we're hearing. The audio keeps breaking up, so we can't tell if it's a recording."

"Understood," Hood said. "Bob, I've got a bad feeling about this. Fenwick goes to the Iranian mission, and then an Iranian rig is attacked."

"I know," Herbert said. "I tried to call him, but there was no answer. I'm wondering if the NSA knew about this attack, and Fenwick took intelligence to the mission in New York."

"If Fenwick had intel, wouldn't Iran have tried to prevent the attack?" Hood asked.

"Not necessarily," Herbert told Hood. "Teheran has been itching for a reason to establish a stronger military presence in the Caspian Sea. An attack by Azerbaijan could give them that reason. It's no different than historians who say that Franklin Roosevelt allowed Pearl Harbor to be attacked so we'd have a reason to get into World War Two."

"But then why all the deception with the president?" Hood asked.

"Plausible deniability?" Herbert replied. "The president has been getting misinformation."

"Yes, but Jack Fenwick would not undertake something of this magnitude on his own," Hood said.

"Why not?" Herbert asked. "Ollie North ran an uberoperation during Iran-Contra—"

"A military officer might have the balls for that but not Jack Fenwick," Hood said. "I had a look at his dossier. The guy is Mr. Support Systems. He's instituted backup systems for backup systems at the NSA. Got congress to jack up the budget fifteen percent for next year. The CIA only got an eight percent bump and we got six."

"Impressive."

"Yeah," Hood said. "And he just doesn't strike me as the kind of guy to take this kind of chance. Not without backup."

"So?" Herbert said. "Maybe he's got it."

Shit, Hood thought. *Maybe he does.*

"Think about it," Herbert went on. "He got double the increases everyone else got. Who has that kind of sway with congress? Not President Lawrence, that's for sure. He's not conservative enough for the budget group."

"No, he's not," Hood agreed. "Bob, find out if Matt can get into Fenwick's phone records and calendar. See who he might have talked to and met with over the past few days and weeks."

"Sure," he said. "But it's going to be tough to draw any conclusions from that. The NSA head meets with practically everyone."

"Exactly," Hood said.

"I don't follow."

"If Fenwick were part of a black-ops situation, he would probably meet with his team away from the office. Maybe by seeing who he stopped meeting with, officially, we can figure out who he's been seeing on the sly."

"Nice one, Paul," Herbert said. "I wouldn't have thought of that."

"But that isn't what has me worried," Hood went on. The phone beeped. "Excuse me, Bob. Would you bring Mike up to date on this?"

"Will do," Herbert said.

Hood switched lines. Sergei Orlov was on the other end.

"Paul," Orlov said, "good news. We have your man."

"What do you mean you have him?" Hood asked. The Russian operative was only supposed to keep an eye on him.

"Our operative arrived in time to save him from joining his comrades," Orlov said. "The assassin was dispatched and left in the hospital room. Your man was taken from the hospital to another location. He is there now."

"General, I don't know what to say," Hood told him. "Thank you."

"Thank you is good enough," Orlov said. "But what do we do now? Can he help us get the Harpooner?"

"I hope so," Hood told him. "The Harpooner must still be there. Otherwise, he would not have had to draw these people out and assassinate them. General, did you hear what happened in the Caspian?"

"Yes," Orlov said. "An Iranian oil rig was destroyed. The Azerbaijanis are probably going to be blamed, whether they did it or not. Do you know anything more about it?"

"Not yet," Hood said. "But the operative you saved might. If the Harpooner's behind this attack, we need to know. Can you arrange for the American agent to call me here?"

"Yes," Orlov said.

Hood thanked him and said he would wait by the phone.

Orlov was correct. Suspicion would fall on Azerbaijan. They were the ones who disputed Iran's presence in that region of the sea. They were the ones who had the most to gain. But the Harpooner had done most of his work for Middle Eastern nations. What if Azerbaijan wasn't behind the attack? What if another nation was trying to make it seem that way?

Hood got back on the phone with Herbert. He also patched in Mike Rodgers and briefed them both. When he was finished, there was a short silence.

"Frankly, I'm stumped," Herbert said. "We need more intel."

"I agree," Hood said. "But we may have more intel than we think."

"What do you mean?" Herbert asked.

"I mean we've got the NSA working with Iran," Hood said. "We have a president who was kept out of the loop by the NSA. We have a terrorist who works with Iran taking out CIA agents in Azerbaijan. We have an attack on an Iranian oil installation off the coast of Azerbaijan. There's a lot of information there. Maybe we're not putting it together in the right way."

"Paul, do we know who in the CIA first found out the Harpooner was in Baku?" Rodgers asked.

"No," Hood said. "Good point."

"I'll get someone to find that out ASAP," Herbert said.

Hood and Rodgers waited while Herbert made the call. Hood sat there trying to make sense of the facts, but it still was not coming together. *Concerned, confused, and tired.* It was a bad combination, especially for a man in his forties. He used to be able to pull all-nighters without a problem. Not anymore.

Herbert got back on. "I've got someone calling the director's office, Code Red-One," he said. "We'll have the information soon."

Code Red-One signified an imminent emergency to national interest. Despite the competitiveness between the agencies, CR1s were generally not denied.

"Thanks," Hood said.

"Paul, do you know the story about the Man Who Never Was?" Rodgers asked.

"The World War Two story? I read the book in high school," Hood said. "He was part of the disinformation campaign during World War Two."

"Correct," Rodgers said. "A British intelligence group took the body of a homeless man, created a false identity for it, and planted papers on the body that said the Allies would invade Greece, not Sicily. The body was left where the Germans would find it. This helped divert Axis forces from Sicily. I mention this because a key player in the operation was a British general named Howard Tower. He was key in the sense that he was also fed misinformation."

"For what reason?" Hood asked.

"General Tower's communiqués were intercepted by the Germans," Rodgers said. "British Intelligence saw to that."

"I'm missing something here," Herbert said. "Why are we talking about World War Two?"

"When Tower learned what had happened, he put a gun barrel in his ear and pulled the trigger," Rodgers said.

"Because he was used?" Hood asked.

"No," Rodgers said, "because he thought he'd screwed up."

"I'm still not getting this," Herbert admitted.

"Paul, you said the president was pretty upset when you spoke with him," Rodgers went on. "And when you met with the First Lady, she described a man who sounded like he was having a breakdown."

"Right," Hood said.

"That may not mean anything," Herbert said. "He's president of the United States. The job has a way of aging people."

"Hold on, Bob. Mike may be onto something," Hood said. There was something gnawing at Hood's stomach. Something that was getting worse the more he thought about it. "The president did not look tired when I saw him. He looked disturbed."

"I'm not surprised," Herbert said. "He was being kept out of the loop and made an apparent faux pas about the UN. He was embarrassed."

"But there's another component to this," Hood told him. "There's the cumulative psychological impact of disinformation. What if plausible deniability and bureaucratic confusion aren't the reasons the president was misled? What if there's another reason?"

"Such as?" Herbert asked.

"What if disinformation isn't the end but the means?" Hood said. "What if someone is trying to convince Lawrence that he's losing his grip?"

"You mean, what if someone is trying to gaslight the president of the United States?" Herbert declared.

"Yes," Hood replied.

"Well, it's going to take a lot of convincing before I buy that," Herbert said. "For one thing, anyone who tried that would never get away with it. There are too many people around the president—"

"Bob, we already decided that this is something Jack Fenwick would not, probably could not, do on his own," Hood said.

"Yes, but to make it work, he'd need a small army of people who were very close to the president," Herbert said.

"Who?" Hood asked. "The chief of staff?"

"For one," Herbert said. "He's privy to most of the same briefings the president receives."

"Okay," Hood said. "Gable's already on my list of unreliables. Who else? Who would be absolutely necessary for a plan like this to work?"

Before Herbert could answer, his phone beeped. He answered the call and was back in less than a minute.

"Don't tell me, 'I told you so,' " Herbert said.

"Why?" Hood asked.

"A high-level official at the CIA in Washington got the intel about the Harpooner from the NSA," Herbert told them. "The NSA didn't have anyone in Baku, so they notified the CIA. The CIA sent David Battat."

"Whom the Harpooner knew just where to find," Rodgers said. "Instead of killing him, the Harpooner poisoned him somehow. And then Battat was used to bring out Moore and Thomas at the hospital."

"Apparently," Herbert said.

"Paul, you asked a question a moment ago," Rodgers said. "You wanted to know who else would be necessary for a psy-ops maneuver to work against the president. That's a good question, but it's not the first one we need to answer."

"No?" Hood said. "What is?"

"Who would benefit the most from the mental incapacitation of the president?" Rodgers asked. "And at the same time, who would be in a perfect position to help make some of the disinformation happen?"

Hood's stomach was growling now. The answer was obvious.

The vice president of the United States.

THIRTY-TWO

Washington, D.C.
Monday, 11:24 P.M.

Vice President Charles Cotten was in the ground-floor sitting room of the vice presidential residence. The mansion was located on the sprawling Massachusetts Avenue grounds of the United States Naval Observatory. It was a twenty-minute drive from here to the vice president's two offices: one in the White House and the other in the neighboring Old Executive Office Building. It was just a short walk from the mansion to the National Cathedral. Lately, Cotten had been spending more time than usual at the cathedral.

Praying.

An aide knocked and entered. The woman told the vice president that his car was ready. The vice president thanked her and rose from the leather armchair. He entered the dark, wood-paneled hallway and headed toward the front door. Upstairs, Cotten's wife and children were asleep.

My wife and children. They were words Cotten never thought would be part of his life. When he was a senator from New York, Cotten had been the ultimate lady's man. A new, gorgeous date to every function. The press referred to these younger women as "Cotten candy." There were regular jokes about what went on below the

Cotten belt. Then he met Marsha Arnell at a Museum of Modern Art fund-raiser in Manhattan, and everything changed. Marsha was twenty-seven, eleven years his junior. She was a painter and an art historian. She was telling a group of guests about late–twentieth-century art and how the work of commercial artists like Frank Frazetta, James Bama, and Rich Corben defined a new American vision: the power of the human form and face blended with landscapes from dream and fantasy. Cotten was hypnotized by the young woman's voice, her ideas, and her vital and optimistic view of America.

They were married four months later.

For nearly ten years, Marsha and their twin girls had been the foundation of Charles Cotten's life. They were his focus, his heart, and their future was never far from his thoughts.

They were the reason the vice president had conceived of this plan. To preserve America for his family.

The fact was, the United States was at risk. Not just from terrorist attacks, though more and more those were becoming a very real threat. The danger facing the United States was that it was on the verge of becoming irrelevant. Our military could destroy the world many times over. But other nations knew that we would never do that, so they did not fear us. Our economy was relatively strong. But so were the economies of many other nations and alliances. The Eurodollar was strong, and the new South American League and their SAL currency was growing in power and influence. Central America and Mexico were talking about a new confederacy. Canada was being tempted to join the European economy. Those unions, those nations, did not face the kind of suspicion and resentment that greeted America the world over. The reason? America was a giant everyone wanted to see brought down. Not destroyed; they needed us too much for international policing. They simply wanted us humbled and humiliated. We were a meddling thug to our enemies and an overbearing big brother to our supposed allies.

These were not concerns that bothered other nations during times of international depression or world war. It was all right to invade France to free the French of Hitler. But it was not okay to fly over France to bomb Libya, the home of a different despot. It was all right to maintain a military presence in Saudi Arabia to protect the nation from Saddam Hussein. But it was not all right to fly jets from Riyadh to protect American troops in the region.

We were not respected, and we were not feared. That had to change. And it had to change long before Michael Lawrence was scheduled to leave the White House in three years. That would be too late to act.

The problem had not been caused by Michael Lawrence. He was simply the latest bearer of the torch of arrogant isolationism. When he was in the Senate, Cotten had felt that there needed to be a United States that was better integrated with the world. The one that Teddy Roosevelt had described. The one that carried a big stick and was not afraid to use it. But also one that knew how to speak softly. An America that knew how to use and exert diplomacy and economic pressure. One that had the resolve to use quiet assassination and blackmail instead of mounting very public and unpopular miniwars.

When the senator was tapped to share a ticket with presidential candidate Michael Lawrence, Cotten accepted. The public liked Lawrence's "I'm for the people" slogan and style, his perception as a man who had come back from the political wilderness to serve them. But he had wanted to balance his relatively up-front and independent manner with someone who knew how to work the back rooms of Congress and the corridors of power abroad.

Cotten left the mansion and slid into the car. The driver shut the door for him. They rolled into the dark, still night. Cotten's soul was on fire. He was not going to enjoy what he and his allies were about to do. He remembered when he had first approached them and others individually. Seemingly casual remarks were dropped. If they were ignored, he let the subject drop. If not, he pursued it with more pointed remarks. Cotten realized that was what it must be like for a married man to ask a woman to have an affair. Go too far with the wrong individual, and everything could be lost.

Each man had become involved for the same reason: patriotism. The creation of an America that led the world community rather than reacted to it. An America that rewarded peace with prosperity and punished warmongers not with a public pummeling and credibility but with quiet, lonely death. Lawrence was not willing to cross the line from legal war to illegal murder, even though lives would be saved. But the dawn of the twenty-first century was not a time for warfare. It bred short-term misery and long-term hatred. The world was becoming too small, too crowded for bombs. As distasteful as this was, a change had to come. For the nation and for the sake of its children. For the sake of his children.

The car moved swiftly through the empty streets. Washington was always so deserted at night. Only the spies and plotters were afoot. It seemed strange to think of himself in that capacity. He had always been a straight shooter. If you felt passionately about something, you spoke your mind. If you didn't feel passionately, then it probably was not worth doing. But this was different. This operation had to be kept very quiet. Kept only among those who were actively involved in its planning and execution.

Now this was it, Cotten thought. The last leg of the operation. According to the president's staff, announcing a UN intelligence initiative that did not exist had seriously rattled Lawrence. It had shaken him more than the other canards Fenwick and Gable had fed him and subsequently denied—usually during a cabinet session or meeting in the Oval Office.

"No, Mr. President," Cotten would say softly, seemingly embarrassed for the confusion of the president, "there was never a Pentagon report that Russia and China exchanged artillery fire over the Amur River. Sir, we had not heard that the FBI director had threatened to resign. When did this happen? Mr. President, don't you recall? We had agreed that Mr. Fenwick would share this new intelligence with Iran."

The question of sharing intelligence with Iran had been important to the final stage of the operation. Jack Fenwick had told the Iranian ambassador that according to United States intelligence sources, an attack would come from Azerbaijan. They weren't sure what the target would be, but it would probably be a terrorist attack in the heart of Teheran. Fenwick had assured Iran that if they retaliated, the United States would stay out of it. This nation wanted to nurture closer ties with the Islamic Republic of Iran, not stand in the way of its self-defense.

Lawrence, of course, would be pushed to behave in a less accommodating manner. And when he realized where his confused perceptions had taken the nation, he would be forced to resign.

The fact that Lawrence had known nothing about the meeting was irrelevant. At tonight's meeting with the so-called "Eyes Only Group"—Gable, Fenwick, and the vice president—the men would convince the president that he had been kept informed. They would show him memos that he had seen and signed. They would show him the calendar his secretary kept on the computer. The appointment had been added after she left for the day. Then they would jump right into the current crisis. They would trust and the president would lead. By morning, Michael Lawrence would be publicly committed to a path of confrontation with two of the most volatile nations on earth.

The following morning, with the help of unnamed NSA sources, the *Washington Post* would run a front-page, above-the-fold article about the president's mental health. Though the newspaper piece would be hooked to the UN fiasco, it would also contain exclusive details about some of the president's increasingly dramatic and fully documented lapses. The nation would not tolerate instability from the commander-in-chief. Especially as he was about to send the nation to war.

Things would happen very quickly after that. There

was no constitutional provision for the president to take a leave of absence. And there was no short-term cure for mental illness. Lawrence would be forced to resign, if not by public pressure then by act of congress. Cotten would become president. The United States military would immediately back down in the Caspian Sea to avoid a confrontation with Iran and Russia. Instead, through intelligence operations, they would prove that Iran had masterminded the entire operation in the first place. Teheran would protest, but the government's credibility would be seriously compromised. Then, through diplomacy, the United States would find ways to encourage moderates in Iran to seize more power. Meanwhile, spared a pounding from Iran and Russia, Azerbaijan would be in America's debt.

After the clouds of war drifted away, President Cotten would make certain of something else. That Azerbaijan and America shared in the oil reserves of the Caspian Sea. The Middle East would never again hold the United States hostage. Not in their embassies nor at the gas pump.

With order restored and American influence and credibility at its peak, President Charles Cotten would reach out to the nations of the world. They would be invited to join us in a permanent peace and prosperity. When their people experienced freedom and economic reward for the first time, they would cast those governments out. Eventually, even China would follow suit. They had to. People were greedy, and the old-line Communists would not live forever. If the United States stopped provoking them, providing the government with a public enemy, Beijing would weaken and evolve.

This was the world that Charles Cotten wanted for America. It was the world he wanted for his own children. He had thought about it for years. He had worked to achieve it. He had prayed for it.

And very soon, he would have it.

THIRTY-THREE

Baku, Azerbaijan
Tuesday, 8:09 A.M.

David Battat was lying on a hard twin bed in the small, sparsely furnished studio apartment. There was a window to his left. Though the blinds were drawn, the room brightened as light leaked through the slats.

Battat was shivering but alert. His abductor, hostess, or savior—he had not yet decided which—was in the kitchenette off to the right. She had been making eggs, sausage, and tea when the phone rang.

Battat hoped the call was brief. The food smelled good, but the thought of tea was even better. He needed to warm himself inside. Do something to stop the trembling. He felt as though he had the flu. He was weak and everything he saw or heard seemed dreamlike. But his head and chest were also very tight. More than from any sickness he could remember. Hopefully, once he had tea and something to eat, he would be able to focus a little better, try to understand what had happened back at the hospital.

The woman walked over to the bed. She was carrying the phone. She stood about five-foot-nine and had a lean, dark face framed by thick, black, shoulder-length hair. Her cheekbones were pronounced, and her eyes were blue. Battat was willing to bet there was Lithuanian blood in her. She handed the receiver to Battat.

"There is someone who wishes to speak with you," she said in thickly accented English.

"Thank you," said Battat. His own voice was a weak croak. He accepted the cordless phone. He did not bother to ask her who it was. He would find out soon enough. "Hello?"

"David Battat?" said the caller.

"Yes—"

"David, this is Paul Hood, the director of Op-Center."

"Paul Hood?" Battat was confused. Op-Center found him here and was calling him now to ask about—that? "Sir, I'm sorry about what happened," Battat said, "but I didn't know that Annabelle Hampton was working with—"

"This isn't about the United Nations siege," Hood interrupted. "David, listen to me. We have reason to believe that the NSA set you and your colleagues up."

It took a moment for Battat to process what Hood had said. "They set us up to be murdered? Why?"

"I can't tell you that now," Hood replied. "What's important is that for the present, you're out of danger."

The young woman walked over with a cup of tea. She set it on the night table beside the bed. Battat used an elbow to drag himself into a sitting position. She helped him by putting strong hands under his arm and literally lifting him from the bed.

"What I need to know is this," Hood went on. "If we can locate the Harpooner, do you feel up to helping us take him down?"

"If there's a way for me to get the Harpooner, I'm up

for it," Battat said. Just the thought of that energized him.

"Good," Hood told him. "We're working with a Russian intelligence group on this. I don't know when we'll have additional information. But when we do, I'll let you and your new partner know."

Battat looked over at the young woman. She was standing in the kitchenette spooning eggs onto two plates. The last time he was in the field, Russians were the enemy. It was a strange business they were in.

"Before I go, is there anything else you can tell us about the Harpooner?" Hood asked. "Anything you might have seen or heard while you were looking for him? Anything Moore or Thomas might have said?"

"No," Battat said. He took a sip of tea. It was stronger than he was used to. It was like a shot of adrenaline. "All I know is that someone put me in a choke hold from behind. The next thing I knew, I was on the ground. As for Moore and Thomas, they were as mystified as I was."

"Because—?"

"The Harpooner had let me live," Battat said.

"Assuming it was the Harpooner," Hood said. "Listen. Use the time you have to rest. We don't know where the Harpooner may turn up or how much time you may have to get to him. But we need you to be ready to move out."

"I'll be ready," Battat said.

Hood thanked him and hung up. Battat placed the phone on the night table. Then he took another swallow of tea. He still felt weak, but he was trembling a little less than before.

The young woman walked over with a plate for him.

Battat watched her as she set the plate on his legs and placed a cloth napkin and utensils on the night table. She looked tired.

"My name is David Battat," he said.

"I know," she said.

"And you are—?" he pressed.

"In Baku, I am Odette Kolker," she said. There was finality in the young woman's voice. It told him two things. First, that she was definitely not an Azerbaijani recruited by the Russians. And second, that Battat would not be getting her real name. Not from her, anyway.

"I'm pleased to meet you," Battat said, extending his hand. "I'm also extremely grateful for everything you've done."

"You're welcome," she said.

The young woman shook Battat's hand firmly but per- functorily. As she did, Battat noticed several small bloodstains on the sleeve of her off-white police blouse. There were no lacerations on her hand or forearm. The blood did not appear to be hers.

"Are you really a policewoman?" Battat asked.

"Yes," she replied.

"Were you working the night shift?" he asked.

"No," she replied. "I was called in to do this." She smiled slightly. "And I cannot collect overtime for it."

Battat sipped more tea and smiled back. "I'm sorry they had to wake you." He moved the plate to the night table and started to throw off the cover. "I probably shouldn't be taking your bed—"

"No, it's all right," she said. "I'm expected on duty in less than an hour. Besides, I'm accustomed to having unexpected guests."

"A hazard of the business," he said.

"Yes," Odette observed. "Now, if you'll excuse me, I'm going to eat. You should do the same. Eat and then rest."

"I will," Battat promised.

"Do you need salt or anything else?"

"No thank you," he said.

Odette turned and walked slowly toward the kitchenette.

Less than an hour ago, she had killed a man. Now she was serving Battat breakfast. This was a strange business. A very strange business indeed.

THIRTY-FOUR

Washington, D.C.
Tuesday, 12:10 A.M.

"Hello, Paul."

Sharon's voice was thick and cold on the other end of the phone. Hood glanced at the clock on his computer. "Hi," he said warily. "Is everything okay?"

"Not really," she replied.

"I just got back from the hospital."

"What happened?"

"The short version," she said, "is that Harleigh freaked out about ninety minutes ago. I called an ambulance—I didn't know what else to do."

"You did the right thing," Hood said. "How is she?"

"Dr. Basralian sedated her, and she's sleeping now," Sharon went on.

"What does he think is wrong?" Hood asked. "Is it physical—?"

"He isn't sure," she said. "They're going to run tests in the morning. The doctor said that sometimes a traumatic event can have physical repercussions. It can affect the thyroid, cause it to get hyper, or create a surplus of adrenaline. Anyway, I didn't call so you'd drop what you're doing and go to see her. I just wanted you to know."

"Thank you," Hood said. "I'll still get over as soon as I can."

"No need for that," Sharon told him. "Everything's quiet. I'll let you know if there's a change."

"All right," Hood said. "If that's what you want."

"I do. Just some down-time. Tell me, Paul. Is there a problem?" Sharon asked.

"With what?"

"The world," Sharon said.

"Always," Hood replied.

"I tried the motel first," Sharon told him. "When you weren't there, I figured you must be putting out a fire somewhere."

Hood was not exactly sure how to take that remark. He tried not to read anything into it.

"There's a problem in the Middle East," Hood said. "Could be a bad one."

"Then I won't keep you," Sharon said. "Just don't kill yourself, Paul. You're not a kid anymore. You need sleep. And the kids need you."

"I'll take care of myself," he promised.

Sharon hung up. When Hood and his wife were together, Sharon used to be frustrated and angry whenever he worked long hours. Now that the two of them were apart, she was calm and concerned. Or maybe she was holding it all together for Harleigh's sake. Whatever the reason, it was a sad, sad joke being played on the Hood family.

But Hood did not have time to consider the injustice of it all or even the condition of his daughter. The phone rang a moment after he hung up. The call was from another concerned wife.

The president's.

THIRTY-FIVE

Saint Petersburg, Russia
Tuesday, 8:30 A.M.

General Orlov was proud that his operative had been able to save the American. Proud, but not surprised.

Odette—Natalia Basov—had been working with him for three years. The thirty-two-year-old was a former decryption expert who had begun her career with the GRU, Soviet military intelligence. Her husband Viktor was an officer in the Spetsnaz, the Russian special forces. When Viktor was killed on a mission in Chechnya, Basov became deeply depressed. She wanted to get out from behind a desk. Because the GRU was being dismantled and its components downsized, Basov was sent to see Orlov. Orlov was happy to put her in the field. Not only was Basov skilled in electronic intelligence, her husband had taught her the self-defense techniques of the *systema,* the lethal martial arts style of the Spetsnaz. Orlov himself had studied the basics as a way of staying in shape. The *systema* did not rely on practiced moves or on physical strength. It taught that during an assault, your own defensive motion dictated what the counterattack should be. If you were struck on the right side of the chest, you instinctively turned the right side away to avoid the blow. As a result, your left side automatically came forward. Thus, your attack would be with the left arm. And it would not be a single blow. It would be a trinity. Perhaps a fist to the chin, an elbow to the jaw, and a swipe with the back of the hand, all in quick succession. While that was going on, you were positioning yourself to unleash the next trinity. Typically, an opponent did not get more than a first chance to strike. Multiple opponents were too busy avoiding their falling comrades to move in.

Basov had mastered the form well. And she had proven to be a valuable asset in Azerbaijan. Orlov's people had created a false identity for her, and she had obtained a job with the police force. That put her in a job to watch and question people, other officers, guards, and night watchmen at plants and military bases. To learn what was happening in Baku's corridors of power and in the military. Being a beautiful woman made men more inclined to talk to her, especially in bars. And underestimate her.

Basov said that she and her guest were safe, but they were not what bothered Orlov right now. What concerned him was finding the Harpooner. Basov had told Orlov that the Baku police radio was reporting an explosion in the harbor. A boat had blown up, killing everyone on board. Orlov was willing to bet that the boat had belonged to the Harpooner. That was his way—to destroy all the evidence along with some or all of his coworkers. The dead men would probably be blamed for the rig attack. Orlov wondered who they were. Azerbaijanis? Iraqis? Russians? There were any number of people he could have recruited for a job like that. Just as long as they did not know what usually happened to his employees.

Most of Orlov's staff began arriving at half-past eight. The general had left e-mail for the two key members of his intelligence team, Boris and Piotr, to come and see him as soon as possible. If the Harpooner had been responsible for the attack in the Caspian, he probably would not attempt to leave Baku immediately. In the past, the Harpooner apparently waited a day or two after an attack. And when he finally moved, he often passed through Moscow. No one knew why. Unfortunately, by the time authorities learned he was in the city, he had vanished. General Orlov did not want that to happen again. The question was how to find him. And Paul Hood might have unwittingly given them a clue.

Boris Grosky was a sullen, gray-haired intelligence veteran who missed the Cold War. Piotr Korsov was an eager newcomer who had studied at Technion in Haifa, Israel. He was openly thrilled to be working in a field he loved and for a man who had helped pioneer space travel. The men entered the windowless office within a minute of one another. They sat on the couch across from Orlov's desk, Boris drinking tea and Korsov sitting with a laptop on his knees.

Orlov briefed the men. Grosky became noticeably more interested when the general mentioned that the NSA and CIA might somehow be involved in the Caspian operation.

"What I want to know is this," Orlov said. "We have eavesdropped on cell phone communications between American intelligence operatives before. We've gotten through many of their secure lines."

"We've gotten through most of them," Grosky pointed out.

"They try to keep you out by altering the signal from second to second," Korsov said. "The shifts are all within just a few megahertz in the superhigh frequency. We've learned how to ride most of the shifts."

"The difficult part is decoding the messages, which are scrambled electronically," Grosky added. "The American agencies use very complex codes. Our computers aren't always up to the task of decrypting the calls."

"Do the same callers usually use the same signals, the same patterns?" Orlov asked Korsov.

"Usually," Korsov told him. "Otherwise, there would be audio crossover. Callers would keep bumping into one another."

"Do we keep records of the calls?" Orlov asked.

"The conversations?" Grosky asked. "Yes. We keep working on them, trying to decode—"

"I mean the signals," Orlov interrupted.

"Absolutely," said Grosky. "We send them up to the Laika so it can keep a lookout for those signals."

The Laika was the Russian Op-Center's sentry satellite. Named for the pioneering Soviet space dog, the Laika was in a high geostationary orbit over Washington, D.C. It could intercept signals from the United States, all of Europe, and parts of Asia.

"So, if the Harpooner spoke with an intelligence unit in Washington, we might have picked up the signal if not the content," Orlov said.

"That's right," said Kosov.

"Very good," said Orlov. "Go to the computer records for the past two weeks. Look up communiqués between Azerbaijan and the National Security Agency in Washington. Get me all the information you have."

"Even if we haven't decrypted them," said Kosov.

"Yes," Orlov replied. "I want to know exactly where the Harpooner or his people might have been calling from."

"When you know that, what will you do?" Grosky asked.

"I'll call the American Op-Center and ask them to go through any satellite imaging they have for the region," Orlov said. "The Harpooner had to move explosives and personnel into position. If we can pinpoint his location, there may be a photographic record of it—"

"And clues to where he might be," Grosky said.

Orlov nodded.

"We'll have that information for you as soon as possible," Kosov said eagerly. "It would be a coup if we could catch that monster."

"It would be," Orlov agreed.

The men left. Orlov put in a call to Paul Hood to bring him up to date.

Catching the Harpooner would be a highlight of his career. But more than that, he wondered if this close cooperation between Op-Centers could become increasingly routine. If the trust and sharing could lead to less suspicion and greater international security.

That would be the real coup.

THIRTY-SIX

Washington, D.C.
Tuesday, 12:30 A.M.

"Paul, I'm glad I found you," Megan Lawrence said. "I think you should come here. There's something going on."

The First Lady's voice was steady when she got on the line, but Hood knew her well enough to know that it was Megan's "I have to be strong" voice. He had heard that voice during the campaign when there were hard questions from the press about an abortion she had had before she met the president. As she had years before, Megan was pulling this strength from deep inside. She would crash only when it was safe to do so.

"Talk to me," Hood said. He was drawing on his own emotional and psychological reserves to deal with the First Lady's problem. The call from Sharon had shaken him.

"We were just getting into bed when Michael received a call from Jack Fenwick," Megan said. "Whatever Fenwick said rattled my husband very much. His voice was calm while they talked and then afterward, but I watched this look come over him."

"What kind of look?" Hood asked.

"It's difficult to describe," she said.

"Was it guarded, startled, doubtful?" Hood asked.

"All of that," Megan replied.

Hood understood. That was what he saw in the Oval Office. "Where is the president now?" he asked.

"He went down to meet with Fenwick, the vice president, and Red Gable," Megan said.

"Did he say what the meeting was about?" Hood asked.

"No. But he told me not to wait up," she said.

It was probably about the Caspian situation. A small, nonconspiratorial part of Hood said that this might not be anything to worry about. On the other hand, the president was meeting with people who had fed him misinformation before. Perhaps that was what Megan had seen in her husband's expression. The fear that it might be happening again.

"Paul, whatever is going on, I think Michael needs to have friends around him," Megan said. "He should be with people he knows well and can trust. Not just policy advisers."

Hood's aide Stef Van Cleef beeped. She said there was a call from General Orlov. Hood told her to apologize to the general for the delay. He would take it in just a moment.

"Megan, I don't disagree," Hood said. "But I can't just invite myself to a meeting in the Oval Office—"

"You have the security clearance," she said.

"To get into the West Wing, not the Oval Office," he reminded her. Hood stopped. His eyes were on the beeping light on the phone. Maybe he would not have to get himself invited.

"Paul?"

"I'm here," Hood said. "Megan, listen to me. I'm going to take a call, and then I'm going to the White

House. I'll call your private line later and let you know how things are going."

"All right," Megan said. "Thank you."

Hood hung up and took the call from Orlov. The Russian general briefed him on the plan to try to locate the Harpooner. Orlov also told him about the destruction of the boat in the harbor. He suspected that Azerbaijani officials would find bodies in the water, either the Harpooner's hirelings or people who were abducted to impersonate hirelings.

Hood thanked Orlov and informed the general that he would have Op-Center's full cooperation. Hood indicated that he would be away from the office for a while and that he should contact Mike Rodgers with any new information. When Hood hung up, he conferenced Herbert and Rodgers on his cell phone. He updated them as he hurried to the parking lot.

"Do you want me to let the president know you're coming?" Rodgers asked him.

"No," Hood said. "I don't want to give Fenwick a reason to end the meeting early."

"But you're also giving Fenwick and his people more time to act," Rodgers pointed out.

"We have to take that chance," Hood said. "If Fenwick and Gable are launching some kind of endgame, I want to give them time to expose it. Maybe we can catch them in the act."

"I still think it's risky," Rodgers said. "Fenwick will press the president to act before other advisers can be consulted."

"That could be why this was timed the way it was," Herbert pointed out. "If there's a plot of some kind, it was designed to happen when it was the middle of the night here."

"If this is tied to the Caspian situation, the president will have to act quickly," Rodgers went on.

"Mike, Bob, I don't disagree with what you're saying," Hood told them. "I also don't want to give these bastards a chance to discredit anything I may have to say before I get there."

"That's a tough call," Herbert said. "Real tough. You don't have a lot of information on the situation overseas."

"I know," Hood said. "Hopefully, we'll have more intel before too long."

"I'll be praying for you," Herbert said. "And if that doesn't work, I'll be checking other sources."

"Thanks," Hood said. "I'll be in touch."

Hood sped through the deserted streets toward the nation's capital. There was a can of Coke in the glove compartment. Hood kept it there for emergencies. He grabbed the can and popped the tab. He really needed the caffeine. Even warm, the cola felt good going down.

Rodgers was correct. Hood was taking a chance. But Hood had warned the president about Fenwick. The rerouted phone call, the visit to the Iranian mission, failure to communicate with Senator Fox and the COIC. Hopefully, Lawrence would look very carefully at whatever data was being presented to him. The president might also take the time to run the information through Op-Center, just to make sure it was valid.

But Hood's hopes did not change the fact that the president was under an unusual amount of stress. There was only one way to be certain what Michael Lawrence would do. That was for Hood to get there with new intelligence. And while Hood was there, to help the president sift through whatever information Fenwick was presenting to him.

And there was one more thing Hood had to do. Pray that Mike Rodgers was not right.

That there was still time.

THIRTY-SEVEN

Baku, Azerbaijan
Tuesday, 9:01 A.M.

Maurice Charles settled into his small room at the Hyatt. The room had a queen-sized bed and a tall cabinet that held the TV and minibar. There was a desk to the left of them and a night table on either side of the bed. An armchair was tucked into a corner opposite the desk. There was very little room, which was fine with Charles. He did not like suites. There was too much open space. Too many places for people to hide.

The first thing Charles did was to tie a nylon rope to one of the legs of the desk. It was located near the window. The room was on the third floor of the ten-story hotel. If Charles were cornered there for any reason, the police would find it difficult to climb from the ground or rappel from the roof without making noise. That left only the door as a means of getting in. And he was prepared to deal with that. He carried cans of shaving cream that were actually filled with highly flammable liquid methanol. Spilled under the doorway and set aflame, it burned hot and fast and drove people back. That would give Charles time to shoot anyone who was waiting for him outside the window, then use the rope to climb out. Methanol was also a fatal poison. The liquid's fumes were so potent that even brief exposure to the vapors could cause blindness.

Charles turned on the light beside the bed and drew the heavy drapes. Next, he picked the locks between his room and the adjoining room. That was another route of escape in case he needed it. Then he pulled over the desk chair. He braced the back of the wooden chair under the knob of the door between his room and the next. He would be able to remove the chair quickly to escape. But if anyone on the other side tried the door, they would think it was locked.

The security arrangements took under a half hour. When they were finished, Charles sat on the bed. He went to his luggage and took out his .45. He placed it on the floor beside the bed. He pulled a Swiss army knife from his pocket and lay it on the night table. He also brought over a bag of several stuffed animals he had bought when he first came to Baku. All of the animals had costumes. If Charles were ever questioned, the plush toys were for his daughter. There were photos of a young girl in his wallet. It was not his daughter, but that did not matter. Then he opened the Zed-4. There was one last call to make.

The call was to the abandoned van. The microchip he had placed in the gas tank was a remote detonator. It had been nicknamed a Kamikaze Cell Phone by its Taiwanese inventor. The KCP had no function other than to pick up the signal, do its job, and then die. This particular KCP had been programmed to heat to 145 degrees Fahrenheit when triggered. Some chips could be programmed to emit high-pitched sounds to interfere with electronic signals or even confuse bloodhounds.

Other chips could be used to create magnetic bursts that would cause radar or navigational tools to go haywire.

This chip would melt and leave no trace of itself. It would also set the gas tank afire. The police and fire department would be forced to respond at once to calls about a burning van. They would arrive in time to save some of the vehicle along with what little evidence Charles had left for them to find. That included the traces of Charles's blood. The heat of the fire would cause the water content of the blood to evaporate, leaving clear stains on the metal door handle, glove compartment knob, and other sections of the van that had not burned. The police would conclude that the wounded terrorist had tried to destroy the van and the evidence before leaving. They would assume that their quick response had enabled them to save what they were not supposed to see.

Charles punched in the number of the KCP. He waited while his signal traveled twenty-five miles into space and bounced back to a street three blocks away. There were two short clicks and then the dial tone returned. That meant the call had been completed. The chip had been designed to disconnect from the Zed-4 as it began to heat up.

Charles hung up. He put everything into his backpack except for the .45. As he did, he heard sirens. They stopped exactly where they were supposed to.

By the burning van.

Comforted by the unparalleled feeling of a job well done, Maurice Charles made the final preparations for his stay. He removed one of the pillows from the bed and put it on the floor between the bed and the window, directly in front of the nightstand. Then he lay down and looked to his right, toward the bed. The hem of the bedspread reached nearly to the floor. Beneath and beyond the bed, he could see the front door. If for some reason anyone came in, Charles would see their feet. That was all he had to see to stop them.

Charles kept his clothes and shoes on in case he had to leave in a hurry, but they did not distract him. Nothing did now. This was the time he enjoyed most. When he had earned his rest and his pay.

Soon, even the sound of the police and fire sirens did not penetrate his deep, rewarding sleep.

THIRTY-EIGHT

Saint Petersburg, Russia
Tuesday, 9:31 A.M.

At 9:22 A.M., Piotr Korsov e-mailed General Orlov a brief data file. The file contained a list of the secure calls that had been intercepted between Azerbaijan and Washington during the past few weeks. Most of those calls had been between the American embassy and either the CIA or the NSA. The Russian Op-Center had been unable to decrypt any of the conversations, but Orlov was able to scratch them off his list. Those calls were pretty much routine and not likely suspects for calls made by the Harpooner.

Over the past few days, there had also been calls to the NSA from Gobustan, a village to the south of Baku. They were all made before the attack on the oil rig. The calls from the embassy to the United States had a slightly different bandwith from the Gobustan calls. That meant the calls were made from different secure phones. In a note attached to the file, Korsov said he was watching for new calls made from either line.

Orlov was not very hopeful. The Harpooner probably would not signal his allies to tell them he had been successful. Whoever he was in league with would hear about that from their own intelligence sources.

The very fact that a secure satellite uplink had played

any part in this business was personally disturbing to Orlov. That was the kind of technology his space flights had helped to pioneer—satellite communications. The fact that they were being so expertly abused by terrorists like the Harpooner made him wonder if the technology should have been developed at all. It was the same argument people had made for and against splitting the atom. It had produced plentiful and relatively clean atomic power, but it had also bred the atomic bomb. But Orlov had not had a hand in that work. Just in this.

Then again, Orlov thought, as Boris Pasternak wrote in one of his favorite novels, *Doctor Zhivago*, "I don't like people who have never fallen or stumbled. Their virtue is lifeless and it isn't of much value. Life hasn't revealed its beauty to them." Progress had to allow monsters like the Harpooner to surface. That was how it showed the creators where the flaws were.

Orlov had just finished reviewing the material when his private internal line beeped. It was Korsov.

"We picked up a ping," Korsov said excitedly.

"What kind of ping?" Orlov asked. A *ping* was how his intelligence officers described any kind of electronic communication.

"The same one we recorded as having been sent from Gobustan," Korsov replied.

"Was the call made from Gobustan?"

"No," Korsov replied. "It was made from Baku to a site very close by. A site that was also in Baku."

"How close?" Orlov asked.

"The caller and receiver were less than a quarter mile," Korsov told him. "We can't measure distances less than that."

"Maybe the Harpooner was calling accomplices who have another secure line," Orlov suggested.

"I don't think so," Korsov told him. "The phone call only lasted three seconds. As far as we can tell there was no verbal communication."

"What was sent?"

"Just an empty signal," Krosov said. "We've fed cartographical data into the computer. Grosky is overlaying the signal and trying to pinpoint the exact location now."

"Very good," Orlov said. "Let me know as soon as you have it."

As soon as Orlov hung up, he put in a call to Mike Rodgers to let him know about the apparent NSA-Harpooner connection and the possible location of the Harpooner. Then he called Odette. He hoped that the American she had saved was ready to move out. Orlov did not want to send Odette against the Harpooner unassisted, but he would if he had to. Because more than that, he did not want to lose the Harpooner.

As Orlov punched in Odette's number, he began to feel hopeful and upbeat. The technology that he had helped put into space was actually a two-edged sword. The Harpooner had been using a secure satellite uplink to help destroy lives. Now, with luck, that uplink would have an unexpected use.

To pinpoint the Harpooner and help destroy him.

THIRTY-NINE

Teheran, Iran
Tuesday, 10:07 A.M.

The chief of the Supreme Command Council of the Armed Forces of the Islamic Republic of Iran had been called at home shortly after dawn. Teheran maintained listening posts on many of their oil rigs in the Caspian Sea. From there, they eavesdropped electronically on foreign shipping and on military sites along the Caspian coast. Each post sent a pulse every five minutes to indicate that the electronics were still on-line. The sudden silence of Post Four was the first indication anyone in Teheran had that something was wrong in the Caspian.

An F-14 Tomcat was immediately dispatched from the Doshan Tapeh Air Base outside of Teheran. The Tomcat was one of ten that remained of the seventy-seven that had been a part of the shah's state-of-the-art air force. The fighter confirmed that the oil rig had been destroyed. Salvage experts and military engineers were immediately parachuted into the region by a Kawasaki C-1 transport. While rescue patrol boats hurried to the site from Caspian fleet headquarters in Bandar-e Anzelli, the engineers found burn marks on the platform that were consistent with powerful high explosives. The fact that the underside had been struck suggested a submarine attack that had somehow eluded sonar detection. At nine-thirty A.M., the salvage experts found something more. The body of Russian terrorist Sergei Cherkassov.

The report galvanized the often fractious officers of the SCCAF as well as the minister of the Islamic Revolutions Guards Corps, the minster of foreign affairs, the minister of the interior, and the minister of intelligence. The moderates had joined the extremists, and by ten A.M., the order had been given: the IRI military was ordered to defend Iranian interests in the Caspian at any and all cost.

On the sea, the initial thrust was to be an antisubmarine defense. That was spearheaded by antisubmarine aircraft and helicopters. Marine battalions in the region were also mobilized. The second wave would consist of destroyers and frigates, which were to be stationed around the remaining rigs. Chinese-made Silkworm missiles were rushed to the forces defending the Caspian.

In the air, Chinese-made Shenyang F-6s began regular patrols from both the Doshan Tapeh Air Base and the Mehrabad Air Base. Three surface-to-air missile battalions in the region were also put on high alert.

At the same time, Iranian embassies in Moscow and Baku were ordered to notify the Russian and Azerbaijani governments that while the attack was under investigation, any further moves against Iranian interests would be regarded as a declaration of war by those governments. Iranian diplomats were informed by both governments that they had had no hand in the attack on the Iranian oil facility. Representatives of Moscow and Baku added that Iran's increased military presence was unwelcome. Both nations indicated that their own navies and air forces would be placed on alert and would increase patrols in the region.

By late morning, waters that had given lives to fishermen and oilmen the night before were rich with something else.

The promise of death.

FORTY

Washington, D.C.
Tuesday, 1:33 A.M.

Mike Rodgers was in his office when General Orlov
called. After hearing what the Russian had to say, Rodgers immediately called Paul Hood in his car and gave
him the new information about the Harpooner.

"How certain is General Orlov about the NSA-
Harpooner connection?" Hood asked.

"I asked him that," Rodgers told Hood. "Orlov answered that he is very certain. Though I'm not sure the
president is going to put a lot of credence in what a
Russian general thinks."

"Especially if several of the president's top advisers
refute that information," Hood said.

"Paul, if Orlov is correct, we're going to have to do
more than tell the president," Rodgers said. "There's going to have to be a massive housecleaning in the NSA.
We can't have American intelligence agencies hiring terrorists who have attacked American interests, taken
American lives."

"Didn't we do that with the German rocket scientists
after World War Two?" Hood asked.

"The operative phrase is, '*after* World War Two,'"
Rodgers said. "We didn't hire German scientists to work

for us while they were still building missiles to attack Great Britain."

"Good point," Hood said.

"Paul, this is the guy that helped kill Bob Herbert's wife," Rodgers said. "If Orlov's intel is true, the NSA has to be held accountable for this."

"I hear you," Hood said. "Look, I'll be at the White House soon. Work on trying to get me any kind of backup you can. See if Bob can dig up signal intelligence that backs up Orlov's claims."

"He's working on that now," Rodgers said.

Hood hung up, and Rodgers got up. He poured coffee from the pot that sat on a cart in the back of his room. It was an aluminum cart from the 1950s. He'd picked it up at a Pentagon garage sale ten years before. He wondered if the sounds of crisis still resonated somewhere deep in its molecular structure. Arguments and decisions about Korea, the Cold War, Vietnam.

Or were they arguments about whose turn it was to treat for coffee and Danish? Rodgers wondered. That was part of war, too, of course. The moments of downtime that let decision makers catch their breath. Do something real instead of theoretical. Remind themselves that they were talking about people's lives and not just statistics.

When he sat back down, Rodgers started going through the files of the NSA's top officials. He was looking for people who had previous ties with Jack Fenwick or had ever investigated Middle Eastern terrorist groups. The NSA could not have contacted the Harpooner unless someone in one of those groups had helped. If it turned out that Orlov was right, Rodgers wanted to be ready to help with the purge. A purge of Americans who had collaborated with a man who had murdered American men and women, soldiers, and civilians.

He wanted to be ready with a vengeance.

FORTY-ONE

Washington, D.C
Tuesday, 1:34 A.M.

The White House is an aging monument in constant need of repair. There is peeling paint on the southern columns and splitting wood on the third-floor terraces.

But in the West Wing, especially in the Oval Office, there is a sense of constant renewal. To outsiders, power is a large part of the appeal of the Oval Office. To insiders, it is the idea that an intense new drama presents itself every hour of every day. Whether it's small, cautious maneuvering against a political rival or the mobilization of the military for a massive offensive and possible casualties, each situation starts, builds, and ends. For someone who thrives on outthinking an adversary or on extrapolating short- and long-term results from quiet decisions, the Oval Office is the ultimate challenge. It clears the game board every few minutes and offers new contests with new rules. Some presidents are aged and drained by the process. Other presidents thrive on it.

There was a time until very recently when Michael Lawrence was invigorated by the problems that crossed his desk. He was undaunted by crises, even those that required quick military action and possible casualties. That was part of the job description. A president's task was to minimize the damage caused by inevitable aggression.

But something had changed over the past few days. Lawrence had always felt that however stressful situations got, he was at least in control of the process. He could chair meetings with confidence. Lately, that was no longer the case. It was difficult for him even to focus.

Lawrence had worked with Jack Fenwick and Red Gable for many years. They were old friends of the vice president, and Lawrence trusted Jack Cotten. He trusted his judgment. Lawrence would not have selected him as a running mate otherwise. As vice president, Cotten had been more closely involved in the activities of the NSA than any previous vice president. Lawrence had wanted it that way. For years, the CIA, the FBI, and military intelligence had had their own agendas. The Executive Branch needed its own eyes and ears abroad. Lawrence and Cotten had more or less appropriated the NSA for that task. The military could still utilize the NSA's chartered assets, which were the centralized coordination and direction of U.S. government intelligence technical functions and communications. Under Cotten, its role had quietly been expanded to increase the breadth and detail of intelligence that was coming directly to the president. Or, rather, to Fenwick and the vice president and then to the president.

The president stared at the open laptop on his desk. Jack Fenwick was talking about Iran. Data was downloading quickly from the NSA. Fenwick had some facts and a good deal of supposition. He also had an edge. He appeared to be going somewhere, though he had not yet indicated where.

Meanwhile, Lawrence's eyes stung, and his vision was foggy. It was difficult to concentrate. He was tired, but he was also distracted. He did not know who to believe or even what to believe. Was the data from the NSA real or falsified? Was Fenwick's intelligence accurate or fabricated?

Paul Hood suspected Fenwick of deception. Hood appeared to have the evidence for it. But what if it were Hood's evidence that wasn't trustworthy? Hood was going through an extremely stressful time. He had resigned his post at Op-Center, then returned. He had been at ground zero of the explosive UN hostage crisis. His daughter was suffering from an extreme case of post-traumatic stress disorder. Hood was in the process of getting a divorce.

What if it were Hood who had the agenda, not Fenwick, the president wondered. When Fenwick had arrived at the White House before, he admitted that he had been to the Iranian mission. He admitted it openly. But he insisted that the president had been informed. The vice president corroborated that fact. So did the calendar on the president's computer. As for the call regarding the United Nations initiative, Fenwick insisted that was not placed by him. He said the NSA would investigate. Could it have been placed by Hood?

"Mr. President?" Fenwick said.

The president looked at Fenwick. The national security adviser was seated in an armchair to the left of the desk. Gable was to the right, and the vice president was in the center.

"Yes, Jack?" the president replied.

"Are you all right, sir?" Fenwick asked.

"Yes," Lawrence replied. "Go on."

Fenwick smiled and nodded and continued.

The president sat up taller. He had to focus on the issue at hand. When he got through this crisis, he would schedule a short vacation. Very soon. And he would invite his childhood friend and golfing buddy, Dr. Edmond Leidesdorf, and his wife. Leidesdorf was a psychiatrist attached to Walter Reed. The president had not wanted to see him officially with this problem because the press would find out about it. Once that happened, his political career would be over. But they had played golf and gone sailing before. They could talk on a golf course or boat without raising suspicion.

"The latest intelligence puts the Russian terrorist Sergei Cherkassov at the scene of the explosion," Fenwick continued. "He had escaped from prison three days before the attack on the rig. His body was found at sea. There were burn marks consistent with flash explosives. There was also very little bloating. Cherkassov had not been in the water for very long."

"Do the Azerbaijanis have that information?" the president asked.

"We suspect they do," Fenwick replied. "The Iranian naval patrol that found Cherkassov radioed shore on an open channel. Those channels are routinely monitored by the Azerbaijanis."

"Maybe Teheran wanted the rest of the world to have the information," the president suggested. "It might turn them against Russia."

"That's possible," Fenwick agreed. "It's also possible that Cherkassov was working for Azerbaijan."

"He was being held in an Azerbaijani prison," the

vice president said. "They might have allowed him to escape so that he could be blamed for the attack."

"How likely is that?" the president asked.

"We're checking with sources at the prison now," Fenwick said. "But it's looking very likely."

"Which means that instead of the attack turning Iran against Russia, Azerbaijan may have succeeded in uniting both nations against them," the vice president said.

Fenwick leaned forward. "Mr. President, there's one thing more. We suspect that creating a union between Russia and Iran may actually have been the ultimate goal of the Azerbaijani government."

"Why in hell would they do that?" the president asked.

"Because they are practically at war with Iran in the Nagorno-Karabakh region," Fenwick said. "And both Russia and Iran have been pressing claims on some of their oil fields in the Caspian."

"Azerbaijan wouldn't stand a chance against either nation individually," the president pointed out. "Why unite them?"

Even as he said it, the president knew why.

To win allies.

"How much of our oil do we get from that region?" the president asked.

"We're up to seventeen percent this year with a projection of twenty percent next year," Gable informed him. "We're getting much better prices from Baku than we are from the Middle East. That was guaranteed by the trade agreement we signed with Baku in March 1993. And they've been very good about upholding their end of the agreement."

"Shit," the president said. "What about the other members of the Commonwealth of Independent States?" he asked. "Where will they stand if two of their members go to war?"

"I took the liberty of having my staff put in calls to all of our ambassadors before I came over here," the vice president said. "We're in the process of ascertaining exactly where everyone stands. But a preliminary guess is that it will pretty much be split. Five or six of the poorer, smaller republics will side with Azerbaijan in the hopes of forming a new union with a share of the oil money. The other half will go with Russia for pretty much the same reason."

"So we risk a wider war as well," the president said.

"But this is more than just the possibility of us losing oil and watching a war erupt," Fenwick pointed out. "It's Iran and the Russian black market getting their hands on petrodollars that scares me."

The president shook his head. "I'm going to have to bring the joint chiefs in on this."

The vice president nodded. "We're going to have to move quickly. It's midmorning in the region. Things are going to happen very quickly. If they get ahead of us—"

"I know," the president said. He was suddenly energized, ready to deal with the situation. He looked at his watch and then at Gable. "Red, would you notify the joint chiefs to be here at three? Also, get the press secretary out of bed. I want him here as well." He looked at the vice president. "We'll need to alert the thirty-ninth Wing at Incirlik and the naval resources in the region."

"That would be the *Constellation* in the North Arabian

Sea and the *Ronald Reagan* in the Persian Gulf, sir," Fenwick said.

"I'll put them on alert," the vice president said. He excused himself and went to the president's private study. It was a small room that adjoined the Oval Office on the western side. That was also where the president's private lavatory and dining parlor were located.

"We'll also have to brief NATO command," the president told Gable. "I don't want them holding us up if we decide to act. And we're going to need a complete chemical and biological workup of the Azerbaijani military. See how far they'll go if we don't join in."

"I already have that, sir," Fenwick said. "They've got deep reserves of anthrax as well as methyl cyanide and acetonitrile on the chemical side. All have surface-to-surface missile delivery systems. Most of the reserves are stored in or near the NK. We're watching to see if any of them are moved."

The president nodded as his intercom beeped. It was his deputy executive secretary Charlotte Parker.

"Mr. President," said Parker, "Paul Hood would like to see you. He says it's very important."

Fenwick did not appear to react. He turned to Gable and began talking softly as he pointed to data on his notepad.

Are they talking about the Caspian or about Hood? the president wondered. Lawrence thought for a moment. If Hood were the one who had lost his way— either intentionally or because of external pressures— this would be the time and the place to find out.

"Tell him to come in," said the president.

FORTY-TWO

Saint Petersburg, Russia
Tuesday, 9:56 A.M.

"We have the Harpooner's location!" Korsov shouted.

Orlov looked up as Korsov rushed into his office. The young intelligence officer was followed by Boris Grosky, who looked less glum than Orlov had ever seen him. He did not look happy, but he did not look miscrable. Korsov was holding several papers in his hands.

"Where is he?" Orlov asked.

Korsov slapped a computer printout on Orlov's desk. There was a map and an arrow pointing to a building. Another arrow pointed to a street several blocks away.

"The signal originated at a hotel in Baku," Korsov said. "From there it went to Suleyman Ragimov Kuchasi. It's an avenue that runs parallel to Bakihanov Kuchasi, the location of the hotel."

"Was he calling someone with a cell phone?" Orlov asked.

"We don't believe so," Grosky said. "We've been monitoring police broadcasts from the area to find out more about the oil rig explosion. While we were listening, we heard about a van explosion on Suleyman Ragimov. The blast is being investigated now."

"It doesn't sound like a coincidence," Korsov added.

"No, it doesn't," Orlov agreed.

"Let's assume the Harpooner was behind that," Korsov said. "He might want to see it from his hotel room—"

"That might not be necessary, as long as he could hear it," Orlov said. "No. The Harpooner would be worried about security if he were staying in a hotel room. Do we have any way of fine-tuning the location of the signal?"

"No," Korsov said. "It was too brief, and our equipment is not sensitive enough to determine height in increments under two hundred feet."

"Can we get a diagram of the hotel?" Orlov asked.

"I have that," Korsov said. He pulled a page from the pile he was holding and laid it beside the map. It showed a ten-story hotel.

"Natasha is trying to break into the reservations list," Grosky said. He was referring to the Op-Center's twenty-three-year-old computer genius Natasha Revsky. "If she can get in, she will give us the names of all single male occupants."

"Get single females as well," Orlov said. "The Harpooner has been known to adopt a variety of disguises."

Grosky nodded.

"You feel very confident about this?" Orlov asked.

Korsov had been leaning over the desk. Now he stood like a soldier, his chest puffed. "Completely," he replied.

"All right," Orlov said. "Leave the hotel diagram with me. This was very good work. Thank you both."

As Grosky and Korsov left, Orlov picked up the phone. He wanted to talk to Odette about the hotel and then get her on site. Hopefully, the American would be strong enough to go with her.

The Harpooner was not a man to tackle alone.

FORTY-THREE

Baku, Azerbaijan
Tuesday, 10:07 A.M.

Odette Kolker was cleaning up the breakfast plates when the phone beeped. It was the apartment phone, not her cell phone. That meant it was not General Orlov who was calling.

She allowed her answering machine to pick up. It was Captain Kilar. The commander of her police unit had not been in when she phoned the duty sergeant to let him know that she would be out sick. Kilar was calling to tell her that she was a good and hardworking officer, and he wanted her to get well. He said that she should take whatever time she needed to recuperate.

Odette felt bad about that. She was hardworking. And though the Baku Municipal Police Department paid relatively well—twenty thousand manats, the equivalent of eight thousand American dollars—they did not pay overtime. However, the work Odette did was not always for the BMP and the people of Baku. The time she spent at her computer or on the street was often for General Orlov. Baku was a staging area for many of the arms dealers and terrorists who worked in Russia and the former Soviet republics. Checking on visa applications, customs activity, and passenger lists for boats, planes, and trains enabled her to keep track of many of these people.

After putting away the few dishes, Odette turned and looked back at her guest. The American had fallen asleep and was breathing evenly. She had placed a cool washcloth on his head and he was perspiring less than when she had brought him home. She had seen the bruises on his throat. They were consistent with choke marks. Obviously, the incident in the hospital was not the first time someone had tried to kill him. There was also a tiny red spot on his neck. A puncture wound, it looked like. She wondered if this illness were the result of his having been injected with a virus. The KGB and other Eastern European intelligence services used to do that quite a bit, typically with lethal viruses or poison. The toxin would be placed inside microscopic pellets. The pellets were sugar-coated metal spheres with numerous holes in their surface. These would be injected by an umbrella tip, pen point, or some other sharp object. It would take the body anywhere from several minutes to an hour or two to eat through the sugar coating. That would give the assassin time to get away. If this man had been injected, he probably was not supposed to die by the virus. He had been used to draw his colleagues out into the open. The hospital ambush had been well organized.

Just like the ambush that killed her husband in Chechnya, she thought. Her husband, her lover, her mentor, her dearest friend. They all perished when Viktor died on a cold, dark, and lonely mountainside.

Viktor had successfully infiltrated the Chechan mujihadin forces. For seven months, Viktor was able to obtain the ever-changing radio frequencies with which different rebel factions communicated. He would write this information down and leave it for a member of the KGB field force to collect and radio to Moscow. Then the idiot KGB officer got sloppy. He confused the frequency he was supposed to use with the one he was reporting about. Instead of communicating with his superiors, he broadcast directly to one of the rebel camps. The KGB officer was captured, tortured for information, and killed. He had not known Viktor's name but he knew which unit her husband had infiltrated and when he had arrived. The rebel leaders had no trouble figuring out who the Russian agent was. Viktor would always leave his information under a rock which he would chip in a distinctive fashion. While he was out one night, supposedly standing watch, Viktor was brought down by ten men, then taken into the mountains. There, his Achilles tendons were severed and his wrists were slashed. Viktor bled to death before he could crawl to help. His last message to her was painted on a tree trunk with his own blood. It was a small heart with his wife's initials inside.

Odette's cell phone beeped softly. She picked it up from the kitchen counter and turned her back toward her guest. The woman spoke softly so she would not wake him.

"Yes?"

"We believe we've found the Harpooner."

That got Odette's attention. "Where?"

"At a hotel not far from you," Orlov said. "We're trying to pinpoint his room now."

Odette moved quietly toward the bed. She was required to check her service revolver when she left police headquarters every night. But she kept a spare weapon in the nightstand. It was always loaded. A woman living alone had to be careful. A spy at home or abroad had to be even more careful.

"What's the mission?" Odette asked.

"Termination," Orlov said. "We can't take a chance that he'll get away."

"Understood," Odette said calmly. The woman believed in the work she was doing, protecting the interests of her country. Killing did not bother her when doing it would save lives. The man she had terminated just a few hours before meant little more to her than someone she might have passed in the street.

"Once we've narrowed down the guests who might be the Harpooner, you're going to have to make the final call," Orlov said. "The rest depends on what he does, how he acts. What you see in his eyes. He's probably going to have showered but still look tired."

"He's been a busy bastard," Odette said. "I can read that in a man."

"The chances are he won't open the door to the hotel staff," Orlov went on. "And if you pretend to be a housekeeper or security officer, that will only put him on guard."

"I agree," she said. "I'll find a way to get in and take him by surprise."

"I spoke to our profiler," Orlov said. "If you do get to him, he'll probably be cool and even pleasant and will appear to cooperate. He might attempt to bribe you or get you to be overconfident. Try to get your guard down so he can attack. Don't even listen. Make your assessment and do your job. I wouldn't be surprised if he also has several traps at the ready. A gas canister in an air duct, an explosive device, or maybe just a magnesium flash to blind you. He might have rigged it to a light switch or a remote control in his heel, something he can activate when he ties his shoe. We just don't know enough about him to say for certain how he secures a room."

"It's all right," Odette assured him. "I'll make the ID and neutralize him."

"I wish I could tell you to go in with a squad of police," Orlov said apologetically. "But that isn't advisable. A shout, rerouted traffic, anything out of the ordinary can alert him. Or the Harpooner may sense their presence. If he does, he may get away before you can even get to him. I'm sure he has carefully planned his escape routes. Or he may try to take hostages."

"I understand," Odette said. "All right. Where is the Harpooner registered?"

"Before I tell you that, how is your guest?" Orlov asked.

"He's sleeping," Odette replied. She looked down at the man on the bed. He was lying on his back, his arms at his side. His breathing was slow and heavy. "Whatever he's suffering from was probably artificially induced," she said. "Possibly by injection."

"How is his fever?"

"Down a bit, I think," she said. "He'll be okay."

"Good," Orlov said. "Wake him."

"Sir?" The order took her completely by surprise.

"I want you to wake him," Orlov told her. "You're bringing him with you."

"But that's not possible!" Odette protested. "I don't even know if the American can stand."

"He'll stand," Orlov said. "He has to."

"Sir, this is not going to help me—"

"I'm not going to have you face the Harpooner without experienced backup," Orlov said. "Now, you know the drill. Do it."

Odetted shook her head. She knew the drill. Viktor had taught it to her. Lit matches were applied to the soles of the feet. It not only woke up the ill or people who had been tortured into unconsciousness, but the pain kept them awake and alert as they walked.

Odette shook her head. By definition, field work was a solo pursuit. What had happened to Viktor underscored the danger of working with someone even briefly. Even if the American were well, she was not sure she wanted a partner. Ill, he would be more of a burden than an asset.

"All right," Odette said. She turned her back on the American and walked toward the kitchenette. "Where is he?"

"We believe the Harpooner is in the Hyatt," Orlov told her. "We're trying to have a look at their computer records now. I'll let you know if we learn anything from the files."

"I'll be there in ten minutes," Odette promised. "Is there anything else, General?"

"Just this," Orlov said. "I have grave reservations about sending you after this man. I want you both to be careful."

"We will," Odette said. "And thank you."

She hung up and hooked the cell phone on her belt. She removed the gun and ankle holster from the night table and slipped them on. Her long police skirt would cover the weapon. She slipped a silencer in her right pocket. She had brought a switchblade to the hospital. That was still tucked in her left skirt pocket. If she did not need it for self-defense, she would need it as a throwaway. If she were stopped for any reason, perhaps by hotel security, Odette could say that she was visiting a friend—the checkout who, of course, would no longer be there. Odette would be able to say that she knocked on the wrong door and the Harpooner attacked her. With her help—using information provided by Orlov and the Americans—the police would connect the dead man with the terrorist attack.

Hopefully, though, it would not be necessary to explain anything to anyone. With surprise on her side, Odette might be able to catch the Harpooner relatively unprepared.

Odette walked on slightly bent knees and tiptoed to the front door of the apartment. The hardwood floors creaked loudly underfoot. It was strange, Odette thought. It had never been necessary for her to be quiet here before. Until today, there had never been anyone but her in this bed. Not that she regretted that. Viktor had been all she ever wanted.

Odette opened the door. Before leaving, she looked back at the sleeping American.

The woman felt bad about lying to General Orlov. Though the coin of her profession was subterfuge and deceit, she had never lied to Orlov. Fortunately, this was a win-win situation for her. If she succeeded in bringing down the Harpooner, Orlov would be angry with her—but not very. And if she failed, she would not be around to hear Orlov complain.

Odette stepped into the corridor and quietly shut the door behind her. If she blew this assignment, she would probably have to listen to Viktor complain. Listen for all eternity.

She smiled. That, too, was a win situation.

FORTY-FOUR

Washington, D.C.
Tuesday, 2:08 A.M.

A stoic secret service agent opened the door to the Oval Office and admitted Paul Hood. The large, white door closed with a small click. The sound seemed very loud to Hood as he crossed the carpet toward the president's desk. So did the sound of Hood's heart. He had no way of knowing for certain whether Fenwick was a rogue figure or working as part of a team. Either way, convincing others about possible involvement in an international conspiracy of some kind was going to be extremely difficult.

The mood in the room was hostile. Hood could feel that even before he saw the faces of the vice president, Fenwick, and Gable. None of the men looked back at him, and the president's expression was severe. Mike Rodgers once said that when he first joined the military, he had a commanding officer with a very singular expression of disapproval. He looked at you as though he wanted to tear heads off and use them for punting practice.

The president had that look.

Hood quickly made his way between the armchairs to the president's desk. The Washington Monument was visible through the windows behind the president. The tower was brightly moonlit in the flat, black night. Seeing it then gave Hood the flash of courage he needed.

"I'm sorry to intrude, Mr. President, gentlemen," Hood announced. "This couldn't wait."

"Things never can wait with you, can they?" Fenwick asked. He glanced back at the green folder in his lap.

A preemptive strike, Hood thought. *The bastard was good.* Hood turned and looked at the NSA chief. The short, slender man had deep-set eyes beneath a head of thick, curly white hair. The whiteness of his hair emphasized the darkness of his eyes.

"Your team has a history of rushing blindly into evolving crises, Mr. Hood. North Korea, the Bekaa Valley, the United Nations. You're a lighted match waiting for the wrong tinderbox."

"We haven't blown one yet," Hood pointed out.

"Yet," Fenwick agreed. He looked at Lawrence. "Mr. President, we need to finish reviewing our data so that you can make a decision about the Caspian situation."

"What does Maurice Charles have to do with the Caspian situation?" Hood demanded. He was still looking at Fenwick. He was not going to let the man wriggle away.

"Charles? The terrorist?" Fenwick asked.

"That's right," Hood said. Hood said nothing else. He wanted to see where this went.

The president looked at Fenwick. "Did the NSA know that Charles was involved with this?"

"Yes, Mr. President, we did," Fenwick admitted. "But we don't know what his involvement was. We've been looking into that."

"Maybe I can point you in the right direction, Mr.

Fenwick," Hood said. "Maurice Charles was in touch with the NSA both before and after the attack on the Iranian oil rig."

"That's bullshit!" Fenwick charged.

"You seem sure of that," Hood said.

"I am!" Fenwick said. "No one in my organization would have anything to do with that man!"

Hood had expected Fenwick to 3D the charge: disavow, deny, and delay. But neither the vice president nor Gable had jumped in to defend him. Perhaps because they knew it was true?

Hood turned to the president. "Sir, we have every reason to believe that Charles, the Harpooner, was involved in the destruction of that rig."

"Evidence from whom?" Fenwick demanded.

"Unimpeachable sources," Hood replied.

"Who?" Vice President Cotten asked.

Hood faced him. The vice president was a calm and reasonable man. Hood was going to have to bite the bullet on this one. "General Sergei Orlov, commander of the Russian Op-Center."

Gable shook his head. Fenwick rolled his eyes.

"The Russians," the vice president said dismissively. "They may have been the ones who sent Cherkassov into the region to attack the rig. His body was found in the water nearby."

"Moscow has every reason not to want us involved in the region," Gable said. "If Azerbaijan is chased out of the Caspian, Moscow can lay claim to more of the oil reserves. Mr. President, I suggest we table this side of the problem until we've dealt with the larger issue of the Iranian mobilization."

"We've reviewed the data Orlov provided, and we believe it's accurate," Hood stated.

"I'd like to see that data," Fenwick said.

"You will," Hood promised.

"You wouldn't also have given General Orlov any secure codes to help him listen in on alleged NSA conversations, would you?"

Hood ignored that. "Mr. President, the Harpooner is an expert at creating and executing complex cover stories. If he's involved in this operation, we have to look carefully at any evidence that comes in. We should also inform Teheran that this action may have nothing to do with Baku."

"Nothing?" Fenwick said. "For all we know, they may have hired the Harpooner."

"You may be right," Hood said. "What I'm saying is that we have no evidence of anything except the fact that the Harpooner is in the region and was probably involved in the attack."

"Secondhand evidence," Fenwick said. "Besides, I spent a day trying to open a dialogue with Teheran about an intelligence exchange. The bottom line is that they don't trust us, and we can't trust them."

"That is not the bottom line!" Hood snapped. He stopped. He had to watch that—showing anger. He was frustrated, and he was extremely tired. But if he lost control, he would also lose credibility. "The bottom line," Hood continued evenly, "is that misinformation has been passed regularly between the NSA, the CIOC, and the Oval Office—"

"Mr. President, we need to move on," Fenwick said calmly. "Iran is moving warships into the Caspian region. That is a fact, and it must be dealt with immediately."

"I agree," said the vice president. Cotten looked at Hood. There was condescension in the vice president's eyes. "Paul, if you have concerns about the actions of personnel at the NSA, you should bring your proof to the CIOC, not to us. They will deal with it."

"When it's too late," Hood said.

"Too late for what?" the president asked.

Hood turned to the president. "I don't know the answer to that, sir," Hood admitted. "But I do believe you should hold off making any decisions about the Caspian right now."

Fenwick shook his head. "Based on hearsay from Russians who may themselves be moving planes and ships into the region."

"Mr. Fenwick has a point," the president said.

"The Russians may indeed have designs on the Caspian oil," Hood agreed. "That in itself doesn't repudiate General Orlov's intelligence."

"How long do you need, Paul?"

"Give me another twelve hours," Hood said.

"Twelve hours will give Iran and Russia time to position ships in the Azerbaijani oil regions," Gable said.

The president looked at his watch. He thought for a moment. "I'll give you five hours," he said.

That was not what Hood wanted, but it was obviously all he was going to get. He took it.

"I'll need an office," Hood said. He did not want to waste time running back to Op-Center.

"Take the Cabinet Room," the president said. "That

way I know you'll be done by seven. We'll be moving in then."

"Thank you, sir," Hood said.

Hood turned. He ignored the other men as he left the Oval Office. The hostility was much greater now than when he had come in. Hood was certain he had hit a bull's-eye. Just not with enough firepower.

It would have been too much to expect the president to buy everything he was telling him. Even after their earlier conversation, Lawrence was still obviously struggling with the idea that Jack Fenwick could be a traitor. But at least the president had not dismissed the idea entirely. Hood had been able to buy himself some time.

Hood walked down the quiet, green-carpeted hallway of the West Wing. He made his way past two silent secret service officers. One was posted outside the Oval Office. The other was standing down the hall between the doorway that led to the press secretary's office on the northwest end of the corridor and door to the Cabinet Room on the northeast side.

Hood entered the oblong room. There was a large conference table in the center of the room. Beyond it, in the northern end of the room, was a desk with a computer and a telephone. Hood went over and sat down.

The first thing Hood would do was contact Herbert. He had to try to get more information about the Harpooner's contacts with the NSA. Yet even having the exact time and location of the calls would probably not persuade the president that there was a conspiracy.

Hood needed proof. And right now, he did not know how he was going to get it.

FORTY-FIVE

Saint Petersburg, Russia
Tuesday, 10:20 A.M.

When he was a cosmonaut, General Orlov had learned to read voices. Often, that was the only way he learned whether there was a problem with a flight. Ground control had once told him that all was well with his Salyut space station mission. In fact, pitting from micrometeoroid dust and a chemical cloud dumped by the spacecraft's own thrusters had corroded the solar array. The panels had been so seriously compromised that the station was going to lose power before a Kosmos ship from Earth was due to ferry them home.

The first hint of trouble came from the voice of the liaison in ground control. His cadence was a little different from usual. Orlov already had an ear for voices from the years he spent as a test pilot. Orlov insisted on being told what the problem was with the Salyut. The entire world heard the conversation, embarrassing the Kremlin. But Orlov was able to shut down noncritical systems and conserve power rather than wait for scientists to figure out how to realign the remaining panels while also shielding them from further corrosion.

Orlov trusted Natalia Basov. Completely. But he did not always believe her, which was not the same thing. There was something in her tone of voice that worried him. It was as if she had been concealing something. Just like the liaison at ground control.

Several minutes after they spoke on her cell phone, Orlov called the phone registered to Odette Kolker at her apartment. It rang a dozen times and no one answered. Orlov hoped that meant she had taken the American with her. Twenty minutes later, he called back again.

This time a man with a slurred voice answered. In English.

Orlov looked at the readout on the telephone to make sure he had the correct number. He did. The woman had left without the American.

"This is General Sergei Orlov," he said to the man. "Is this Mr. Battat?"

"Yes," Battat replied groggily.

"Mr. Battat, the woman who rescued you is my subordinate," Orlov went on. "She has gone out to try and apprehend the man who attacked you on the beach. You know who I am talking about?"

"Yes," Battat replied. "I do."

"She has no backup, and I'm worried about her and about the mission," Orlov said. "Are you well enough to get around the city?"

There was a short delay. Orlov heard grunts and moans.

"I'm on my feet, and I see my clothes hanging behind the door," Battat replied. "I'll take one step at a time. Where did she go?"

Orlov told the American he had no idea what Odette's plan was, or if she even had one. Orlov added that his team was still trying to get into the hotel computer to find out which rooms were occupied by single males.

Battat asked Orlov to call him a taxi, since he did not really speak the language.

Orlov said he would do that and thanked him. He gave Battat his telephone number at the Op-Center and then hung up.

Orlov sat still. Save for the faint buzz of the fluorescent light on his desk, his underground office was dead silent. Even space was not this quiet. There were always creaks as metal warmed and cooled or bumps as loose objects struck equipment. There were sounds of coolant moving through pipes and air rushing through vents. And every now and then there was someone talking in his headphone, either from Earth or somewhere else in the ship.

Not here. This was a lonelier-feeling place by far.

By now, Odette had probably reached the hotel and gone inside. He could phone her and order her back, but he did not think she would listen. And if she was intent on going through with this, he did not want to rattle her. She needed to know she had his support.

Orlov was angry at Odette for having disobeyed orders and lying to him. His anger was tempered by an understanding of what had driven the woman. Her husband had been a loner as well. A loner who had died because of someone else's carelessness.

Still, she would not stand in the way of Orlov's job. And that job was not just to capture or kill the Harpooner.

It was to make certain that Odette did not end up like Viktor.

FORTY-SIX

Baku, Azerbaijan
Tuesday, 10:31 A.M.

There was a great deal of traffic, and it took Odette twice as long as she expected to reach the Hyatt Hotel. She parked on a side street less than a block from the employees' entrance. She did not want to park out front. There was still a sniper out there somewhere, the person who had shot the American diplomat outside the hospital. The killer might be bird-dogging the hotel for the Harpooner. He might have seen her car at the hospital and could recognize it again.

It was a sunny morning, and Odette enjoyed the brief walk to the front of the hotel. The air tasted richer and seemed to fill her lungs more than usual. She wondered if Viktor had felt this way while he was in Chechnya. If simple moments had seemed more rewarding when there was a real risk of losing it all.

Odette had been to the rear entrance of the hotel twice before. Once was to help a cook who had burned himself in a skillet fire. Another time was to quiet a man who was complaining about charges on his dinner bill. She knew her way around the back. Unfortunately, she didn't think she would find the Harpooner here. Odette assumed that when the Harpooner came and went, he used the front entrance. Sneaking out a delivery door or first-

floor window might call attention to himself. Smart terrorists hid in plain sight.

And smart counterterrorists waited for them rather
than charging into their lair, she thought.

But Odette had no idea when the Harpooner would
be leaving. It could be the middle of the night. It could
be early afternoon. It could be three days from now. She
could not be here the entire time. She also had no idea
whether or not he would be disguised. And for all she
knew, he might even hire a prostitute to pose as his
daughter, wife, or even his mother. There were some old
prostitutes in Baku. Some very young ones, too. Odette
had arrested a number of them.

There were many possibilities, all of which made it
imperative that Odette get to the Harpooner before he
left. The question was how to find him. She had no idea
what his name was or what name he might be using.

Except for the Harpooner, Odette thought. She
laughed to herself. Maybe she should run down the halls
shouting that name. Watch to see which doors did not
open. Anyone who did not need to see what the uproar
was about had to be the Harpooner.

Odette rounded the corner and walked toward the
front of the hotel. There was a kiosk around the corner.
A newspaper extra was already announcing the Iranian
buildup in the Caspian Sea. There were aerial reconnaissance photos of Iranian ships setting sail. Baku had
always been relatively insulated from military action.
This was something new for the nation's capital. That
would help to explain the traffic. Most people lived in
the suburbs. Many of them probably came to work,

heard the news, and were getting out of town in the event of attack.

There was just one person standing beneath the gold and green awning. A doorman in a green blazer and matching cap. There were no tour buses, though that was not surprising. They usually left by nine A.M. Tourists who had entered the country as part of a group probably could not opt for early departure and had almost certainly gone ahead with their plans. In any case, checkout was not until noon. People who did want to leave were probably on the phones trying to book plane, train, or car reservations—

Of course, she thought. *The phone.*

Orlov had said that the Harpooner made a call using a secure phone. That would mean he probably had not made any calls using the hotel phone. She would look for a single male occupant with no phone charges on his bill.

Odette entered the hotel. She looked away from the front desk as she crossed the lobby. She did not want to risk being seen by the manager or any of the clerks who might recognize her. The first thing she did was turn to the right, toward the corridor that led to housekeeping. The long, simple office was located in the back of the hotel. There was a desk with a supervisor in the front of the office. Behind her was an array of cleaning carts. To her right was a Peg-Board with keys for all the rooms. A row of master keys was located on the bottom. These were given out to the cleaning staff each morning. Two keys remained.

Odette asked the elderly clerk if she could have more shampoo. Smiling pleasantly, the clerk rose and went to one of the carts. While the woman's back was turned, Odette took one of the master keys from the wall. The clerk returned with three small bottles of shampoo. The woman asked if she needed anything else. Odette said that she did not. Thanking her, Odette returned to the lobby and walked to the bank of telephone booths that lined an alcove in the back.

As she was walking, her phone beeped. She tucked herself into one of the booths, shut the door, then answered it.

Orlov said his team had broken into the hotel computer and they had five possibilities. Odette wrote down the names and room numbers.

"We might be able to narrow it down a little more," Orlov told her. "If someone wanted to get out of the country quickly, he would assume a nationality the Azerbaijani would not want around."

"Iranian," Odette said.

"No," Orlov countered. "Iranians might be detained. Russian is more likely. And there are two Russians at the hotel."

Odette said she might be able to narrow it down even further by checking the room telephone records.

"Good thinking," Orlov said. "Hold on while we're checking. Also, Odette, there's one thing more."

Odette felt her lower belly tighten. There was something about the general's voice.

"I spoke with Mr. Battat a few minutes ago," Orlov said.

Odette felt as if she'd run into a thick, low-lying tree branch. Her momentum died and her head began to throb. She did not think she had done wrong, leaving a sick man at home. But she had disobeyed an order and could think of nothing to say in her defense.

"The American is on his way to the hotel," General Orlov continued evenly. "I told him to look for you in the lobby. You're to wait until he arrives before you try to take down your man. Do you understand, Odette?"

"Yes, sir," she replied.

"Good," Orlov said.

The woman held on as Orlov's staff checked the records. Her palms were damp. That was less from nervousness than from having been caught. She was an honest woman by nature, and Orlov's trust was important to her. She hoped he understood why she had lied. It was not just to protect Battat. It was to allow herself to concentrate on the mission instead of on a sick man.

According to the hotel's records, two of the five men staying there had not made any calls from the room. One of them, Ivan Ganiev, was Russian. Orlov told her they were also checking the computer's housekeeping records. According to the last report, filed the day before, Ganiev's room, number 310, had not been cleaned in the three days he had been there.

Meanwhile, Orlov went to his computer and asked for a background check on the name. It came up quickly.

"Ganiev is a telecommunications consultant who lives in Moscow. We're checking the address now to make sure it's valid. He doesn't appear to work for any one company," Orlov said.

"So there's no personnel file we can check for his education or background," she said.

"Exactly," Orlov said. "He's registered with the Central Technology Licensing Bureau, but all it takes to get a license is a bribe. Ganiev does not have family in Moscow, does not appear to belong to any organizations, and receives his mail at a post office box."

That made sense, Odette thought. No mail collecting in the postbox, no newspapers piling up on the stoop. None of the neighbors would be certain whether he was there or not.

"Hold on, we have his address," Orlov added. He was silent for a moment. Then he said, "It's him. It has to be."

"Why do you say that?"

"Ganiev's residence is a block from the Kievskaya metro stop," Orlov told her.

"Which means—?"

"That's where we've lost the Harpooner on at least two other occasions," Orlov said.

Battat walked into the lobby just then. He looked like Viktor did after ten rounds of boxing in the military amateurs. Wobbly. Battat saw Odette and walked toward her.

"So it looks as though he's our man," Odette said. "Do we proceed as planned?"

This was the most difficult part of intelligence work. Making a determination about life and death based on an educated guess. If General Orlov were wrong, then an innocent man would die. Not the first and certainly not the last. National security was never error-free. But if he were correct, hundreds of lives might be spared. Then there was the option of attempting to capture the Harpooner and turn him over to Azerbaijani authorities. Even if it could be done, there were two problems with that. First, the Azerbaijanis would find out who Odette

really was. Worse, they might not want to try to extradite
the Harpooner. It was an Iranian rig he had attacked.
And Russian buildings. And American embassies. The
Azerbaijanis might want to make some kind of arrangement with him. Release him in exchange for his cooperation, for help in covert actions of their own. That was
something Moscow could not risk.

"You're going to wait for the American to arrive?"
Orlov asked.

"He's here now," Odette said. "Do you want to speak
with him?"

"That won't be necessary," Orlov said. "The Harpooner will probably be traveling with high-tech equipment to go with his cover story. I want you to take some
of it and any money he's carrying. Pull out drawers and
empty the luggage. Make it look like a robbery. And
work out an escape route before you go in."

"All right," she said.

There was nothing patronizing about Orlov's tone. He
was giving instructions and also reviewing a checklist
out loud. He was making sure that both he and Odette
understood what must be done before she closed in.

Orlov was quiet again. Odette imagined him reviewing the data on his computer. He would be looking for
additional confirmation that this was their quarry. Or a
reason to suspect it was not.

"I'm arranging for airline tickets out of the country in
case you need them when you're finished," Orlov said.
He waited another moment and then decided as Odette
knew he must. "Go and get him."

Odette acknowledged the order and hung up.

FORTY-SEVEN

Washington, D.C.
Tuesday, 2:32 A.M.

Hood shut the door of the Cabinet Room behind him. There was a coffee machine on a small table in the far corner. The first thing Paul did upon entering was brew a pot using bottled water. He felt guilty doing that in the midst of a crisis, but he needed the caffeine kick. Desperately. Though his mind was speeding, his eyes and body from the shoulders down were crashing. Even the smell of the coffee helped as it began to brew. As he stood watching the steam, he thought back to the meeting he had just left. The shortest way of defusing the crisis on this end was to break Fenwick and whatever cabal he had put together. He hoped he could go back there with information, something to rattle Fenwick or Gable.

"I need time to think," he muttered to himself. Time to figure out how best to attack them if he had nothing more than he did now.

Hood turned from the coffeemaker. He sat on the edge of the large conference table and pulled over one of the telephones. He called Bob Herbert to see if his intelligence chief had any news or sources he could hit up for information about the Harpooner and possible contact with the NSA.

He did not.

"Unless no news is news," Herbert added.

Herbert had already woken several acquaintances who either worked for or were familiar with the activities of the NSA. Calling them in the middle of the night had the advantage of catching them off guard. If they knew anything, they would probably blurt it out. Herbert asked if any of them had heard about U.S. intelligence overtures to Iran.

None of them had.

"Which isn't surprising," Herbert said. "Something of that magnitude and delicacy would only be conducted at the highest executive levels. But it's also true that if more than one person knows about an operation over there, then everyone has heard at least a piece of the story. Not so here."

"Maybe more than one person at the NSA doesn't know about this," Hood said.

"That could very well be," Herbert agreed.

Herbert said he was still waiting to hear from HUM-INT sources in Teheran. They might know something about this.

"The only solid news we have is from Mike's people at the Pentagon," Herbert said. "Military Intelligence has picked up signs of Russian mobilization in the Caspian region. Stephen Viens at the NRO has confirmed that. The Slava-class cruiser *Admiral Lobov* is apparently aleady heading south and the Udaloy II–class destroyer *Admiral Chebanenko* is joining it along with several corvettes and small missile craft. Mike expects air cover over the Russian oil installations to commence within a few hours."

"All from something that started with the Harpooner—or whoever first hired him," Hood said.

"Eisenhower was the first to use the metaphor in 1954," Herbert said. "He said, 'You have a row of dominoes set up; you knock over the first one and what will happen to the last one is that it will go over very quickly.' He was talking about Vietnam, but it applies to this."

Herbert was right. You could count on the fact that dominoes not only fell, but they dropped quickly. And the only way to stop dominoes falling was to get far enough ahead of the chain and remove a few tiles.

After hanging up, Hood poured himself coffee, sat down in one of the leather seats, and called Sergei Orlov. The fresh, black coffee was a lifesaver. In the midst of chaos even a small respite seemed enormous.

The general brought Hood up to date on the situation with the Harpooner. Hood could hear the tension in the Russian's voice as he explained what the overall plan was. Hood related to Orlov's concern completely. There was worry for his operative Odette and a desperate desire to end the career of a notorious terrorist. Hood had been in that place. And he had both won there and lost there. This was not like a film or novel where the hero necessarily won.

Hood was still on the phone with General Orlov when the door opened. He glanced up.

It was Jack Fenwick. The time to think was over.

The NSA head entered the room and shut the door behind him. The Cabinet Room was a large room, but it suddenly seemed small and very close.

Fenwick walked over to the coffee and helped himself. Hood was nearly finished with the call. He ended the conversation as quickly as possible without seeming to hurry. He did not want Fenwick to hear anything. But he also did not want to show the NSA chief a hint of desperation.

Hood hung up. He took a swallow of coffee and glanced over at Fenwick. The man's dark eyes were on Hood.

"I hope you don't mind," Fenwick said. He indicated the coffee.

"Why should I?" Hood asked.

"I don't know, Paul," Fenwick shrugged. "People can get protective about things. Good coffee, by the way."

"Thanks."

Fenwick perched himself on the edge of the table. He was just a few feet from Hood. "We've taken a little break," Fenwick told him. "The president is waiting for the joint chiefs and secretary of state before making any decisions about the Caspian situation."

"Thanks for the update."

"You're welcome," Fenwick said. "I can give you more than an update," he went on. "I can give you a prediction."

"Oh?"

Fenwick nodded confidently. "The president is going to respond militarily. Emphatically. He has to."

Both Op-Center and the NSA had access to photographic reconnaissance from the NRO. No doubt Fenwick knew about the Russians as well.

Hood got up to freshen his coffee. As he did, he remembered what he had been thinking just a few minutes before.

The only way to stop the dominoes falling was to get far enough ahead of the chain and remove a few tiles.

"The question is not what the president will do, what the nation will do. The question is what are you going to do?" Fenwick said.

"Is that why you came here? To pick my brains?"

"I came here to stretch my legs," Fenwick said. "But now that we've gone there, I am curious. What are you going to do?"

"About what?" Hood asked as he poured more coffee. The dance was on. They were each watching their words.

"About the current crisis," Fenwick replied. "What part are you going to play?"

"I'm going to do my job," Hood said. He was either being interviewed or threatened. He had not yet decided which. Nor did he care.

"And how do you see that?" Fenwick asked.

"The job description says 'crisis management,'" Hood said. He looked back at Fenwick. "But at the moment, I see it as more than that. I see it as learning the truth behind this crisis and presenting the facts to the president."

"What truth is that?" Fenwick asked. Though his expression did not change, there was condescension in his voice. "You obviously don't agree with what Mr. Gable, the vice president, and I were telling him."

"No, I don't," Hood said. He had to be cautious. Part of what he was about to say was real, part of it was bluff. If he were wrong it would be the equivalent of crying wolf. Fenwick would not be concerned about anything Hood had to say. And Fenwick could use this to undermine Hood's credibility with the president.

But that was only if he were wrong.

"I've just been informed that we captured the Harpooner at the Hyatt Hotel in Baku," Hood said. He had to present it as a fait accompli. He did not want Fenwick calling the hotel and warning the terrorist.

"Then it's definitely the Harpooner?" Fenwick said.

Fenwick took a sip of coffee and held it in his mouth. Hood let the silence hang there. After a long moment, Fenwick swallowed.

"I'm glad," Fenwick said without much enthusiasm. "That's one less terrorist Americans have to worry about. How did you get him? Interpol, the CIA, the FBI—they've all been trying for over twenty years."

"We've been following him for several days," Hood went on. "We were observing him and listening to his phone calls."

"Who are *we*?"

"A group comprised of Op-Center, CIA, and foreign resources," Hood replied. "We pulled it together when we heard the Harpooner was in the region. We managed to lure him out using a CIA agent as bait."

Hood felt safe revealing the CIA's role since it was probably Fenwick who had given the information about Battat to the Harpooner.

Fenwick continued to regard Hood. "So you've got the Harpooner," Fenwick said. "What does all this have to do with the truth about what's going on? Do you know something that I don't?"

"The Harpooner apparently had a hand in what happened in the Caspian," Hood said.

"That doesn't surprise me," Fenwick said. "The Harpooner will work for anyone."

"Even us," Hood said.

Fenwick started when he heard that. Just a little, but enough so that Hood noticed. "I'm tired, and I don't have time for guessing games," Fenwick complained. "What do you mean?"

"We're talking to him now," Hood went on. "He seems willing to tell us who hired him in exchange for limited amnesty."

"Of course he does," Fenwick said dismissively. "That bastard would probably say anything to save his hide."

"He might," Hood agreed. "But why lie when only the truth can save his life?"

"Because he's a twisted bastard," Fenwick said angrily. The NSA chief threw his cup into the wastebasket beneath the coffeemaker and got up from the table. "I'm not going to let you advise the president based on the testimony of a terrorist. I suggest you go home. Your work here is finished."

Before Hood could say anything else, Fenwick left the Cabinet Room. He pulled the door shut behind him. The room seemed to return to its former size.

Hood did not believe that Fenwick was concerned about the president getting misinformation. Nor did he believe that Fenwick was overworked and simply venting. Hood believed that he had come very close to exposing a relationship that Fenwick had worked hard to conceal.

A relationship between a high-ranking adviser to the president and the terrorist who had helped him to engineer a war.

FORTY-EIGHT

Baku, Azerbaijan
Tuesday, 10:47 A.M.

When David Battat was six years old, he came down
with the mumps and was extremely sick. He could
barely swallow and his belly and thighs ached whenever
he moved. Which was not so much of a problem because
David had been too weak to move.

Battat felt too weak to move now. And it hurt when
he did move. Not just in his throat and abdomen but in
his legs, arms, shoulders, and chest. Whatever that bastard Harpooner had injected him with was debilitating.
But it was also helpful, in a way. The pain kept him
awake and alert. It was like a dull toothache all over his
body. Whatever energy Battat had now was coming
from anger. Anger at having been ambushed and debilitated by the Harpooner. And now anger at having been
indirectly responsible for the deaths of Thomas and
Moore.

Battat's hearing was muffled and he had to blink to
see clearly. Yet he was extremely aware of his surround-
ings. The elevator was polished brass with green carpet.
There were rows of small bright lightbulbs in the ceiling.
There was a trapdoor in the back, and a fish-eye video
lens beside it.

The elevator was empty except for Battat and Odette.

When they reached the third floor, they stepped out. Odette took Battat's hand, like they were a young couple looking for their room. They checked the room numbers posted on the wall in front of them: 300 to 320 were to the right. That put 310 in the center of a long, brightly lit corridor. They started toward it.

"What are we doing?" Battat asked.

"Checking the stairwell first," Odette said. "I want to make sure the other killer isn't watching the room from there."

"And after that?" Battat asked.

"How would you feel about being married?" she asked.

"I tried it once and didn't like it," Battat said.

"Then you'll probably like this less," she replied. "I'll tell you what I'm thinking when we reach the stairwell."

They headed toward the stairwell, which was located at the opposite end of the corridor. As they neared 310, Battat felt his heart speed up. The "Do Not Disturb" sign was hanging from the door handle. There was something dangerous about the place. Battat felt it as they passed. It was not a physical sensation but a spiritual one. Battat was not prepared to go so far as to say it was palpable evil, but the room definitely had the feel of an animal's lair.

Odette released his hand when they reached the stairwell. She removed the gun from her holster and screwed on the silencer. Then she stepped ahead of Battat and cautiously peered through the window at the top of the door. No one was there. Odette turned the knob and stepped inside. Battat followed. He backed toward the concrete steps and leaned on the iron banister with one arm. It felt good not to have to move. Odette kept a heel in the door so it would not close and lock them out. She faced Battat.

"I'm sure the Harpooner has his room heavily protected from the inside," she said. "Since we probably won't be able to break in, we're going to have to try and draw him out."

"Agreed," Battat said. He was tired and dizzy and had to force himself to focus. "What do you propose?"

"You and I are going to have a lovers' quarrel," she said.

That got his attention. "About what?" he asked.

"It doesn't matter," she said. "As long as we end up arguing about which room is ours."

"One of us will say it's 312 and the other will insist it's 310," Battat said.

"Exactly," Odette replied. "Then we'll open the door to 310."

"How?"

Odette reached into her pocket.

"With this," she said as she pulled out the master key she had taken from the housekeeper. "If we're lucky, the Harpooner will only want to chase us away."

"What if someone else comes from their room or calls hotel security?" Battat asked.

"Then we argue more quickly," Odette said as she took off her jacket and slipped it over her forearm, concealing the gun.

The woman seemed to be growing impatient, a little anxious. Not that Battat blamed her. They were facing both the Harpooner and the unknown. If it were not for the dullness caused by whatever was afflicting him, he would have been experiencing fear on top of his lingering anger.

"This is not a science," she added. "The point of what we're doing is to distract the Harpooner long enough to kill him."

"I understand," Battat said. "What do you want me to do?"

"When I open the door, I want you to push it back hard," she said. "That should startle the Harpooner and also give me a moment to aim and fire. When we're finished, we come back to the stairwell and leave."

"All right," Battat said.

"Are you sure you feel up to this?" Odette asked.

"I'll be able to do what you want me to," he said.

She nodded and gave him a reassuring half smile. Or maybe she was trying to reassure herself.

A moment later, they headed down the hall.

FORTY-NINE

Saint Petersburg, Russia
Tuesday, 11:02 A.M.

Josef Norivsky was the Russian Op-Center's liaison between the country's other intelligence and investigative agencies as well as Interpol. He was a young, broad-shouldered man with short black hair and a long, pale face. He strode into General Orlov's office wearing an expression that was somewhere between fury and disbelief.

"Something is wrong," he said. Norivsky did not disseminate information unless he was sure of it. As a result, when he spoke, he had a way of making any statement seem like a pronouncement.

The intelligence liaison handed Orlov a set of eight-by-ten photographs. Orlov looked quickly at the eleven blurry black-and-white pictures. The shots showed five men in ski masks moving a sixth, unmasked man through a corridor made of cinder blocks.

"These photographs were taken by security cameras at the Lenkoran high-security prison in Azerbaijan," Norivsky explained. "We received them two days ago. The man without the mask is Sergei Cherkassov. The SIS was hoping we could help to identify the others."

The SIS was Azerbaijan's State Intelligence Service.

They still maintained relatively close, cooperative relations with Russian intelligence groups.

"What have you come up with?" Orlov asked as he finished going through the photographs.

"The weapons they're carrying are IMI Uzis," said Norivsky. "They're based on the submachine guns Iran bought from Israel before the Islamic revolution. In and of themselves, they don't necessarily mean anything. Iranian arms dealers could have sold them to anyone. But look how the men are moving."

Orlov went back through the pictures. "I don't follow," he said.

Norivsky leaned over the desk and pointed to the fourth picture. "The men in the ski masks have formed a diamond shape around the Cherkassov. The point man covers the package, the escapee, the man in the rear watches their flank, and the men on the sides cover right and left. The fifth man, the only one who appears in pictures one and two, is ahead of the group, securing the escape route. Probably with a rocket launcher, according to reports." Norivsky stood. "This is the standard evacuation procedure used by VEVAK."

VEVAK was Vezarat-e Etella'at va Amniat-e Keshvar. The Iranian Ministry of Intelligence and Security.

"Why would Iran want to free a Russian terrorist from Azerbaijan?" Norivsky asked. The intelligence chief answered the question himself. "To use his talents? It's possible. But another possibility is that they wanted to dump his body at the attack site. How many bodies were found in the harbor at Baku? Four to six, depending on how the pieces eventually fit together."

"The same number of people who helped him to escape," Orlov said.

"Yes," Nirovsky replied.

"Which may mean they were all working together," Orlov said. "Nothing more than that."

"Except for the presence of the Harpooner," Norivsky pointed out. "We know that he has worked for Iran on many occasions. We know that he can usually be contacted through a series of associates in Teheran. What I'm saying, General, is, what if Iran organized the attack on its own oil rig as an excuse to move warships into the area?"

"That wouldn't explain the involvement of the American National Security Agency," Orlov said.

"But Cherkassov's presence might," Norivsky insisted. "Consider, sir. Iran threatens Azerbaijan. The United States becomes involved in that conflict. It has to. American oil supplies are being threatened. If the foe is only Iran, Americans are not opposed to an air and sea war. They have wanted to strike back at Teheran for decades, ever since the hostage crisis in 1979. But imagine that Russia is brought into the situation. At his trial, Cherkassov admitted working for the Kremlin. That was how he avoided execution. Suppose Azerbaijan or Iran retaliates by attacking Russian oil platforms in the Caspian. Are the people of the United States going to stand for a world war erupting in the region?"

"I don't think they would," Orlov said. He thought for a moment. "And maybe they wouldn't have to stand for it."

"What do you mean?" Norivsky asked.

"The Harpooner was working with the NSA, apparently to orchestrate this showdown," Orlov said. "What if someone in the American government made a deal with Iran before it happened?"

"Does the NSA have that kind of authority?" Norivsky asked.

"I don't believe so," Orlov said. "They would probably need higher-ranking officials working with them. Paul Hood at Op-Center indicated that contacts of that type may have taken place. What if the Americans agreed they would back down at a certain point? Allow Iran to have more of the oil-rich regions in exchange for American access to that oil?"

"A normalization of relations?" Norivsky suggested.

"Possibly," Orlov said. "The American military pushed to brinkmanship then pulled back for some reason. But what reason? That had to have been arranged as well."

Orlov did not know the answer, but he knew who might. Thanking Norivsky, Orlov rang his translator and put in a call to Paul Hood.

FIFTY

Washington, D.C.
Tuesday, 3:06 A.M.

After Fenwick left the Cabinet Room, Hood sat alone at the long conference table. He was trying to figure out what he could tell the president to convince him that something was wrong with the intelligence he was receiving. That was going to be difficult without new information. Hood thought he had convinced him of Fenwick's duplicity earlier. But in the press of developing crises, crisis managers often took the advice of trusted and especially passionate friends. Fenwick was passionate, and Cotten was an old ally. Without hard facts, Hood would not be able to combat that. But what troubled him nearly as much was something the NSA head had said to Hood before leaving the Cabinet Room.

"I'm not going to let you advise the president."

This was not just an international showdown. It was also a territorial fight in the Oval Office. But for what, exactly? It was not just about access to the president of the United States. Fenwick had tried to confuse Lawrence, to embarrass him, to mislead him. Why?

Hood shook his head and rose. Even though he had nothing to add to what he said before, Hood wanted to hear what the joint chiefs had to say. And Fenwick could not bar him from the Oval Office.

As Hood was leaving the Cabinet Room, his phone beeped. It was General Orlov.

"Paul, we have some disturbing information," Orlov said.

"Talk to me," Hood replied.

Orlov briefed him. When he was finished, Orlov said, "We have reason to believe that the Harpooner and Iranian nationals carried out the attack on the Iranian oil rig. We believe the attack may have been the same Iranians who freed the Russian terrorist Sergei Cherkassov from prison. This would make it seem as if Moscow was involved."

"Compelling the United States to lend its support to Azerbaijan as a counterbalance," Hood said. "Do you know if Teheran sanctioned the attack?"

"Very possibly," Orlov replied. "The Iranians appear to have been working for or were trained by VEVAK."

"In order to precipitate a crisis that would allow them to move in militarily," Hood said.

"Yes," Orlov agreed. "And the presence of Cherkassov, we think, was designed to give Iran a reason to threaten our oil facilities. To draw Russia into the crisis. Cherkassov may have had nothing to do with the attack itself."

"That makes sense," Hood agreed.

"Paul, you said before that members of your own government, of the NSA, were in contact with the Iranian mission in New York. That it was a member of the NSA that was in communication with the Harpooner in Baku. Could that agency be involved in this?"

"I don't know," Hood admitted.

"Perhaps the mission put them in contact with the Harpooner," Orlov suggested.

That was possible. Hood thought about it for a moment. Why would Fenwick help Iran to blow up its own rig and then encourage the president to attack Iran? Was this a plot to sucker Iran into a showdown? Was that why Fenwick had concealed his whereabouts from the president?

But Fenwick would have known about Cherkassov, Hood thought. He had to know that Russia would be drawn in as well.

And that still did not explain why Fenwick had made a point of calling the president right before the United Nations dinner. That was a move designed to humiliate Lawrence. To erode confidence in the president's—

Mental state, Hood thought suddenly.

Hood followed the thread. Wasn't that what Megan Lawrence was concerned about? Mental instability, apparent or real, created by a careful pattern of deception and confusion? The president becomes deeply shaken. The United States finds itself on the precipice of war, led there by Fenwick. Lawrence tries to manage the crisis. What happens next? Does Fenwick undermine him somehow? Make him doubt his abilities—

Or does he make the public doubt his abilities? Hood wondered.

Senator Fox was already concerned about the president. Mala Chatterjee had no love for him. The secretary-general would certainly give interviews stating that the president had been completely mistaken about the United Nations initiative. What if Gable or Fenwick were also to leak information about bad judgment the president had shown over the past few weeks?

Reporters would swallow it whole, Hood knew. It would be easy to manipulate the press with a story like that. Especially if it came from a reliable source like Jack Fenwick.

And it wasn't just Fenwick and Gable who were involved in this, Hood now knew for certain.

The vice president had been on the same page as Fenwick and Gable back in the Oval Office. Who stood to benefit most if the president himself and possibly the electorate were convinced that he was unfit to lead the nation in a time of crisis? The man who would succeed him, of course.

"General Orlov, have we heard from our people tracking the Harpooner?" Hood asked.

"They're both at the hotel where he is staying," Orlov reported. "They're moving in on him now."

"To terminate, not capture."

"We don't have the manpower to capture him," Orlov stated. "The truth is, we may not even have the manpower to complete the mission at hand. It's a great risk, Paul."

"I understand," Hood said. "General, are you solid about this information? That the men who attacked the Iranian rig are Iranian?"

"Until their body parts are collected and identified, an educated guess is the best I can do," Orlov said.

"All right," Hood said. "I'm going to take that information to the president. His advisers are pushing him to a military response. Obviously, we have to get him to postpone that."

"I agree," Orlov said. "We're mobilizing as well."

"Call me with any other news," Hood said. "And thank you, General. Thank you very much."

Hood hung up the phone. He ran from the Cabinet Room and jogged down the carpeted hallway toward the Oval Office. Canvas portraits of Woodrow Wilson and First Lady Edith Bolling Wilson looked down from the wall. She had effectively run the country in 1919 when her husband suffered a stroke. But she was protecting his health while looking out for the country's best interests. Not her own advancement. Had we become more corrupt since then? Or had the line between right and wrong become entirely erased? Did presumably virtuous ends justify corrupt means?

This was maddening. Hood had information, and he had a strong, plausible scenario. He had Fenwick turning pale when he said that the Harpooner had been captured. But Hood did not have proof. And without that, he did not see how he was going to convince the president to proceed slowly, carefully, regardless of what Iran did. Nor were the joint chiefs likely to be much help. The military had been itching for a legitimate reason to strike back at Teheran for over twenty years.

He turned the corner and reached the Oval Office. The secret service officer stationed at the door stopped him.

"I have to see the president," Hood told him.

"I'm sorry, sir, you'll have to leave," the young man insisted.

Hood wagged the badge that hung around his neck. "I have blue-level access," he said. "I can stand here. Please. Just knock on the door and tell the president I'm here."

"Sir, my doing that won't help you to see the

president," the secret service agent told him. "They've moved the meeting downstairs."

"Where?" Hood asked. But he already knew.

"To the Situation Room."

Hood turned and swore. Fenwick was correct. He was going to keep him from seeing the president. The only way to get down there was with the next-level access badge, which was red level. Everyone who had that level would be down there. Being seduced and controlled by Jack Fenwick.

Hood walked back toward the Cabinet Room. He was still holding his cell phone and tapping it against his open palm. He felt like throwing the damn thing. He could not phone the president. Calls to the Situation Room went through a different switchboard than the rest of the White House. He did not have clearance for direct dial, and Fenwick would certainly have arranged it so that any calls Hood made would be refused or delayed.

Hood was accustomed to challenges, to delays. But he always had access to the people he needed to talk to and persuade. Even when terrorists had seized the United Nations Security Council, there had been ways to get in. All he needed was the resolve and manpower to do it. He was not accustomed to being utterly stone-walled like this. It was miserably frustrating.

He stopped walking. He looked up at the portrait of Woodrow Wilson, then looked at the painting of Mrs. Wilson.

"Shit," he said.

He glanced down at the phone. Maybe he wasn't as stonewalled as he thought.

Jogging again, Hood returned to the Cabinet Room.

He was willing to bet there was one avenue Jack Fenwick hadn't closed down.

He couldn't have, even if he wanted to.

A queen always beat a Jack.

FIFTY-ONE

Baku, Azerbaijan
Tuesday, 11:09 A.M.

As Odette walked down the hall, she had two concerns.

One worry was that she might be making a mistake about the identity of the man in room 310. That he was not, in fact, the Harpooner. Orlov had given Odette a general idea what the Harpooner looked like. But he had added that the Harpooner probably wore disguises. She had a mental picture of someone tall and aquiline with pale, hateful eyes and long fingers. Would she hesitate to shoot if someone not-so-tall and heavyset with blue, welcoming eyes and stubby fingers opened the door? Would that give him a chance to strike first?

An innocent man would come over and say "Hello," she told herself. The Harpooner might do that to throw off her guard. She *had* to strike first, whoever was in there.

Her other concern was a question of confidence. She had been thinking about the reluctance she heard in General Orlov's voice. Odette wondered what concerned him most. That something would happen to her or that the Harpooner might escape? Probably both. Though she tried to rev up an "I'll show him" mentality, General Orlov's lack of confidence did not boost her own.

It doesn't matter, she told herself. *Focus on the goal*

and on nothing else. The mission was all that mattered. The target was just a few doors down.

Odette and David Battat had agreed that she would start their spat. She was the one who had to open the door and go in. She should control the timing. The couple passed room 314. Odette was holding the key in her left hand. She still had the gun in her right hand, under the jacket, which was draped over her forearm. Battat was holding the switchblade at his side. He seemed to be somewhat more focused than he had been when he arrived. Odette was not surprised.

She was, too.

They passed room 312.

Odette turned to Battat. "Why are you stopping?" she asked him. Odette made sure not to shout just so the Harpooner could hear. Her tone was normal, conversational.

"What do you mean, 'Why am I stopping?'" he asked right back.

Odette moved ahead several steps. She stopped in front of room 310. Her heart was speeding. "Aren't we going inside?"

"Yes," he replied impatiently.

"That's not our room," Odette said.

"Yes it is," Battat said.

"No," Odette said. "This is our room."

"We're in 312," Battat said confidently.

She put the key in the slot of 310. That was the signal for Battat to step over to the room. He walked over and stopped directly behind her. His right shoulder was practically touching the door.

Odette's fingers were damp with sweat. She could actually smell the brass of the key. She hesitated. *This is what you've been waiting for*, she reminded herself. An opportunity to prove herself and to make Viktor proud. She turned the key to the right. The bolt went with it. The door opened.

"I told you this was our room," she said to Battat. Odette swallowed hard. The words had caught in her throat and she did not want to show her fear. The Harpooner might hear it in her voice.

With the door open a sliver, Odette withdrew the key. She slipped it in her pocket and used that moment to listen. The TV was off and the Harpooner was not in the shower. Odette was half hoping he had been in the bathroom, cornered. But she heard nothing. She opened the door a little more.

There was a short, narrow hallway inside. It was cave-dark and utterly still. They had assumed the Harpooner would be hiding in the room, but what if he were not? He could be out for a late breakfast. Or he might have left Baku. Perhaps he kept the room as a safe house in case he needed it.

But what if he's waiting for us? she thought then. And she answered her own question. *Then we'll have to handle the situation.* Viktor used to say that nothing was guaranteed.

"What's wrong, honey?" Battat asked.

The words startled her. Odette looked back at her companion. The American's brow was pinched. He was obviously concerned. She realized that she was probably waiting too long to go in.

"Nothing's wrong," she said. She opened the door a

little farther and reached in with her left hand. "I'm just looking for the light."

Odette pushed the door until it was halfway open. She could see the glowing red numbers of the alarm clock on the night table. There was a jagged line of white light in the center of the drapes. Its brilliance only made the rest of the room seem darker.

Odette's gun was still hidden under her jacket, still behind the half-closed door. She found the light switch with her left hand. She flicked it on. The hall light came on as did the lamps on the night tables. The walls and furniture brightened with a dull yellow orange glow.

Odette did not breathe as she stepped into the hallway. The bathroom was to her right. She turned and looked in. There were toiletries on the counter beside the sink. The soap was opened.

She looked at the bed. It had not been slept in, though the pillows had been moved around. She saw a suitcase on the luggage stand, but she did not see the Harpooner's shoes. Maybe he was out.

"Something's wrong here," Odette said.

"What do you mean?"

"That's not our bag on the luggage rack," she replied.

Battat stepped in behind her. He looked around. "So I was right," he said. "This isn't our room."

"Then why did the key work?" she asked.

"Let's go back downstairs and find out," Battat urged. He was still looking around.

"Maybe the bellman made a mistake and put someone else in here," Odette suggested.

Battat suddenly grabbed Odette's left shoulder. He

roughly shoved her into the bathroom and followed her in.

Odette turned and glared at Battat. He put a finger to his lips and moved very close.

"What's wrong?" she whispered.

"He's in there," Battat said quietly.

"Where?"

"Behind the bed, on the floor," Battat told her. "I saw his reflection in the brass headboard."

"Is he armed?" she asked.

"I couldn't tell," Battat said. "I'm betting he is."

Odette put her jacket on the floor. There was no longer any reason to conceal the gun. Battat was standing a few steps in front of her, near the door. Just then she saw a small round mirror and extender arm attached to the wall to his right. She had an idea.

"Hold this," she whispered and handed Battat the gun. Then she walked around him, popped the mirror from its holder, and moved toward the door. Crouching, she carefully poked the mirror into the corridor. She angled it so that she could see under the bed.

No one was there.

"He's gone," she said quietly.

Odette extended the mirror arm a little farther so she could see more of the room. She angled it slowly from side to side. There was no one in the corners, and she could not see a bulge behind the drapes.

"He's definitely not here," she said.

Battat squatted behind her and looked into the mirror. Odette wondered if the feverish man had really seen anyone or if he had been hallucinating.

"Wait a second," Battat said. "Move the mirror so we can see the head of the bed."

Odette did as he asked. The drapes were moving there. It looked as if they were being stirred by a gentle wind.

"The window's open," Odette said.

Battat rose. He entered the room cautiously and looked around. "Damn."

"What?" Odette asked as she stood.

"There's a rope under the drape," he said and started toward it. "The bastard climbed—"

Suddenly, Battat turned and hurried back into the bathroom.

"Down!" he shouted and shoved Odette roughly to the floor. He dove down beside her, next to the fiberglass bathtub. Quickly, he pulled her jacket over their heads and lay beside her, his arm across her back.

A moment later, the hotel room was lit by a yellow red flare. There was a whooshing sound as the air became superheated. The flare died after a moment, leaving a sickly sweet smell mixed with the stench of burning fabric and carpet. The room smoke detector was squealing.

Odette whipped her jacket from them and knelt. "What happened?" she shouted.

"There was a TIC on the desk!" Battat yelled.

"A what?"

"A TIC," Battat said as he jumped to his feet. "Terrorist in a can. Come on—we've got to get out of here!"

Battat helped Odette up. She grabbed her jacket and the two of them swung into the hallway. Battat shut the door and staggered over to room 312. He was obviously having difficulty staying on his feet.

"What's a terrorist in a can?" Odette asked.

"Napalm with a benzene chaser," Battat said. "It looks like shaving cream and doesn't register on airport X-ray machines. All you have to do is twist the cap to set the timer, and *blam*." The main fire alarm began to clang behind them. "Give me the master key," he said as they reached 312.

Odette handed it over.

Battat opened the door. Smoke was already spilling through the door that connected the room to 310. Battat hurried past it and ran to the window. The heavy drapes were open. He edged toward the window, standing back just enough so that he could see out but not be seen from below. Odette stepped up behind him. Battat had to lean against the wall to keep from falling. They looked out at the empty parking lot.

"There," Battat said, pointing.

Odette moved closer. She looked out.

"Do you see him?" Battat asked. "In the white shirt, blue jeans, carrying a black backpack."

"I see him," Odette replied.

"That's the man I saw in the room," Battat said.

So that's the Harpooner, she thought. The monster cut an unimposing figure as he walked unhurriedly from the hotel. But his easygoing manner only made him seem even more noxious. People might be dying in the fire he set to cover his escape. Yet he did not care. Odette wished she could shoot him from here.

"He's probably going to keep moving slowly so he won't attract attention," Battat told her. He gave the gun back to her. He was panting, having trouble standing. "You've got enough time to catch up to him and take him out."

"What about you?"

"I'd only slow you down," he said.

She hesitated. An hour ago, she had not wanted him to be part of this. Now she felt as if she was deserting him.

"You're wasting time," Battat said. He gave her a gentle push and started toward the door. "Just go. I'll get to the stairwell and make my way back to the embassy. I'll see if I can do anything from there."

"All right," she said, then turned and hurried toward the door.

"He'll be armed!" Battat yelled after her. "Don't hesitate!"

She acknowledged with a wave as she left the room.

The hallway was filling with smoke. The few guests who had been in their rooms were filing into the hallway to see what was happening. Housekeeping staff and security personnel were beginning to arrive. They were helping everyone toward the stairwell.

Odette told one of the security men that someone needed help in 312. Then she rushed ahead to the stairwell.

In less than a minute, she was in the street. The parking lot was on the other side of the building. She ran toward it.

The Harpooner was gone.

FIFTY-TWO

Washington, D.C.
Tuesday, 3:13 A.M.

Paul Hood returned to the Cabinet Room and shut the door. He took a calming breath. The room smelled of coffee. He was glad. It covered the stink of treason. Then he took out his Palm Pilot, looked up a number, and went to the phone to enter it. This was not something that Hood wanted to do. It was something he had to do. It was the only way he could think of to prevent what was effectively shaping up as a coup d'état.

The phone was answered right after the second ring. "Hello?" said the voice on the other end.

"Megan, it's Paul Hood."

"Paul, where are you?" asked the First Lady. "I've been worried—"

"I'm in the Cabinet Room," he said. "Megan, listen. Fenwick is definitely involved in a conspiracy of some kind. My feeling is that he, Gable, and whoever else is in this have been trying to gaslight the president."

"Why would anyone want to make my husband think he's lost his mind?" she asked.

"Because they've also set in motion a confrontation with Iran and Russia in the Caspian Sea," Hood told her. "If they can convince the president or the public that he's not equipped to handle the showdown, he'll have to resign. Then the new president will either escalate the war or, more likely, he'll end it. That will win him points with the people and with Iran. Maybe then we'll all divide up the oil wells that used to belong to Azerbaijan."

"Paul, that's monstrous," Megan said. "Is the vice president involved with this?"

"Possibly," Hood said.

"And they expect to get away with it?"

"Megan, they are very close to getting away with it," Hood informed her. "The Caspian situation is revving up, and they've moved the strategy sessions from the Oval Office to the Situation Room. I don't have security clearance to go down there."

"I'll phone Michael on the private number and ask him to see you," Megan told him.

"That won't be enough," Hood said. "I need you to do something else."

Megan asked him what that was. Hood told her.

"I'll do it," she said when he was finished. "Give me five minutes."

Hood thanked her and hung up.

What Hood had proposed was a potentially dangerous tactic for him and for the First Lady. And under the best of circumstances, it was not going to be pleasant. But it was necessary.

Hood looked around the room.

This was not like rescuing his daughter. That had been instinctive. He had to act if she were to survive. There had been no choice.

This was different.

Hood tried to imagine the decisions that had been made in this room over the centuries. Decisions about war, about depressions, about human rights, about foreign policy. Every one of them had affected history in some way, large or small. But more important than that, whether they were right or wrong, all of them had required a commitment. Someone had to believe they were making the proper decision. They had to risk anything from a career or national security to the lives of millions on that belief.

Hood was about to do that. He was about to do both, in fact. But there was a proverb that used to hang in the high school classroom where Hood's father taught civics. It was appropriate now:

"The first faults are theirs that commit them. The second theirs that permit them."

As Hood turned and left the Cabinet Room, he did not feel the weight of the decision he made. Nor did he feel the danger it represented.

He felt only the privilege of being able to serve his country.

FIFTY-THREE

Baku, Azerbaijan
Tuesday, 11:15 A.M.

It had been a long time since Maurice Charles had to make a sudden retreat from a safe site. It infuriated him to run from a place he had carefully prepared. But it infuriated him even more to run from anyone or anything. It did not even matter to him at the moment how someone had found out where he was. From their accents, the intruders were Russian and American. Perhaps Moscow and Washington had been tracking him without him knowing it. Perhaps he had slipped up somewhere. Or maybe one of his associates had made a mistake.

But Charles did not believe the couple had been there by accident. For one thing, he had taken both of the keys to room 310 when he checked in. The front desk did not have a third key to give out. When the click of the bolt being opened woke him up, he knew something was not right. For another thing, Charles had watched the woman's feet, listened to her speak as she came in. Everything about her entrance was tentative. If she truly thought this were her room, she would have strode in and turned on the light. Women were always eager to prove things when they believed they were correct.

Yet, as angry as Charles was, he refused to give in to his rage. The immediate task was to cover his tracks so he could get away. That meant eliminating the couple who had come to his room. He had not considered calling the assassins he had used the night before. He did not want it to be known that he had run into trouble. That would be bad for his reputation and bad for business.

He had gotten a good look at the couple's feet and pants. That would be enough to identify them. He had his gun and his knife. They would not survive the morning.

Charles had walked halfway into the parking lot before turning around. If the couple were looking out a window to find him, he wanted them to see him. He wanted them to come rushing downstairs to stop him from getting away. That would make them easier to spot. It would also tell him whether or not they had backup. If they had called for help, cars or other personnel would converge on the parking lot within moments. If that did not happen, he could dispatch them and then get out of the city by train as he had planned.

After giving the couple a chance to see him, Charles doubled back to the hotel. He entered by the side door, which led past a row of shops. There were fire sirens approaching the hotel but no police sirens. No other cars came speeding into the lot. That did not mean Charles was home free. But it did suggest that the man and woman had been acting without immediate backup near or on site. Losing himself in a crowd that was fleeing a fire should be easy. First, however, he had to finish his business with the intruders.

FIFTY-FOUR

Washington, D.C.
Tuesday, 3:17 A.M.

During the administration of Harry Truman, the White House was virtually gutted and rebuilt due to the weakened condition of its centuries-old wooden beams and interior walls. The Trumans moved across the street to Blair House and, from 1948 to 1952, new foundations were laid and the decaying wooden struts were replaced by steel girders. A basement was also excavated, ostensibly to provide more storage space. In fact, it was created to provide safe areas for the president and members of his staff and family in the event of nuclear attack. Over the years, the basement was secretly expanded to include offices, command headquarters, medical facilities, surveillance posts, and recreational areas. It is now comprised of four levels that go down over two hundred feet.

All four basement levels are only accessible by a pair of elevators. These are located in both the East and West Wings. The West Wing elevator is located a short distance west of the president's private dining room, in a corner that is halfway between the Oval Office and the vice president's office. The carriage is small and wood-paneled and holds six people comfortably. Access to the elevator is gained by thumbprint identification. There is a small green monitor to the right of the door for this purpose. Since the White House recreation areas are down there, all the members of the First Family have access to the elevator.

Hood went to the vice president's office and waited outside. Because the vice president was at the White House, there was a secret service agent standing a little farther along the corridor. The vice president's office was close to the State Dining Room, where the original White House meets the newer, century-old West Wing.

Hood was there less than a minute when Megan Lawrence arrived. The First Lady was dressed in a medium-length white skirt and a red blouse with a blue scarf. She was wearing very little makeup. Her fair skin made her silver hair seem darker.

The secret service agent wished the First Lady a good morning as she passed. Megan smiled back at the young man and then continued on. She embraced Hood warmly.

"Thank you for coming down," Hood said.

Megan put her arm through his and turned toward the elevator. That gave her a reason to stand close to Hood and talk quietly. The secret service man was behind them.

"How are you going to handle this?" she asked.

"It's going to be a tough, uphill fight," Hood admitted. "Back in the Oval Office, the president was very focused. If your husband has had doubts about his ability to function, then what Fenwick and the others have given him is the perfect remedy. A crisis. They couldn't have planned it better. The president seemed to be putting a lot of trust in what Fenwick was telling him. He needed to. It was helping him get his confidence back."

"So you said," the First Lady remarked. "And they're all lies."

"I'm certain of it," Hood assured her. "The problem is, I don't have hard evidence."

"Then what makes you so sure they are lies?" the First Lady asked.

"I called Fenwick's bluff when we were alone in the Cabinet Room," Hood said. "I told him we had the terrorist who orchestrated the situation overseas. I told him the terrorist is going to tell us who he was working for. Meaning Fenwick. Fenwick told me I'll never get the information to the president."

They reached the elevator. Megan gently put her thumb on the screen. There was a faint hum behind it.

"Fenwick will deny he ever threatened you," she pointed out.

"Of course he will," Hood said. "That's why I need you to get the president away from the meeting. Tell him you need to see him for five minutes. If I did that, Fenwick and his people would chew me up. But they'll be very reluctant to attack you. That would turn the president against them."

"All right," Megan replied. The door slid open. The First Lady and Hood stepped in. She pressed button S1—Sublevel One. The door closed, and the elevator began to move.

"There's a guard downstairs," Megan said. "He's going to have to call ahead. I don't have access to the Situation Room."

"I know," Hood replied. "Hopefully, someone other than Fenwick or Gable will answer the phone."

"What if I can only get my husband alone? Just the two of us," Megan asked. "I get his attention. Then what?"

"Tell him what you've noticed over the past few weeks," Hood said. "Talk to him honestly about what we're afraid of, that Fenwick has been manipulating him. Buy me time, even if it's only two or three hours. I need that to get the evidence to stop a war."

The elevator stopped. The door opened. Outside was a brightly lit corridor. The walls were white and lined with paintings of American military officers and famous battles from the Revolution to the present. The Situation Room was located at the end of the corridor behind two black double doors.

A young, blond, fresh-faced marine guard was seated at a desk to the right of the elevator. There was a telephone, a computer, and a lamp on the desk. On a metal stand to his left were several security monitors.

The guard rose and looked from Hood to Megan. "Good morning, Mrs. Lawrence," he said. "Up kind of early for a swim," he added with a smile.

"Up kind of late, Corporal Cain," she smiled back. "This is my guest, Mr. Hood. And I'm not going for a swim."

"I didn't think so, ma'am," he replied. The guard's eyes shifted to Hood. "Good morning, sir."

"Good morning," Hood said.

"Corporal, would you please phone the president?" Megan said. "Tell him I need to speak with him. Privately, in person."

"Certainly," the guard said.

Cain sat and picked up the phone. He punched in the extension of the Situation Room.

Hood did not often pray, but he found himself praying that someone other than one of Fenwick's people was there to answer the phone.

A moment later, the guard said, "The First Lady is here to see the president."

The guard fell silent then. Hood and Megan stood still in the quiet corridor. The only sound was a high faint whine that came from the security monitors.

After a moment, the guard looked up. "No, sir," he said. "She's with a gentleman. A Mr. Hood." The guard fell silent again.

That wasn't a good sign. Only one of Fenwick's people would have thought to ask that question.

After several seconds the guard said, "Yes, sir," and hung up. He rose and looked at the First Lady. "I'm sorry, ma'am. I've been told that the meeting can't be interrupted."

"Told by whom?" she asked.

"Mr. Gable, ma'am."

"Mr. Gable is trying to keep Mr. Hood from delivering an important message to the president," Megan said. "A message that may prevent a war. I need to see my husband."

"Corporal," Hood said. "You're a military man. You don't have to take orders from a civilian. I'm going to ask you to place the call again. Ask to speak to an officer, and repeat the First Lady's message."

"If Mr. Gable gives you trouble, I will take responsibility," Megan said.

Corporal Cain hesitated, but only for a moment. He picked up the phone and remained standing as he punched in the extension.

"Mr. Gable?" he said. "I would like to speak with General Burg."

General Otis Burg was the chairman of the Joint Chiefs of Staff.

"No, sir," Cain said after a moment. "This is a military matter, sir. A security issue."

There was another pause. Hood tasted something tart in the back of his throat. He realized, after a moment, that it was blood. He was biting his tongue. He relaxed.

A few seconds later, Corporal Cain's voice and demeanor changed. His posture was stiffer, his tone formal. He was speaking with General Burg.

Cain repeated the request. Several seconds after that, the young Corporal hung up. He looked at the First Lady.

"Your husband will see you both," he said proudly.

Megan smiled and thanked him.

Hood and Megan turned and hurried down the corridor to the Situation Room.

FIFTY-FIVE

Baku, Azerbaijan
Tuesday, 11:22 A.M.

Unsteadily, David Battat made his way down the stairwell.

Because of the late morning hour, not many people were exiting the hotel. Several of the people who did pass Battat asked if he needed help. The American told them that he had inhaled some smoke but would be all right. Hugging the iron banister, he made his way slowly down the concrete stairs. When Battat reached the lobby, he leaned against a wall near the house phones. He did not want to sit down. He was weak and dizzy and afraid he would not get back up. One of the hotel staff members, an assistant manager, asked him who he was and what room he was staying in. He said he was not a guest but had been visiting a friend. The young woman told him that firefighters wanted everyone to go outside. Battat said he would go out as soon as he caught his breath.

Battat looked across the lobby. It was crowded with people, mostly hotel staff, along with about fifty or sixty guests. The guests were concerned about their belongings and asking questions about security. They did not seem in a hurry to leave. There was no smoke in the lobby, and firefighters were just pulling into the circular drive in front of the hotel.

Battat was concerned about how Odette was making out. He had been proud of her when she left the hotel. If she had been afraid, she did not show it. He wished he were a little steadier. He did not like the idea of her having to face the Harpooner alone.

There was a side exit down the corridor to Battat's right. The parking lot was to the right, the front of the hotel to the left. Since the fire trucks were out front, he felt he stood a better chance of catching a taxi in the parking lot. If not, there was a major thoroughfare beyond the parking lot. He had seen it from the upstairs window. He could probably catch a bus there.

Pushing himself off the wall, Battat shuffled down the carpeted hallway. He felt feverish again, though he did not feel worse than he had before. His body was fighting whatever he had been injected with. That probably meant it was viral rather than chemical. He could finally get medical attention and start to shake this.

Battat's vision was misty as he moved past the bank of telephones. There were several shops beyond, their picture windows reflecting each other. There was no one inside, either customers or employees. The displays of shirts and trinkets, of luggage and toys, all seemed to merge as Battat neared. He tried to blink them clear. He could not. The sickness plus the exertion had worn him down much more than he thought. Battat gave serious thought to going back to the lobby and asking the fire department medics for a ride to the hospital. He had been afraid to go there lest someone recognize him from the night before and ask about the dead man in his room. But he was beginning to doubt that he could make it from the hotel, let alone reach the embassy.

Suddenly, someone appeared in Battat's line of vision. The American stopped and squinted. It was a man wearing jeans and a white shirt. There were straps around his shoulder.

A black backpack.

Oh Christ, Battat thought as the man approached. He knew who it was. And he had no doubt that the man recognized him. And knew why he was in such a weakened condition. After all, it was probably this same man who had injected him with the toxin on the beach.

The Harpooner.

The assassin had just walked in through the side door. He was about twenty feet away. He was holding what looked like a knife in his right hand. Battat would not be able to fight him. He had to try and get back to the lobby.

Battat turned, but he moved too fast. His vision blurred and he stumbled against one of the shop windows. He quickly pushed off with his shoulder. He staggered ahead. If he could just get to the lobby, even if he fell square on his face, someone might get to him before the Harpooner could.

Battat reached the bank of phones. He extended his left arm, used it to move himself along the wall. Push, step, push, step.

He was halfway along the bank when he felt starched fabric slide along the front of his throat. A sleeve. A strong arm pulled back, putting Battat into a choke hold.

"The last time we met, I needed you alive," the assassin whispered harshly. "Not this time. Unless you tell
me who you're working with."

"Up yours," Battat gasped.

Battat felt a knee against the small of his back. If the
Harpooner intended to kill him standing up, he was going to be disappointed. Battat's legs gave out and he
dropped to the floor. The Harpooner immediately released Battat and swung around in front of him. He
straddled Battat and dropped a knee on his chest. Battat
felt a sharp jab in his side and exhaled painfully. One
or more of his ribs had been broken. The Harpooner
brought the knife to the left side of the American's
throat. He pressed the sharp tip just below the ear.

"No," the Harpooner hissed as he glared down at Battat. "This is going up yours."

Battat was too weak to fight. He was aware that he
was going to be cut from ear to ear and then left to
drown in his own blood. But there was nothing he could
do about it. Nothing.

Battat felt a pinch in his throat. A moment later, he
heard a soft pop and blood sprayed into his eyes. He
thought it would hurt more, having his throat pierced.
But there was no pain after the initial pinch. He did not
feel the blade moving through his skin. And he was still
able to breathe.

An instant later, Battat heard a second pop. He
blinked hard to clear the blood from his eyes. He
watched as the Harpooner just hovered there, crouched
on his chest. Blood was pumping from a wound in his
throat. There was no drama in his face, no great gesture
befitting the size of his crimes. Just a momentary look

of confusion and surprise. Then the killer's eyes shut, the knife fell from his hand, and the Harpooner tumbled to the floor between Battat and the phone bank.

Battat lay there. He did not know exactly what had happened until Odette appeared from behind. She was holding her silenced pistol in front of her and looking down at the Harpooner.

"Are you all right?" she asked Battat.

He reached up and felt his throat. Except for a trickle of blood on the left side, it felt intact.

"I think I'm okay," Battat said. "Thank you."

Battat managed to half wriggle, half crawl away as Odette bent and examined the Harpooner. The woman kept the gun pointed at the Harpooner's head as she felt his wrist for a pulse. Then she held her fingers under his nose, feeling for breath. But she had struck him once in the throat and once in the chest. His white shirt was already thick and dripping with blood.

"I'm glad you followed him," Battat said. He pulled a handkerchief from his pocket and pressed it to his own wound.

"I didn't," Odette said as she rose. "I lost him. But then I thought he might come back to try to cover his tracks. And I knew which one of us he would recognize."

Just then, a housekeeper in the lobby saw the body and screamed. Battat looked back. She was pointing at them and shouting for help.

Odette stepped around the corpse to help Battat to his feet. "We've got to get out of here," she said urgently. "Come on. My car isn't far—"

"Wait," Battat said. He bent over the Harpooner's

body and began working on the straps of the backpack. "Help me get this off. There may be evidence we can use to identify his partners."

"You just get on your feet," Odette said as she pulled out her knife. "I'll do that."

Battat pulled himself up, using the ledge under the phones while Odette cut the backpack free. Then, lending Battat her shoulder, Odette led the American down the hall.

They were nearly at the door when someone yelled at them from behind.

"Stop!" a man yelled.

Battat and Odette turned. An elderly hotel security officer was standing just beyond the phone bank. Odette let Battat lean against one of the shop windows while she pulled her badge from her back pocket. She held it toward the security officer.

"I'm Odette Kolker of Metropolitan Squad Three," she said. "The man on the floor is a wanted terrorist. He started the fire in 310. Make sure the room is sealed off. I'm taking my partner to the hospital to see that he gets proper care. Then I'll be back."

Odette did not wait for the man to answer or for other security personnel to arrive. She turned and helped Battat from the building.

She did that well, Battat thought. Gave the man a mission, made him feel important, so he would not interfere with them.

The brisk, clear air and sharp sunshine helped give Battat yet another fresh start. This was the last one, though. He knew that for certain. The American's legs were rubbery, and he was having trouble holding his head up. At least his neck was not bleeding badly. And the handkerchief was keeping most of that inside, where it belonged.

Only after they had made their way through the parking lot to the rear of the hotel did it hit Battat. Odette had done it. She had not only saved his life but she had stopped the Harpooner. She had killed a terrorist who had eluded all of Europe's top security agencies. He was proud to have had a small hand in this. The only downside was that Odette probably would not be able to remain in Baku after this. It was going to be tough to explain this to her police superiors. And if the Harpooner had allies, they might come looking for her. It was probably a good time for Odette to assume another identity.

Five minutes later, Battat was seated in the passenger's seat of Odette's car. They pulled from the curb and headed toward the American embassy. It would be a short ride, but there was something that could not wait. The Harpooner's backpack was in Battat's lap. There was a small padlock on the flap. He borrowed Odette's knife and cut the flap away. He looked inside.

There were some documents as well as a Zed-4 phone. He had worked one of those when he was in Moscow. They were more compact and sophisticated than the American Tac-Sats.

Battat removed the phone from the case. There was an alphanumeric keypad along with several other buttons. Above them was a liquid crystal display on top. He pushed the menu button to the right of the display.

For the Harpooner's sake, the instructions were in English.

And for the first time since David Battat arrived in Baku, he did something he had missed.

He smiled.

FIFTY-SIX

Washington, D.C.
Tuesday, 4:27 A.M.

The Situation Room was a brightly lit chamber with a low ceiling, white walls, and soft, fluorescent lighting. There was a conference table in the center of the room and chairs along three of the four walls. Computer monitors were attached to the arms of the chairs. They provided aides with up-to-the-minute information. The fourth wall was fitted with a ten-foot-long high-definition TV monitor. The screen was linked to the National Reconnaissance Office. Real-time satellite images could be displayed there with magnification of objects up to three feet long. Most of these high-tech improvements were made within the last four years using over two billion dollars that had been allocated to fixing the White House recreation facilities, including the pool and tennis court.

Hood and the First Lady entered through the door that was under the high-definition monitor. The chiefs of the army, navy, and air force and the commandant of the marine corps were sitting along one side of the table with their chairman, General Otis Burg, in the center. Burg was a big, barrel-chested man in his late fifties. He had a shaved head and steel gray eyes that had been hardened by war and political bureaucracy. The joint chiefs' aides were seated behind them. Along the other side of the table were the president, the vice president, NSA head Fenwick, Chief of Staff Gable, and Deputy National Security adviser Don Roedner. Judging by their tense expressions, either it was a difficult meeting or they did not appreciate the interruption. Or both.

Several members of the Joint Chiefs of Staff registered surprise to see Hood with the First Lady. So did the president. He had been in the process of rising to go into an adjoining study and talk with her. The president froze and looked from Megan to Hood, then back to Megan. The new arrivals stopped at the head of the conference table.

"What's going on?" the president asked.

Hood glanced at the joint chiefs, who were a wall of impatience. He still did not know whether the frustration was with him or with the issue at hand. All he knew was that he would not have much time to present his case.

"Sir," Hood said, "there is increasing evidence that the attack on the Iranian oil rig was executed not by Azerbaijanis but by Iranians under the direction of the terrorist known as the Harpooner."

The president sat back down. "Why?" he asked.

"So that Iran could justify moving ships into the region and seize as many oil resources as possible," Hood told him.

"And risk a military showdown with the United States?" Lawrence asked.

"No, sir," Hood replied. He looked at Fenwick. "I believe there is an agreement in place to make sure the United States does not interfere. Then, when the tensions are defused, we simply buy our oil from Teheran.".

"And when was this agreement made?" the president asked.

"Yesterday, in New York," Hood said. "Probably after many months of negotiations."

"You're referring to Jack's visit to the Iranian mission," the president said.

"Yes, sir," Hood replied.

"Mr. Fenwick was not empowered to make such a promise," the president pointed out. "If he did make one, it would not be valid."

"It might be if you were not in office," Hood said.

"This is ridiculous!" Fenwick declared. "I was at the Iranian mission to try and expand our intelligence resources in the Middle East. I've explained that, and I can document it. I can tell you who I met with and when."

"All part of the big lie," Hood said.

"Mr. Roedner was with me," Fenwick said. "I have the notes I made, and I'll be happy to name my contacts. What do you have, Mr. Hood?"

"The truth," he replied without hesitation. "It's the same thing I had when you vowed to keep me from seeing the president."

"What I vowed was to keep you from bothering the president," Fenwick insisted. "Secret deals with Iran. The president being out of office. This isn't the truth, Mr. Hood. It's paranoia!"

The vice president looked at his watch. "Mr. President, forgive me, but we're wasting time. We need to get on with this meeting."

"I agree," said General Burg. "I'm not up to speed on

any of this back-and-forth, and it isn't my job to say which of these gentlemen is full of gravy. But whether we play offense or defense, we have to make some quick decisions if we're going to match Iran's deployment."

The president nodded.

"Then get on with the meeting, Mr. President, General Burg," Hood said. "But please delay taking military action for as long as possible. Give me time to finish the investigation we've begun."

"I asked for evidence to back your claims," the president said, his voice extremely calm. "You don't have that."

"Not yet," Hood said.

"And we don't have the extra time I thought there'd be to investigate. We've got to proceed as if the Caspian threat is real," the president said with finality.

"Which is exactly what they want you to do!" Hood said. He was growing agitated and had to pull himself back. An outburst would undermine his own credibility. "We believe a crisis is being engineered, one that will call into question your ability to govern."

"People have argued about that for years," the president said. "They voted me out of office once. But I don't make decisions based on polls."

"I'm not talking about a policy debate," Hood said. "I'm talking about your mental and emotional state. That will be the issue."

Fenwick shook his head sadly. "Sir, mental health is the issue. Mr. Hood has been under a great deal of stress these past two weeks. His teenage daughter is mentally ill. He's going through a divorce. He needs a long vacation."

"I don't think Mr. Hood is the one who needs a leave of absence," the First Lady said. Her voice was clear and edged with anger. It quieted the room. "Mr. Fenwick, I have watched my husband being misled and misinformed for several weeks now. Mr. Hood looked into the situation at my personal request. His investigation has been methodical, and I believe his findings have merit." She glared at Fenwick. "Or do you intend to call me a liar as well?"

Fenwick said nothing.

The president looked at his wife. Megan was standing straight and stoic at Hood's side. There was nothing apologetic in her expression. The president looked tired, but Hood thought he also seemed sad. He could not tell whether it was because Megan had run an operation behind his back or because he felt he had let her down. The couple was silent. It was clearly an issue they would settle some other time, in private.

After a moment, the president's eyes returned to Hood. The sadness remained. "Your concern is noted and appreciated," the president said. "But I won't jeopardize the nation's interests to protect my own. Especially when you have no evidence that they're at risk."

"All I want is a few hours," Hood said.

"Unfortunately, we don't have a few hours," the president replied.

For a moment, Megan looked as though she was going to hug her husband. She did not. She looked at Fenwick and then at the joint chiefs. "Thank you for hearing us out," she said. "I'm sorry to have interrupted." She turned and started toward the door.

Hood did not know what else to say. He would have

to go back to the Cabinet Room and work with Herbert and Orlov. Try to get the proof the president needed and get it quickly.

He turned to follow the First Lady from the Situation Room. As he did, there was a gentle beep from somewhere in the room. A cell phone. The sound had come from the inside pocket of Fenwick's suit.

He shouldn't be able to get a signal in here, Hood thought. The walls of the Situation Room were lined with chips that generated random electrical impulses or impedence webs. The IWs were designed to block bugs from broadcasting to anyone on the White House grounds. They also blocked cell phone calls with one exception: transmissions relayed by the government's Hephaestus satellite array.

Hood turned back as the NSA chief had slipped a hand into his jacket. Fenwick took out the phone and shut off the ringer.

Bingo.

If it got through IW security, it had to be a Hephaestus call. Highest security. Who wouldn't Fenwick want to talk to right now?

Hood leaned over the NSA chief and pulled the phone from his hand. Fenwick reached for it, but Hood stepped away.

"What the hell are you doing?" Fenwick demanded. He pushed the chair back and rose. He walked toward Hood.

"I'm betting my career on a hunch," Hood said. He flipped open the cover and answered the call. "Yes?"

"Who is this?" asked the caller.

"This is Jack Fenwick's line at the NSA," Hood said. He walked toward the president. "Who's calling?"

"My name is David Battat," said the clear voice on the other end.

Hood felt the world slide off his shoulders. He held the cell phone so the president could listen as well. Fenwick stopped beside them. The NSA head did not reach for the phone. He just stood there. Hood saw just where the weight of the world had shifted.

"Mr. Battat, this is Paul Hood of Op-Center," said Hood.

"Paul Hood?" Battat said. "Why are you answering this line?"

"It's a long story," Hood said. "What is your situation?"

"A helluva lot better than Mr. Fenwick's," Battat said. "We just took down the Harpooner and recovered his secure phone. This number was the first one that came up on the Harpooner's instant-dial menu."

FIFTY-SEVEN

Washington, D.C.
Tuesday, 4:41 A.M.

Paul Hood stepped to a corner of the room to finish speaking with Battat. It was important that he get all the information he could about the Harpooner and what had happened.

While Hood did that, President Lawrence stood. He glanced over at his wife, who was standing by the door. He gave her a little smile. Just a small one to show that he was okay and that she had done the right thing. Then Lawrence turned to Fenwick. The NSA chief was still standing beside him. His arms were stiff at his side and his expression was defiant. The other men remained seated around the table. Everyone was watching Lawrence and Fenwick.

"Why did the Harpooner have your direct number and the Hephaestus access code?" the president asked. There was a new confidence in his voice.

"I can't answer that," Fenwick said.

"Were you working with Iran to orchestrate a takeover of Azerbaijani oil deposits?" the president asked.

"I was not."

"Were you working with anyone to organize a take-over of the Oval Office?" the president asked.

"No, sir," Fenwick replied. "I'm as puzzled as you are."

"Do you still believe that Mr. Hood is a liar?"

"I believe that he's misinformed. I have no explanation for what is going on," Fenwick said.

The president sat back down. "None at all."

"No, Mr. President."

The president looked across the table. "General Burg, I'm going to get the secretary of state and our UN ambassador working on this right away. How would you feel about coordinating a midlevel alert for the region?"

Burg looked at his colleagues in turn. No one voiced a protest. The general looked at the president. "Given the confusion about just who we should be fighting, I'm very comfortable with yellow status."

The president nodded. He looked at his watch. "We'll reconvene in the Oval Office at six-thirty. That will give me time to work with the press secretary to get something on the morning news shows. I want to be able to put people at ease about our troops and about the status of our oil supply." He regarded vice president Cotten and Gable. "I'm going to ask the attorney general to look into the rest of this situation as quietly as possible. I want him to ascertain whether treasonable acts have been committed. Do any of you have any thoughts?"

There was something challenging in the president's voice. Hood had just finished up with Battat and turned back to the table. He remained in the corner, however. Everyone else was still.

The vice president leaned forward and folded his hands on the table. He said nothing. Gable did not move.

Fenwick's deputy, Don Roedner, was staring at the conference table.

"No suggestions at all?" the president pressed.

The heavy silence lasted a moment longer. Then the vice president said, "There will not be an investigation."

"Why not?" asked the president.

"Because you will have three letters of resignation on your desk by the end of the morning," Cotten replied. "Mr. Fenwick's, Mr. Gable's, and Mr. Roedner's. In exchange for those resignations, there will be no charges, no prosecution, and no explanation other than that members of the administration had a difference of policy opinion."

Fenwick's forehead flushed. "Three letters, Mr. Vice President?"

"That's correct, Mr. Fenwick," Cotten replied. The vice president did not look at the NSA chief. "In exchange for complete amnesty."

Hood did not miss the subtext. Nor, he was sure, did the president. The vice president was in on this, too. He was asking the others to take a fall for him— though not a big one. Quitting an administration, high-ranking officials often tumbled upward in the private sector.

The president shook his head. "I have here a group of administration officials who apparently conspired with an international terrorist to steal oil from one nation, give it to another, reap foreign policy benefits, and in the process steal the office of president of the United States. And you sit there arrogantly declaring that these men will be given de facto amnesty. And that one of them, it appears, will remain in office, in line for the presidency."

Cotten regarded Lawrence. "I do declare that, yes," he said. "The alternative is an international incident in which the United States will be seen as having betrayed Azerbaijan. A series of investigations and trials that will ghost this administration and become its sole legacy. Plus a president who was unaware of what was going on among his closest advisers. A president who his own wife thought might be suffering from a mental or emotional breakdown. That will not boost public confidence in his abilities."

"Everyone gets off," the president said angrily. "I'm supposed to agree to that?"

"Everyone gets off," the vice president repeated calmly.

"Mr. Vice President, sir?" General Burg said. "I just want to say if I had my weapon here, I would shoot you in the ass."

"General Burg," the vice president replied, "given the pitiful state of our military, I'm confident you'd miss." He regarded the president. "There was never going to be a war. No one was going to shoot at anyone or be shot at. Peace would have been reached with Iran, relations would have been normalized, and Americans would have had a guaranteed fuel supply. Whatever one may think of the methods, this was all done for the good of the nation."

"Any time laws are broken, it is not for the good of the nation," the president said. "You endangered a small, industrious country trying to get its footing in a post-Soviet world. You sought to undo the will of the American electorate. And you betrayed my faith in you."

Cotten rose. "I did none of those things, Mr. President," he replied. "Otherwise, I would be resigning. I'll see you all at the six-thirty meeting."

"You will not be needed there," the president said.

"Ah," said the vice president. "You would prefer I go on the *Today Show* to discuss administration policy in the Caspian region."

"No," the president replied. "I would prefer that you draft your letter of resignation to submit with the others."

The vice president shook his head. "I won't do that."

"You will," the president replied. "And attribute your resignation to mental exhaustion. I won't make you a martyr to an anticonstitutional fringe. Find some other line of work, Mr. Cotten."

"Mr. President, you are pushing the wrong man," Cotten warned.

"I don't think so," the president replied. His eyes and voice grew steely. "You're correct, Mr. Cotten. I don't want a national or international scandal. But I'll suffer those before I leave a traitor in the line of succession to the office of president. Either you resign or, in exchange for that amnesty, I will urge Mr. Fenwick and his associates to tell the attorney general what they know about your involvement in this operation."

Cotten was silent. Red and silent.

The president reached for the phone in front of him. He pushed a button. "Corporal Cain?"

"Yes, Mr. President?"

"Please have an unarmed detail report to the Situation Room at once," Lawrence told him. "There are some gentlemen who need to be escorted to their offices and then from the grounds."

"Unarmed, sir?" Cain repeated.

"That's right," Lawrence said. "There won't be any trouble."

"Right away, sir."

"Wait outside the door when you're finished," the president added. "The men will be joining you in just a moment."

"Yes, sir."

The president hung up. He regarded the four men. "One more thing. Information about your participation in these events must not leave this room. Amnesty will not be based on anything I intend to do for you. Pardoning you would be a sin. It will be based solely on the absence of news."

The men turned and walked toward the door.

Megan Lawrence stepped aside.

Hood's eyes met hers. The First Lady was glowing with pride. They were obviously thinking the same thing.

She was the only Lawrence who would be stepping aside this day.

FIFTY-EIGHT

Saint Petersburg, Russia
Tuesday, 12:53 P.M.

In most intelligence agencies it's often difficult to tell night from day. That's because conspiracy and espionage never rest, so the counterterrorists and spybusters also work around the clock. Most are usually fully staffed. The distinction is even less noticeable in the Russian Op-Center because the facility is below ground. There are no windows anywhere.

But General Orlov always knew when it was afternoon. He knew because that was when his devoted wife called. She always rang shortly after lunchtime to see how her Sergei's sandwich was. She phoned even today, when she had not had time to prepare a bag lunch before he left.

Unfortunately, the call was brief. It often was. They usually had longer conversations when he was in space than they did at the Op-Center. Two minutes after Masha called, Orlov received a call from Odette. He told Masha he would have to call her back. She understood. Masha always understood.

Orlov switched lines. "Odette, how are you?" the general asked eagerly.

"I'm very well," the woman replied. "We accomplished our mission."

Orlov was unable to speak for a moment. He had been worried about Odette and concerned about the mission. The fact that she was safe and triumphant left him choked with pride.

"We terminated with complications," Odette went on, "but we got away. There were no other injuries."

"Where are you now?" Orlov asked.

"At the U.S. embassy," she said. "Mr. Battat is getting medical care. Then I'll be going to the police station. I had to show my badge to a hotel worker, but I think I'll be able to work it out with my superior. The Harpooner set a fire. I can tell the captain that I went there to see if I could help."

"So you don't want to leave, then?" Orlov asked.

"I think there will be some interesting problems because of all this," she said. "I'd like to stay for a while."

"We'll talk about it," Orlov said. "I'm proud of you, Odette. And I know someone else would be, too."

"Thank you," she said. "I think Viktor was looking out for me today. So was David Battat. I'm glad you asked him to come along."

Odette gave Orlov additional information about what had happened. They arranged to talk again in six hours. If it became necessary for Odette to leave Baku, there was an Aeroflot flight she could catch at eight P.M.

Orlov took a moment to savor the victory's many rewards. First, having won the battle against a tenacious enemy. Second, having made the right decision to send Odette and Battat into the field together. And finally, having been able to help Paul Hood. Not only did it repay an old debt, but it hopefully opened the door to future close collaborations.

Odette said that Battat had spoken with Paul Hood. There was nothing Orlov could add to that. Orlov would call him in a few minutes. First, however, he wanted to brief the staff members who had been involved in the hunt.

He was about to send for Grosky and Kosov when the men came to his office door. Kosov was carrying a rolled-up blueprint.

"General," said the outgoing Kosov, "we have some news."

"Good news?" Orlov asked.

"Yes, sir," Kosov said. "That information the Americans gave us about the Harpooner's Russian identity has proved very useful."

"In what way?" Orlov asked.

"It suggested to us how he has been able to come to Moscow and disappear without ever being seen," Kosov said. He stepped forward and unrolled the blueprint on Orlov's desk. "This is a map of the old Soviet army railroad routes," he said. "As you know, they go underground well outside of Moscow and stop at various points beneath the city."

"It was designed that way so troops could be moved into place clandestinely, to put down riots or even foreign attacks," Grosky added.

"I know about these," Orlov said. "I've traveled in them."

"But what you may not know about is this one," Kosov said.

The intelligence analyst used a pen to point to a faint red line. It led from Kievskaya metro stop to several other stations around the city. Kosov was right. Orlov did not know what it was.

"This is unmarked, as you can see, even though it links up to the main trunk," Kosov continued. "We thought it might be a service tunnel of some kind, but we looked at an older map from the GRU files just to make certain. It was the old Stalin tunnel. If the German army had ever reached Moscow during World War II, Stalin would have been evacuated through this system. Only his closest military advisers know that it existed." Kosov stepped back and folded his arms. "We believe, sir, that all we need to do to catch our rat is to put video cameras at the entrance and exit. Sooner or later, the Harpooner is certain to show up there."

Orlov looked at the map for a moment, then sat back. "You may have solved a very perplexing riddle," he said. "Excellent work."

"Thank you, sir," Kosov beamed.

"Fortunately," Orlov went on, "the Harpooner was killed earlier today. The only rats that will be using the tunnel are the four-legged kind."

Grosky's mouth twisted slightly at one end. Kosov's expression seemed to fall entirely.

"But we could not have taken him without you, and I will say so in my report to the president's director of intelligence review," Orlov promised. He rose and extended his hand to each man in turn. "I am proud of you both and deeply grateful."

Kosov's disappointment evaporated quickly. Grosky's mouth remained bent. But even Grosky's perpetual sourness couldn't spoil the moment. An inexperienced woman, a sick man, and two former enemies had joined forces to win a big one.

It was an extraordinary feeling.

FIFTY-NINE

Washington, D.C.
Tuesday, 5:04 A.M.

After the vice president and his team had been ushered away, the president asked Hood to wait for him. Hood stepped outside the Situation Room as the president and Megan stood alone behind the conference table, talking. The president took his wife's hands in his. He seemed composed, once again in control.

The Joint Chiefs of Staff filed out quickly after Cotten's group had been led off. They headed quickly toward the elevator. Before leaving, General Burg paused and turned to Hood. He shook the intelligence leader's hand.

"What you did in there was good work, smart work," the general said. "It was also ballsy. My congratulations, Mr. Hood. I'm proud to be associated with you. Proud to be an American."

Coming from anyone else under almost any other circumstance, that sentiment might have sounded corny. But the system had worked, despite the formidable forces and pressures rallied against it. General Burg had every reason to feel proud. Hood did.

"Thank you, General," Hood said sincerely.

After the Joint Chiefs left, the hall was quiet, save for the whispered conversation of the president and First

Lady. Hood was relieved but still a little shell-shocked by everything that had just happened. He did not believe that the press would accept the given explanations for a mass resignation of the vice president and top administration officials. But that was a battle for other warriors and another day. Hood and his team had saved the presidency and defeated the Harpooner. Right now, all he wanted to do was hear what the president wanted to say, get back to the hotel, and go to sleep.

The president and First Lady emerged a few minutes later. They looked tired but content.

"Did your man in Baku have anything else to say?" the president asked as he walked toward Hood.

"Not really, sir," Hood said. "He's at the American embassy now. We'll talk again. If there's any other intel, I'll let you know at once."

The president nodded as he stopped next to Hood. Megan was standing beside him.

"I'm sorry to have kept you waiting, but Mrs. Lawrence and I wanted to thank you together," the president said. "She told me you've been working on this nonstop since Sunday night."

"It's been a long day and a half," Hood admitted.

"You're more than welcome to sleep upstairs, if you'd like," the president said. "Or a driver will take you home."

"Thank you, sir," Hood said. He looked at his watch. "Rush hour doesn't start until six, so I should be all right. I'll just roll down the window and enjoy the fresh air."

"If you're certain," the president said. He offered his hand. "I've got work to do. Megan will make sure you get back upstairs. And thank you again. For everything."

Hood accepted the president's hand. "It's been an honor, sir."

After the president left, Megan faced Hood. There were tears in her eyes. "You saved him, Paul. While I stood there, I watched him pull back from wherever they had taken him."

"He did that by himself," Hood said. "And without your heads-up, I wouldn't have acted on any of this."

"For once in your life, Paul, give the self-effacement a rest," Megan said. "You took all the risks in there. If things had gone the other way, you would have been ruined."

Hood shrugged.

Megan grimaced. "You're exasperating. Michael is right about one thing, though. You're tired. Are you sure you won't rest awhile before you head back?"

"I'm sure," Hood said. "There are still a few things we have to tie up, and I want to call Sharon."

"How's that going?" Megan asked.

"As good as could be expected," Hood said. "Harleigh's in the hospital so we're focused on that."

Megan touched his arm. "If you want to talk, I'm here."

Hood thanked her with a smile. They left together, and then Hood headed for his car. A plane rumbled in the distance. Hood looked up as he unlocked his car door. The first hint of daylight was appearing on the other side of the White House grounds.

Somehow, that seemed fitting.

SIXTY

*Washington, D.C.
Tuesday, 6:46 A.M.*

Hood was surprisingly alert when he reached his office.

Mike Rodgers was gone. He had left a voice mail message two hours before about a military situation that was developing along the Pakistan-India border. Rodgers said he had gone home to get some rest before going off to a meeting at the Pentagon. Although General Rodgers was officially attached to Op-Center, he was called upon to assess flashpoints in different corners of the world.

Bob Herbert was still awake and "at the switch," as he described it. He came to Hood's office and quickly brought Hood up to speed on the little additional intelligence that Orlov had on the Harpooner and his movements. Then Herbert asked Hood how things had gone at the White House.

Herbert listened intently to his chief's matter-of-fact recitation of the facts. When Hood was finished, the intelligence head sighed. "I've been sitting here collecting intelligence while you were out there, in the field, saving America and the Constitution from a demagogue."

"Some guys have all the luck," Hood said dryly.

"Yeah," Herbert said. "But you're not the one I envy."

"Oh?"

Hood thought for a moment. Then, just before Herbert said it, Hood knew what was coming.

"I wish I had been the one who pulled the plug on the Harpooner," Herbert said. His voice was a low monotone. His eyes were staring. His mind was somewhere else. "I'd have done it slowly. Very slowly. I would have made him suffer the way I've suffered without my wife."

Hood did not know what to say, so he said nothing.

Herbert looked at him. "I've got a lot of vacation time coming, Paul. I'm going to take it."

"You should," Hood said.

"I want to go to Baku and meet this woman Odette," Herbert said. "I want to see where it happened."

"I understand," Hood told him.

Herbert smiled. His eyes were damp. "I knew you would." His voice cracked. "Look at me. You're the one who's had his ass on the firing line twice in the past two weeks. But I'm the one cracking up."

"You've been carrying this pain and frustration for nearly twenty years," Hood said. "It's got to come out." He snickered humorlessly. "I'll break, too, Bob. One day the UN thing, the White House—it's all going to hit me and I'll come apart big time."

Herbert smiled. "Just hold on till I'm back from vacation so I can pick up all the cogs and wheels."

"It's a deal," Hood said.

Herbert wheeled around the desk and hugged Hood warmly. Then he turned his chair around and left the office.

Hood put in a quick call to General Orlov, thanking

him for everything he had done and suggesting that they work out a way to integrate their two systems on some level. Create an Interpol for crisis management. Orlov was all for the idea. They agreed to talk about it the following day.

After hanging up with Orlov, Hood looked at the computer clock. It was still too early to call home. He decided to go to the hotel and phone Sharon and the kids from his room. There would be no other calls, no distractions.

Hood left his office and headed back upstairs. He greeted members of the day team as they arrived: Darrell McCaskey, Matt Stoll, and Liz Gordon. He told them each to go see Bob Herbert for an update. Hood said he would brief them more fully later in the day.

By the time he reached the parking lot, he was starting to crash. The caffeine had made its way through his system. Hood's body was definitely winding down. As he neared his car, he saw Ann Farris. She was just pulling through the gate. The press liaison saw him, waved, and drove over.

She rolled down the window. "Is everything all right?" she asked.

Hood nodded. "Just tired," he said. "Bob is still there. He'll brief you. There's nothing we have to press release, though. Not yet."

"Where are you headed?" she asked.

"Back to the hotel," he said. "I've got to get some rest."

"Hop in and I'll run you over," she said. "You don't look like you should be driving."

"I don't know when I'll be coming back," Hood told her. "I need the car."

"You'll be coming back this afternoon," Ann said. "I know you. A two- or three-hour power nap, and then you'll be back. Just call when you wake up, and I'll come and get you."

The offer sounded inviting. He did not feel like driving anymore.

"All right," Hood said.

Hood went to the passenger's side and slid in. He shut his eyes and had to be nudged awake when they arrived. He was groggy. Ann left her car out front and walked him to his room.

She returned a few minutes later, climbed behind the wheel, and sat there for a moment.

"Screw this," she said. Instead of driving off, she moved the car to the main lot. Then she went back inside.

Hood had just finished his short chat with Sharon. His wife had said that there had been no change in anything.

Hood removed his shoes and tie and was unbuttoning his shirt when there was a knock on the door. It had to be a bellboy with a fax from the office or his attorney. No one else knew he was here. He fished a dollar from his wallet and opened the door. He was surprised to see Ann.

"Thanks," she said, "but I didn't come back for my tip."

He smiled and let her in.

Ann was still wearing her jacket, but she looked different. There was something more accessible about her. It was in the eyes, he decided.

Hood shut the door behind her. As he did, he was surprised by something else. He was glad that she had come back.

EPILOGUE

Baku, Azerbaijan
Tuesday, 3:00 P.M.

Throughout the late morning and early afternoon, the surprises kept coming for Ron Friday, each one more startling than the last.

First, Friday was surprised to find David Battat at the embassy. The CIA operative was being nursed to health by the embassy medic. He looked in remarkably good health and even better spirits.

Next, Friday was even more surprised to hear that a local policewoman had been responsible for killing the Harpooner. Friday himself would not have known how to find him or what he looked like. He could not imagine how a policewoman had gotten to him. Maybe it was an accident or they were mistaken. Perhaps someone else had been mistaken for the Harpooner. In any case, authorities were speculating that he had been the man behind the attack on the Iranian oil rig. Prodded by the United States, military mobilization was being delayed while an investigation was under way.

But the biggest surprise was the call from Jack Fenwick's executive secretary, Dori. Her boss, Don Roedner, Red Gable, and the vice president were all resigning later that morning. Dori did not know anything about the operation Fenwick had been running and was stunned by the announcement. Friday was stunned, too. He could not imagine how everything had come unraveled. He could not imagine what his old mentor must be feeling. He wished he could speak with him, say something reassuring.

But Friday had not been able to reach Fenwick on his cell phone. Someone else answered, and he quickly hung up. He did not know whether the NSA chief would be investigated and whether that investigation would ever get to him. Friday did not generally report to Fenwick directly. He reported to T. Perry Gord, assistant deputy director of South Asian affairs. There was no reason it should reach him. Gord knew nothing about Fenwick's other activities.

Still, after weighing whether or not to remain in Baku, Friday decided it would be best to leave. He would go somewhere that was a little bit off the radar. Someplace the international press would not be paying so much attention to over the next few weeks.

Fortunately, there was a situation developing on the India-Pakistan border that fell within Gord's jurisdiction. Rather than send someone over from Washington, Friday arranged to have himself transferred to the embassy in Islamabad in order to do on-site intelligence gathering. There was a Pakistan International Airlines flight leaving Moscow the following morning. He would fly from Baku tonight and make certain that he was on it.

It would have been nice, he thought, *if it had all worked out for Fenwick.* With Cotten in the White House, Fenwick would have had unprecedented access and power. And any one of the few people who had taken part in the changeover would have been rewarded. Not just for their contribution but for their silence. On the other hand, one of the reasons Friday had gone into intelligence work was for the challenge. The danger. He had done his job. And he had enjoyed doing it, taking out a CIA operative who had CIA swagger. The kind that had helped to keep Friday back his whole life. That swagger did not prevent Thomas Moore from walking into a neat little NSA trap.

All right, Friday thought. Things had not worked out. It was on to the next project.

That, too, was one of the things Ron Friday enjoyed about intelligence work. It was never the same. He never knew who he might be working with—or against. In Islamabad, for example, it was not just a question of getting a good man to the flashpoint. It was getting the right man there quickly. Gord had heard through the grapevine that someone from Op-Center was being brought in to consult on the India-Pakistan situation and was probably going to be sent to the region. Over the past few years, Op-Center had taken over a great deal of the work Fenwick's team used to handle. That had resulted in ongoing budget and personnel battles at the NSA. Fenwick got the monies he wanted but it had turned a heated rivalry into a ferocious one.

Friday carefully disassembled and packed a rifle. He took along two boxes of shells. Because he was going to Islamabad with diplomatic credentials, his luggage would not be checked.

Showing up Op-Center was important. But as Friday

had demonstrated in Baku and elsewhere, outperforming
a rival was not the only way to bring them down.

Whoever this man Mike Rodgers was, he would learn
that the hard way.